# Murder on Third Avenue

By

# Richard Scott

**Winter Island Press**
Salem, Massachsetts

vi

Copyright © 1994 by Richard T. Scott
E-book edition 2011
Published byWinter Island Press
Cover design and photos by Richard Scott
Contact the author at richard.scott2000@comcast.net

For Jeanne

Other books by Richard Scott

**The Reluctant Assassin** (A Tony Dantry espionage novel)
    *paper and ebook*
**The Eager Assassin** (A Tony Dantry espionage novel)
    *ebook*
**Salem, the Novel**  (historic fiction)
    *paper and ebook*
**The Second Assassination** (historic mystery novel)
    *ebook*

# Murder on Third Avenue

## Part 1
### ONE

The office that served as Carson Williamson's base of operations was huge. In point of fact, Carson Williamson's office was the largest in the entire 35-story Harmon Hall Building—for the simple reason that Carson Williamson was president and CEO of the venerable publishing giant for which the building had been named. It was a big job, and he loved it.

In the Harmon Hall Building on Third Avenue Carr Williamson was king. When things were going well, as they had been of late, he felt like a king, too. Not that anyone around him would ever sense this, for Williamson was not that kind of egoist. He was very much aware that his success derived as much from good fortune as it did from sheer brilliance on his part. Not that he wasn't bright. In conversations and in meetings he'd always been one or two thoughts ahead of most of his colleagues. He'd always been good at games, and business was just one more game that he was good at. And for playing the game of business as well as he did, the board compensated him in excess of $5,000,000 each year. Yes, things were going quite well for the small-town boy from Western Pennsylvania. He planned to enjoy the ride, and go as far as it would take him.

As was his practice, he'd gotten to work earlier than his staff this Monday morning. A little before eight. He liked to get started early. Gave him an edge. He could meet with key staffers between eight and nine and not have to worry about interruptions. It also set the tone for the entire staff. Everyone knew he was in early, so others, especially those who reported directly to him, felt a tacit pressure to get in early, too, and to be sharp. Williamson felt no compunction about asking people to meet with him at eight A.M.—or even 7:30 on some occasions. They were making good money, and they should expect to work as long as, and within reason, at the convenience of, the boss.

At 49, Williamson was at the pinnacle of his career. CEO of one of the largest and most prestigious publishing companies in America, he thoroughly enjoyed his position. Since being named to head up the company, he'd "stolen" a few bestselling authors from other houses, and he'd brought in several new promising writers who'd really taken off. He'd also started a highly successful reference division and expanded virtually every other profitable unit in the company. And he'd gotten rid of — either by selling off or writing off — several unprofitable divisions. He'd done all this in just three years, and improved the bottom line at the same time. Harmon Hall had never been so profitable, nor more visible in the industry.

"Excuse me Mr. Williamson," said Betsy Conway, his assistant, interrupting his thoughts. He looked up and across the expansive office toward the open door. Betsy had long ago proven to be invaluable. She'd been with him in his previous job when he was senior v.p. for sales and marketing at a major competitor. When he landed the CEO position at Harmon Hall, he'd asked her to follow him. She stood now in the doorway. "Your wife's on the phone. Says it'll only take a minute."

He looked at his watch. Exactly 9:00 a.m. Laura rarely called him at the office. She knew he had a full schedule every day, and she didn't like to bother him unless it was fairly important. Not that he normally minded it when she called, but when she did, it was often when he was in the middle of something, and he knew that at these times he sounded more abrupt than he intended.

"Hi, what's up?" he said, trying not to sound impatient.

"Did I get you at a bad time?"

"No, this is fine. What's up?"

"I just wanted to remind you that today is Jennifer's birthday."

"Damn. I'd completely forgotten. What're we getting her?"

"New skis, remember?" said his wife patiently. And I'm sure you also remember that we've got a reservation for eight o'clock at Château du Lac. It was all she could talk about this morning. She's really looking forward to it."

He'd completely forgotten, but he replied without missing a beat, "What happened to my little girl who couldn't get enough of McDonald's?"

"Your little girl is 17. She's gotten wise like the rest of us."

"Yeah, and her new-found wisdom is going to cost us in the next few years," he parried. "By the way, I assume, in my unforgivable and typically presumptuous way, that you've gotten the skis?"

"Of course. If I waited for you, your daughter would ski on her bare feet. All you have to do is show up tonight. Don't disappoint her, Carr. She worships you." Then she added teasingly, "Why, I don't know. You're such a loser." "You called me first thing in your day to tell me that?"

"No, but I didn't want you to forget Jennifer's birthday and dinner tonight." She paused for a moment, "Carr, as long as I have you on the phone... we haven't had a chance to talk at home very much lately. I hope you'll be home at a decent hour the rest of the week. I haven't seen much of you recently. This job of yours..."

"Laura, the late nights bother me as much as they do you, believe me. Look, I'll do the best I can. In the meantime let me get back to what's ahead of me today so I can make dinner tonight."

"I'm sorry if I sound like an old shrew, Carr, but you know it's true. It seems like we never get to see each other anymore—except to exchange a quick peck on the cheek in the morning as you rush off. Oh, I'm sorry, I know you're busy. I guess I'm just jealous."

Carr felt a flush in his temples. "What d'you mean by that?"

"It's your *job*. I know, it's the job of a lifetime, and you've earned it, but damn it, Carr, it's become your whole life."

*Does every wife use the same script writer?* At times like this, and it seemed as if such times were becoming more and more common, Carr Williamson found himself visualizing a recurring and surprisingly vivid image of himself in the dungeon of some unnamed castle in medieval England. He was looking down upon himself—in the manner of the out-of-body near-death experiences he'd read about in books by Raymond Moody and Betty Eadie. He could clearly see his physical body, clad only in white loincloth, spread-eagled on the cold, damp surface of the dungeon's torture rack. Each limb was slowly, but inexorably being stretched —— until finally, with a sickening sucking sound, first his arms; then his legs popped out of their sockets, leaving him limbless in excruciating pain, and —— worst of all —— unable to fend for himself ever again. He wasn't even sure if they had the rack in medieval England, but he was certain that his mind was working overtime lately. Fortunately, or maybe unfortunately, he knew why.

There were two possible ways to respond to Laura's complaints about his late nights. He could respond rationally, or he could respond emotionally. He knew she deserved the reasoned response, but in the interest of a newly evolved selective honesty, and despite the dissimulation upon which this honesty rested, he chose the easier, or at least quicker, way.

"I'm sorry, Laura, but my work is what allows you and Jennifer to live as well as you do. I gotta go."

Laura winced, recognizing the all-to-familiar signs of what she perceived as a stressed-out husband. She hated to let it drop like this, but she knew he probably had people waiting to see him, and any prolongation of the conversation would only add to his stress. "Okay, will you be able to get home in time to relax a bit before we go to dinner?"

"I'll try, but I may just get home in time to get to the restaurant in time for our reservation. I'll do my best, Laura. Gotta go."

As he put the phone down he saw that Betsy had materialized in the doorway. Three or four years older than Williamson, Betsy was still an attractive woman. Williamson knew that more than one senior executive at Harmon Hall viewed her exactly that way —— as more than just the efficient assistant to the boss. He could tell by how they looked at her that many of them saw her as an attractive woman in her own right. The younger managers might see her that way, too, but most of them were probably too intimidated by her officious manner to think of her as anything but their boss's assistant.

"Stuart Markham has been waiting," she said.

"Ask him to come in." Markham was editor-in-chief of Harmon Hall. He was also a senior vice president. He'd been asked to be at Carr's office at nine, but because of the call from Laura, he'd been cooling his heels for almost 15 minutes.

"Stuart, sorry to keep you waiting."

"Good morning, Carr. I'm curious as to the subject of our meeting this morning." Markham stood aristocratically in his impeccably tailored double-breasted suit. Nothing in his demeanor indicated that he was annoyed at being made to wait. "When Betsy called yesterday, Cathy couldn't get a word out of her."

That was Markham's way of admitting that he was curious. His aloof mien suggested to anyone he came in contact with that he was above any human frailty, save perhaps arrogance. He was reasonably civil with Williamson, however, but only because Carr was his boss. With the vast majority of people Stuart Markham comported himself in the stuffy and self-important manner of an English country gentleman. It was clear that even his toleration of Williamson was tempered by his knowledge that he predated Carr at Harmon Hall by at least 20 years. It was his company. Like a Down-Easterner's scorn for a new resident, Markham still thought of Williamson as a Johnny-come-lately.

At the very heart of the matter was Markham's thinly disguised resentment of Williamson for winning the job they had both been vying for three years ago. Word was that a majority of the board had been ready to cast their votes for Markham. People who knew Stuart only casually were impressed by his European charm and easy manner in virtually any situation. Carr suspected that many on the board, accomplished people in their own right, were a little star-struck by the array of famous and near-famous authors and celebrities with whom Stuart hobnobbed on a regular basis. And it didn't hurt that Stuart came from an old

New York family of some prominence. His father had been a congressman. Grandfather a highly successful newspaperman. His sister, Alice, was a bestselling novelist. Her books were published by a competitor across the street.

In one easy motion Markham eased his slender six-foot frame into the red leather chair in front of Williamson's enormous desk.

Williamson remained standing for a minute. Probably a bit theatrical, he thought, but you couldn't overdo it with Stuart. As he sat down, he smiled at Markham who, in the meantime, had assumed a cinematically patrician pose with legs crossed and right arm casually thrown over the back of the chair.

*Arrogant prick.* "Stuart, I've got good news. The board's approved your budget for the dictionary."

"Excellent. I was confident they would."

*You sonofabitch!* It bothered Carr to go on. "They okayed your timetable, too. In fact, they didn't change a thing."

"You act surprised, Carr. You must admit it was a good business plan." He smiled smugly; then added with a smirk, "I'm sure you did a good job selling it, though."

"It was your presentation that did it, Stuart. It was a good plan," said Carr, ignoring the implied slight. *Don't let this elitist bastard get to you, Carr. You're the boss for Christ's sake.* "But, $18 million is still a lot of money for one book." As he looked across his desk at Markham, he asked himself for the hundredth time why he didn't get rid of this man. He knew the answer, of course. Markham was the finest book editor in New York, and since New York was the center of the publishing industry in the U.S., that made him the finest book editor in America. Markham's offensive manner aside, Williamson knew that much of the company's success in winning top authors was due to Stuart's editorial ability and to his reputation for having worked with the best authors in the country for nearly three decades.

"Who are you going to put in charge of the project, Stuart?"

"Tony and I discussed it at some length. He thinks Jacqui Dyer would be perfect. I have to say I agree. She's young, Carr, but she's a good editor. Handles people well, too. And she's a good businesswoman. But Tony will keep an eye on her, and I'll be monitoring the project, so don't worry."

"How soon can you get started?"

"Today."

An hour-and-a-half later and after six more phone calls plus a brief, encouraging meeting in his office with the company's head bean counter confirming that both sales and profits were up, and a brief, frustrating meeting with the director of human resources reminding him that the company was still far short of its minority hiring goals, Betsy buzzed to say that Katherine Ferrara was on the line.

"Morning. What's goin' on?" said Williamson with a smile on his face.

"Did you have a nice weekend?" asked the cheerful voice on the other end.

"It was all right. I know how it could have been better."

"Me too. You'll have to work on that. As you know, the ball's in your court."

The conversation was making him feel ambivalent. He felt more alive when he spoke with Kate. At the same time he found himself suppressing any conscious assessment of the merits of what he was doing. Why did she have to push it when everything was fine just the way it was? "I'm well aware of that. Let's not talk about weekends. Let's talk about this week," he said, sounding more businesslike than he'd intended.

"Is the king being presidential?"

*Christ! me and my big mouth.* "Did I get carried away with myself the other night? Remind me never to talk about myself when I'm drinking wine. How about lunch tomorrow?"

"I've got a better idea. Why not dinner tonight?"

"Can't. Laura and I are taking Jennifer out to dinner tonight. Her birthday. Seventeen."

"I understand." She did understand, and even if she didn't she wasn't about to pressure Williamson where his daughter was concerned. Kate Ferrara hadn't become the youngest lawyer and first woman to make partner at the firm of Blythe, Goodstein, and Blum because she was stupid. A moderately patient woman, all five feet six of her, she was reasonably certain that she loved Carr and wanted someday to spend the rest of her life with him. But that could wait. Her career was in overdrive now, and her present social life was all she could handle in light of the demands that career placed on her. She doubted if she'd be able to see Carr more than the two nights a week plus the occasional lunch that they were able to manage now and then. Not without sacrificing her position in the firm. "Of course I understand, Carr. Let's do lunch tomorrow. One. Same place?"

"Same place at one. By the way, before you go, what's the latest on the Schumacher suit?"

"We're filing next week. I'll keep you posted, that is if I can get an appointment to see you."

"We should be able to arrange that."

## TWO

Andy was furious—and yes—humiliated. The latest blow had come this morning, when once again he'd been slighted by his boss, Tony Marcantonio. Tony, unfortunately, was editorial director of the Reference Division. It was two in the afternoon now. Andy had just returned from lunch, if you call eating a hot dog on the street by yourself lunch. That's the way he ate most of his lunches lately. He used to go out with colleagues—couldn't really call them friends—but that hadn't worked out so well. Once in awhile he'd meet an old friend for lunch, but even that didn't happen as much as it used to. He didn't enjoy the kind of conversation most guys engaged in at lunch, or any other time, for that matter. He despised the small talk of most men—gross, preadolescent simple-minded drivel. He hated sports. Obviously wasn't a skirt chaser. Not into traditional male bonding. He smiled at the image. Even though he tried to be cordial on those increasingly rare occasions when he went out to lunch with other guys, he found he simply didn't have a lot in common with most of them. Andy let his gaze drift toward the window. He realized that he had even fewer women friends. But it didn't matter, really, did it. He did have Paul. He turned once more toward his desk.

Then he saw the note. It was from Kelly, his boss's assistant. Just a quick hand scrawl asking him to stop in to see Tony when he got back from lunch. *Well...* he muttered wryly to himself. *To what do I owe this honor?* Andy pulled himself out of his chair and walked down the hall past the six doors that separated his office from the corner office of Tony Marcantonio.

"Good, you're here. Sit down." It was Tony's usual blunt greeting, thought Andy, as he dropped into the comfortable easy chair and looked suspiciously around the spacious office he'd seen so little of in recent months. Must be at least 400-square-feet. Definitely not an E-level, the term Administrative Services used to describe his modest one-window office. Either a B or maybe a C. Corporate bullshit for office size according to job size. Regardless of how they labelled it, it was a very nice corner office with floor-to-ceiling windows on the two outside walls. Trendy modern graphics on the other two walls—plus a built-in mahogany bookshelf displaying many of the company's recent titles. And wall-to-wall carpeting to protect Tony's tender feet. Nice office.

"Andy, I asked you to drop by because I wanted to tell you about a decision I've just made. Wanted you to know about it before I announced it to the staff."

He forced a smile he didn't feel. "Well, you've certainly got my interest," He didn't like the sound of this.

"Here's the situation. We've got the board's approval to do a major unabridged dictionary. Stuart's wanted to do this for some time. As you know, Harmon Hall has never done a monster like this before. Lots of standard-size dictionaries, but never an unabridged one. It'll be the biggest book project this company's ever undertaken—by far. Twenty-eight hundred pages. Four-hundred-fifty-thousand entries. Nothing's ever been done to compare with what we're going to do. Both a print and an electronic version. Budgeted for a little over $18 million. Promotion budget alone comes to over $3 million. This dictionary's going to be a cash cow for Harmon Hall for years to come. We're sort of in the same situation Tandem was in back in the '80s when they did their first unabridged dictionary. Word is, they originally budgeted around $7 mil. But the project quickly got out of hand and eventually ended up costing them over twelve. That's in '80s dollars. Took 'em eight or nine years to complete the project. We're not going to let that happen here. We're doing ours in five years, and we're keeping to budget."

Andy couldn't wait much longer. He only cared about one thing at this point: *Who the hell was going to be in charge?* Finally, as his boss paused for a moment, he said, "Why do you think we can do a better job than Tandem did?" *Jesus, I'm avoiding the question I don't dare ask.*

"It's all in how you organize the project. The first few years they were all fucked up. Finally someone saw what was happening, and they replaced the project editor. By then, it was too late. But there are other differences, too. This becomes our master database. From this baby we can spin off all the other English-language dictionaries we do for years to come. Not to mention the revenue we'll get from licensing rights. But most important of all, think of the electronic versions we can do."

He couldn't get excited about all that—at least not until he knew who was going to be in charge. "Who's going to head up the project?" he asked in a voice hardly above a whisper.

"I've asked Jacqui Dyer to be the project editor. She's got the most dictionary experience, and she's a good organizer."

He felt weak. His pulse started racing. *This can't be.* "You didn't think I could handle it?"

"Not true at all. I had to make a decision, that's all. We've got three senior editors in this division, and I had to consider the strengths of each of them and how the division as a whole would benefit. On balance I think she's the best choice for this job. That doesn't mean you couldn't do it. Not at all. I just think, when you consider everything, she's the right choice. But there's lots else to be done here besides this project."

"Like revising the desk and college dictionaries? "Tony, you know that's not the same,"

"Look, of course it's not the same, but it's important work, and it's got to be done. And I'm counting on you to take the bull by the horns and do the great job I know you're capable of."

*Fucking cheerleader.*

The meeting had gone on for another ten minutes. He'd tried unsuccessfully to persuade Tony to reconsider. In the end he'd left quietly—nursing a splitting headache.

Back in his office he tried to be objective about the company. He knew no company was perfect. But when he looked at things objectively, it did nothing for his spirits. The facts merely proved that what he felt in his gut was not some figment of his imagination. The facts made things seem worse—if that were possible. The facts proved that he was getting screwed by the company, and his nitwitted boss was the prime screwdriver—the perfect company tool. Despite his frustration he smiled inwardly at the analogy.

When he'd joined the company six years ago he'd had high hopes. It certainly wasn't his fault the company was riddled with politics—that people here were more interested in clinging to the right coattails than in simply being right.

During the past six years Andy had learned that intelligence was not valued at Harmon Hall. It was who you knew and who's ass you kissed. Nobody was interested in someone who'd tell it like it is. Everybody lied through their teeth in order to ingratiate themselves with their boss. They chose to call it tact. He knew better. Tact, bullshit! Unadulterated ass-kissing politics. He'd always thought Jacqui was different, though. Obviously he'd been wrong. She was a suck-up just like the rest of them. *Bitch.* He was no politician. He knew that. Probably should have been though. Would have made things a lot easier. Would have been a lot further along in his career.

He felt like an island in a sea of sycophantic yuppies. The only positive thing he could say for the job after six years was that he still got paid—and he certainly did need the money.

Outside it was a gorgeous day. Stark contrast with the way his day was going. Another person under different circumstances might actually enjoy the view. From where he sat he could see the sun reflecting off the middle floors of the glass tower of the monolithic CitiCorp building a few blocks north up on Fifty-Third Street. Just to the left of CitiCorp, if he leaned far to the right, he could make out a slice of a sun-drenched Central Park. Not a bad view, considering... Still, he only had the one window, but what could you expect from an E-level office. E-level offices ranged from 90 to 110 square feet. His, at ten by ten, fell right in the middle at 100 square feet. Senior editors rated E-level offices.

Andy Mack did not consider himself paranoid—despite what his live-in partner, Paul, kept telling him. What could Paul know about Harmon Hall, anyway? Paul didn't work here. Face it, he really was getting screwed. Witness the screwing he'd just gotten down the hall. Being passed over for Jacqui Dyer, of all people. Fucking Jacqui Dyer! *"God, why did they do this to me?* He should have realized something was brewing this morning when Tony deliberately snubbed him by not inviting him to the 10:00 a.m. meeting in the office of senior v.p. of sales and marketing, Mike Clancy. Tony's boss, Stuart Markham, who was editor-in-chief and also a senior v.p., had been there, too. When he'd first heard about the morning meeting, Andy had thought that it was just another example of Tony, as usual, being afraid of being overshadowed by someone with more smarts and more talent. And what better way to prevent that someone from overshadowing you than not inviting him to important meetings.

He now realized that it was more than Tony's insecurities that kept him from inviting Andy. The purpose of the meeting was to put the final nail in

Andy Mack's career coffin. And it wouldn't have taken place if Tony had been more supportive. In fact, it probably took place at Tony's request. . .

If it were just this morning's meeting, he could have forgiven Tony, but this was the latest in a long series of slights and insults. It had started years ago, but got much worse about six months ago when Tony had gotten annoyed because Andy had shown him up in a meeting. As it turned out, it was the last important meeting Andy'd been asked to attend. Andy hadn't intended to show him up. Not at all. Not that it could have been avoided, considering how inept his boss was. All he'd really done was explain how a couple of Tony's facts were wrong. And then he'd shown him how easy it would have been to have gotten them right. Okay, so Markham and Clancy had heard him explain all this to Tony. But Tony had been wrong. And he knew he was wrong. *But he gets pissed off at me!* He should have been pissed at himself for being so stupid.

Andy had come to Harmon Hall right out of college. Started as a rep, and quickly decided he didn't like sales. Fortunately, Allan Larkin, his boss at the time, had understood when he'd asked for a transfer to the editorial department. Larkin had been supportive, had seemed almost as relieved as he was. At the time, editorial had an opening for an assistant editor—he'd skipped right over the entry-level position of editorial assistant. Back then, at least, there were people in this boot-licking company who recognized his potential. He'd risen fairly fast—considering how dumb most of the key people in the company were. First, to associate editor, and then to his present position as senior editor. But then he'd encountered super jock Marcantonio. When Tony wasn't talking about the Knicks or the Giants, he was playing softball with the other moronic juveniles on the company team. For Christ's sake, thought Andy, the guy must be over 40.

When's he going to grow up?.

Since he'd been reporting to Tony Marcantonio, his own career had come to a grinding halt. Just last night Paul had told him that he'd do a lot better if he wouldn't mock Tony behind his back—especially in meetings. Andy knew that Paul meant well, but he also knew that he really didn't understand. He wasn't there day in and day out to see what an idiot Marcantonio was.

He thought he knew himself pretty well. He knew that he never had much patience with the back-slapping, loud, rowdy jock type. He knew he was one of those rare, intellectually-gifted, serious types. Oh, he had a sense of humor. People didn't always get his humor, but that simply proved what he'd known most of his life: He was sharper than 90 percent of the people he met.

He was reminded of the computer term *trivial*. In the world of computers there are trivial programs. Well, he thought smugly, in the world of human beings, most people live what he viewed as trivial lives. God, what a boring agenda most people tolerated. Here at Harmon Hall, where everyone was supposedly educated and relatively smart, you'd expect people to act as if their lives had substance. Instead, most of them lived a trivial, superficial existence—nurturing their puerile shallowness with a steady diet of ball games, rock concerts, next weekend's party, celebrity gazing at the current empty-headed film star, five hours of TV a night, and flipping ga-ga-eyed through *People* Magazine.

He wondered if he were honest with himself he'd consider his own life so substantial. Talk about trivial. For God's sake, where was his career going? Where was his life going? Here he was, 29, and all he could foresee for his next few years in publishing was more of the same. What had happened to all the grandiose plans he'd had for himself back in college?

Back then he was going to make it big in publishing. Well, the first few years had gone more or less as planned. But lately....

And once he was out of the cliquish, arrested-development environment of the residential college, he was going to muster up the courage to come out of the closet. But it had been clear from the start that being avowedly gay was not going to help his career—despite what they said about publishing being so accepting. He quickly found that this vaunted acceptance depended on what department and what company you were in. Oh, there were those who everyone knew were gay, but none of them rose above a certain level in the company. Certainly not this company.

What bothered him most about the whole situation was that he wasn't really sure why he'd stayed in the closet. The reason he gave Paul was that it would have hurt his career. After today, though, could it get much worse? He lived his life as if the reason he gave Paul were, in fact, the real reason. And maybe, hopefully, it was. But somewhere below the surface of the shaky beliefs that he allowed to be tossed up onto the turbulent beach of his consciousness, he harbored thoughts that it might really be a matter of courage, or more accurately, lack of courage. If he'd gotten the job Jacqui got, would he have come out? He didn't know, and that, on top of all his other troubles, bothered him a lot.

# THREE

Williamson left his office at 12:50. He'd be late, damn it. Couldn't be helped. Didn't really have time for this. Wasn't like him at all. At least not until four weeks ago when their business relationship had gone far beyond the limits of professional propriety. Five weeks ago he would have canned a staff member for doing exactly what he was doing. He knew all the arguments against it. He knew also that he couldn't stop now. Kate was not just another attractive woman. She really was something special. *Jesus, even that's a cliché.*

He hated to make a woman wait in a restaurant. Especially a place like this, if you could call Canavan's a restaurant. Sure, the occasional suit would drop in for lunch and a beer...sort of the way British businessmen sometimes stopped in at a pub. But Canavan's on First Avenue definitely was not one of the places people who'd arrived ate their lunch. Hell, it wasn't even the kind of place where people on the way up had lunch. Food wasn't bad,though, considering how the place looked...more like a blue-collar bar with food than like a restaurant. Not the kind of place you'd expect to find the president of one of America's foremost publishing companies.

This, of course, was precisely why he and Kate had chosen the place. The likelihood that they'd be seen there by anyone they knew was remote to say the least. If he were honest with himself though, he'd admit that he didn't come to Canavan's just to avoid being seen. The truth was that the clandestine nature of these lunch-time trysts was itself a high that appealed to the unconventional corner of his mind that had long ago been tamed into submission as he mastered the behavior patterns of upper-middle class America.

At this moment, alternately jogging and walking across town, he didn't feel conflicted about what he was doing. The fact that he was cheating on Laura had been conveniently tucked away in the excitement of the approaching furtive meeting. His only concern now was that he was going to be late. Not that Kate wouldn't understand. Hell, she might even be late herself. Busy corporate lawyers are always running late. But if either of them were late, they'd have less time together at lunch. And he had to be back in his office by 2:30 for a meeting he himself had called a week ago. And since over the past three years he'd established himself as a punctilious and demanding chief, it only undermined the managerial discipline he worked so hard to put in force when he, the boss, was late. Damn. Why hadn't he taken a cab? One of those oppressively hot muggy New York days. Must be 95 degrees, with humidity to match. All he could think of now as he avoided colliding with a senior citizen shuffling slowly in front of him on the crowded sidewalk was that he was going to be a sweaty slob by the time he met Kate. That's not the image he, Carr Williamson, wanted to project.

The interior of the place was cool and inviting. An Irish bar that had taken on airs, Canavan's had a back room that had recently been redecorated in a surprisingly good imitation of an Old World pub. It was now called a dining room. Wasn't a bad job, really. Wood everywhere. Comfortable booths crafted of varnished dark wood or, at least, wood stained to appear dark, hugged three of the room's wood-paneled walls. Framed lithographs, ironically hunting scenes from England, looked down upon each booth. Subdued lighting contributed to the illusion of privacy, giving each booth the warm atmosphere of a secure sanctuary.

He had to squint as he entered the room. Adjusting to the dim lighting, he saw that Kate was already seated. She'd chosen a corner booth—about as private as you could get in this already remote dining room far from the beaten path of corporate America's luncheon haunts.

"Mind if I join you?" he asked, wiping his brow with his monogrammed handkerchief.

"Not at all. I've been looking for a tall handsome gentleman." Then she added with a broad smile, "You'll do."

"Sorry I'm late. My office is a goddamn trap."

"You love it, and you know it."

*Christ, does she look good.* "I suppose I do, but it does get harder every month to divorce myself from the place. Seems to permeate every part of my life. Used to love it. Guess being a workaholic goes with the turf. But I'll tell you something, Katie..."

"Kate, remember."

"Sorry, forgot. Temporary lapse due to corporate overload. As I was saying... What the hell was I saying?"

"Something about how you used to love the corporate game, but..."

"But now I need to put it into some kind of balanced perspective. All work and no play and all that bullshit. I'm not sure what I'm trying to say really." As Williamson trailed off, a perky young waitress materialized at the booth.

"Hi, my name is Wendy. I'll be your waitress. Can I get you something from the bar?"

Kate rolled her cobalt blue eyes upward, and with a grin at Williamson said, "Yes, Wendy, "I'll have some mineral water. Do you have Pellegrino?"

"I'm sorry, we only have Evian and Perrier."

"Perrier will be fine."

"I'll have the same, said Williamson.

"Carr, I think I understand what you're saying about being trapped in your job. I'm sure I don't have to tell you, though, that there's a few million people out there who'd sell their collective souls to trade places with you. You're making great money. You've got prestige, respect, and you're the envy of everyone in the industry." said Kate, her large eyes expressing far more than her words the depth of her feeling for what he was grappling with.

"I know it. It's crazy. How can I expect you to understand when I don't understand myself."

"Oh you're wrong there, my friend. I do understand. Listen, you're the king, and it's lonely at the top," she blurted with a grin.

"Touché," his expression softened. "We'd better order." He was finally relaxing. Looking across the table at his lover his thoughts returned to the previous evening.

Dinner at Château du Lac had not gone well. Everyone, Laura, Jennifer, and Carr had gone to the gracious French restaurant looking forward to a pleasant family evening. He'd only been a few minutes late. That had not been the issue. When they'd been seated at Laura and Carr's favorite table by the window overlooking the reservoir, he'd cheerfully asked,

"So, how's my favorite daughter?"

Laura had responded preemptively, before Jennifer could answer, "If you were home more, you wouldn't have to ask." Laura knew it was a mistake as soon as the words left her mouth.

He'd responded in kind, and the tone for the evening was set. "Dammit, Laura, you know as well as I do how much it bothers me. I work late because I have to. Don't you think I'd like to be home earlier? This is not a nine-to-five kind of job."

"Hey guys," cried Jennifer, "Remember me. My birthday."

After that, Carr and Laura had made an effort to salvage the evening, but the night, if not an unmitigated disaster, had been far from the festive occasion the three members of the Williamson family had hoped for.

"Earth to Starship Enterprise, Earth to Starship. Can you hear me?"

"Sorry," he said sheepishly, "Just thinking about something."

"Hey, I know you've got a lot on your mind, but we only have an hour-and-a-half." She smiled warmly. "Anything you want to tell me?"

"Just last night. We took Jennifer out to dinner for her birthday. Anyway, it was a disaster."

"How so?"

"We weren't there two minutes before Laura and I were at each other tooth and claw."

"I think you mean tooth and nail."

Williamson frowned in mock annoyance.

"I'm sorry," grinned Kate. "Not a good time to be pedantic. Go on. I'll be good."

"She complained, rightfully, I might add, that I was never home anymore, and how was I going to get to know my daughter that way. She meant a lot more than just that, I'm sure, but that itself was enough. Does everyone having an affair get hung up on guilt, or am I unique?"

"I'm sure you're not unique," she asked, concern etched on her face. "Am I detecting cold feet?"

"You're making this even more complicated, Kate."

"By asking a perfectly logical question?"

"Yes, I suppose so. By forcing me to come to grips with things I've been shoving under the rug for the past few weeks. Damn! If this were a business problem I'd have no trouble handling it."

"If this were a business problem, we wouldn't be here, we'd be in your office, and I'd be giving you legal advice my hero. But it's not, and we're not... and I'm not. I can't help you with this one, my sweet, but I do feel my question is a fair one. Are you getting cold feet?"

"No, I don't think so. My problem, I suppose, is

one of guilt. Jennifer is an innocent victim in all this. And I feel responsible."

"And Laura?"

"What do you mean?"

"Do you feel Laura's a victim, too?"

"I'm not sure. I'm trying to be fair minded about all this. I suppose if you take into consideration her lack of consideration for my problems and my needs, I'm as much a victim as she is. She has to share some of the responsibility."

"And me?" asked Kate. "Am I victim or perp?"

"You're definitely not perp," he grinned. "I suppose you're victimized by the situation, too."

"All right, king, what's the bottom line to all of this?

The tautness in his face relaxed a bit, and he smiled, "The bottom line is I care about you, and I have to wrestle with my own problems."

Wendy returned with the drinks and proceeded to recite from memory an elaborate menu of luncheon specials.

"I'll have the bluefish with salsa cruda," said Kate.

"That sounds good. Make it two."

"I said I couldn't advise you on this," she continued, "but I guess we lawyers can only go so long without giving some counsel. You know, my love, that the ball is in your court. There is a solution, and you're going to have to face it someday. Neither of us is in any hurry now, least of all me, but I'll tell you how much I love you. I love you enough to tell you that leading two lives is going to tear you apart eventually. It's not so hard on me because I'm single. I don't have to make up stories for my family -only my colleagues — and yours. You have a family you're lying to, and that duplicity is eating away at you. You're basically an honest person, but our relationship has forced you to do something that goes against the grain."

"Are you suggesting what I think you are?"

"You don't want to hear this right now, and I'm not sure I do either, but I guess what I'm saying is that you're going to have to make a choice soon—for the sake of your own mental and physical health. You can't go on like this. Running a major corporation is a full-time job that very few people could handle. You're one of the few who can, Carr. Running a company well and being a good husband and a good father on top of it would be too much for most men. Throw in a clandestine affair and the equation doesn't work. It's too much for any man, even you. You're going to spend more and more of your time agonizing over what you're doing, and your work's going to suffer at the very least. More than likely, though, you'll suffer, too...a breakdown or a coronary. I'm sorry to sound so negative. You know that's not me normally, but I care, dammit."

"I can handle it. Thanks for the concern, though. That's why I love you."

"You can handle it. God, I thought you were more evolved than that. You can handle it. How long before you break? And do you really want to go on like this? Do you want to handle it? And where's it all heading?"

"I thought you were content with the present arrangement." His eyes focused directly on hers.

"You don't get it, do you? This isn't about me. I'm trying to keep you from destroying yourself. It's you who can't keep this up; not me. You must see that."

The fact of the matter was he did see it. If his ego weren't so big, he'd admit it. He'd grown accustomed to expecting deferential treatment from the people around him. No one but Laura had the temerity to try to examine his thinking, and as of late her steady carping had gotten to be intolerable. It was her constant riding that was what had forced him into this mess in the first place.  No, he knew that wasn't true. He'd gotten himself into it, but by the time he got home late at night or just before he'd leave for work in the morning, he was in no mood for having his life subjected to scrutiny and analysis.  And now Kate was doing it, and with unerring accuracy, too.  Of course she was right.  Of course she was doing it because she loved him.  He knew in his heart that he couldn't go on like this.  But the consequences of changing the equation in the slightest way seemed worse than the admittedly stress-laden status quo.  Was he really prepared to make the final break with Laura?  And how could he tell Jennifer?  How would Howard, his boss, take it?  Christ, he dreaded that as much as anything.  Especially now. Howard Harmon, a robust 64 and grandson of the founder of Harmon Hall Publishing Company, was chairman of the parent company, $12 billion multinational giant Harmon Communications, Inc.

  Just yesterday Howard Harmon had invited Williamson to lunch at the Four Seasons.  Howard had told him then that he was thinking of retiring soon from the chairmanship of Harmon Communications. Jim Crandall, the current president and CEO of the parent company would be kicked upstairs into the chairmanship.  The board and Howard wanted a proactive, imaginative person to replace Crandall as CEO.  Someone like Williamson.  Howard intended to recommend Carr for that position at the appropriate time.  He'd indicated that that time wasn't far off, probably less than a year.  But Howard, despite his renowned ruthlessness in business, was a confirmed family man, and had actually fired a senior manager once because he was having an affair.

  Williamson looked around the noisy dining room, *Thank God the place was off the beaten path.*  He wanted the CEO job at the parent company so much he could taste it.  He couldn't afford to do anything now that might tarnish his image in the eyes of his boss.

"Okay, you're probably right. If I were to make the break tomorrow, would you be ready to make a commitment?" he asked seriously.

"Loosen up. You sound like you're negotiating a publishing contract instead of talking to your lover. Are you asking me to marry you?"

"I suppose I am."

Her eyes softened. "Yes, I would marry you. But don't forget, if you tell Laura tomorrow, it'll be a year or two before you're free. But it would certainly get us one step closer. Are you ready to make the break?"

"I don't know. But you're right, we can't go on this way indefinitely." He went on to tell her about his luncheon with Harmon and how much he really wanted the job that Harmon had dangled in front of him. "Do you think I'm a worm if I hold off making a break with Laura until Howard and the board act on the CEO position?"

"No, you're not a worm, you're a political animal. I don't like it, but I understand. But that doesn't erase what I said before. Leading two lives is taking its toll on you, big fellow, and I don't know if you'll last until the board acts. What good is the job if you're dead?"

"Don't you think you're being a bit melodramatic, Kate?"

"No, I don't. I hope I'm wrong, though."

"Look, can we agree that we'll discuss this again in a month or two. We both know that it can't go on this way indefinitely. But, remember, we've really only been seeing each other a few weeks — even though it seems as if I've known you a lot longer."

"I'd say it can't go on this way any longer than six months or until the board makes its decision -- whichever comes first. Can we agree to that?"

Williamson, feeling inwardly relieved, said "Done. I'll tell Laura two weeks after one of those events occurs. I don't think I should do it the same day the board makes its announcement. Okay?"

"Okay," she gave him a knowing smile. "God, you are a politician. Okay. Let's change the subject. What's new in the king's business realm?"

"You're not going to leave that alone are you?"

"Do you really mind so much?"

"I guess not, as long as we're alone."

"We're always alone. You're having an affair, remember."

"How could I forget? But we're not alone when you function in your official capacity." He was referring to the fact that Kate was the partner at the law firm of Smythe, Goodstein and Blum assigned to the Harmon Hall account. That, of course, was how Carr and Kate had met in the first place, both of them violating every law in the book of professional conduct. It had all started innocently enough. A few meetings with other executives present. Then a few private meetings in his office. Eventually they would meet for lunch to talk over company business and one thing had lead to another. The chemistry had been there from the first day Irving Goodstein had introduced her as the partner of account for Harmon Hall Publishing Company.

"No, we're not alone then," she said with a look of amused exasperation. "I repeat, what's new in the world of business?"

"It's probably not that exciting to most people outside of publishing, but we just decided today to go ahead and build the biggest unabridged dictionary ever published in the U.S. To the best of my knowledge the only one that's larger is the O.E.D., the Oxford English Dictionary, and that's a multi-volume deal published in England. Ours will definitely be the biggest ever done in one volume."

"You said you were going to *build* it. Sounds like a construction job."

Williamson paused to take a bite of his bluefish.

"In a way it is." he said. "This is such a massive job it'll take us five years and about $18 million. Not exciting to the man...excuse me... person on the street, but exciting stuff around here. It'll make a bit of a flap in the industry, too."

"Wouldn't you spread the risk more by publishing ten or 20 regular big novels instead of putting so many eggs in one basket?"

"Now I see why your firm made you partner at such a tender age," grinned Williamson. "Helluva good question. Actually, this is pretty low on the scale of risks. The likelihood of this being highly profitable is much greater than the chances that the next manuscript from all but a handful of famous novelists will make a lot of money. Did that make sense?"

"I think it did," smiled Kate.

"Once it's done, it becomes an active backlist item for many years. But the real value comes from the database we create to produce it in the first place. From that we can spin off numerous other dictionaries and related products. Not to mention the electronic rights and our own electronic versions. In other words it's a license to print money."

"If that's so, why hasn't some other publisher done this?"

"Most publishers lack our resources. A few of our competitors do have the money, but they lack the staff. The kind of staff I'm referring to is dictionary people or lexicographers. Our reference division has some of the top dictionary editors in the country. And we've got quite a few of them, too. One or two of our competitors have highly competent editors, but lack the money. Don't forget, on top of the $18 million it's going to take to create this mother, it'll take several million more to market it in the first two years. There ain't many guys out there with that kind of muscle."

"Consider me sufficiently impressed. You know, Carr, it's good to see you get excited about your work."

"And I'd better get back to that work. Got a meeting in half an hour."

"How's tomorrow evening look? Want some dinner?"

"Your place?" smirked Williamson.

"Certainly not yours."

# FOUR

He wanted to stay, if only to see what else might happen. Wouldn't be too smart, though. Best he leave before Williamson. God, who would have believed it. Son of a bitch, this was great! The president of Harmon Hall Publishing Company cheating on his wife. You had to believe in fate. Why else would he, Andy Mack, be at the same place for lunch on the same day as Williamson. And this place of all places. The improbability of it all was enough to blow your mind. First time in almost a month he'd eaten lunch in a restaurant. And then to see Carson Williamson in Canavan's. No way. But here he was. No mistaking it.

From his inconspicuous perch seated on the brown naugahyde-covered stool at the dark end of the bar, Andy could see with his very own eyes the boss of all bosses, el presidente himself making ga-ga eyes with that bitch lawyer, Not more than 60 feet away.

God must be looking out for you, Andy Mack. Talk about juicy. He couldn't wait to tell Paul who would indeed appreciate this succulent news item. Paul loved this kind of stuff, but he was usually the one with the stories. Tonight, Andy would have the story to top all stories. But there had to be more than just gossip here. Andy had always had the mind of a conspirator. Usually, though, he enjoyed his conspiracies vicariously. This one, however, was too good to be true. Too good to just watch from the sidelines. There must be some way he could use this to his
own advantage.

"Anything else sir?" asked the bartender more respectfully than Andy'd been treated by anyone at Harmon Hall in the past six months.

"No, just the check," said Andy pleasantly. Nice guy, he thought.

On his way back to the office he could think of

nothing else but Carson Williamson and his *liaison dangereux*. However, Andy was anything if not cautious. What if I'm reading it wrong? he asked himself. What if it's just a business lunch? Sure, and it snows in Miami in August, But maybe that's all it was. Just a business luncheon. All he really had was circumstantial evidence. Right, Right. Lots of CEOs eat at a dump like Canavan's. Great place for the corporate elite to meet to eat. Andy smiled. No, this was no innocent business luncheon. And the kiss was no innocent peck on the cheek. Circumstantial, my ass.

Still, he prided himself on not making knee-jerk decisions, but rather on carrying on Hegelian dialectics with himself. Oh, he had knee-jerk reactions. No denying that. But he usually took action only after carefully considering all the options.

Actually he'd gradually come to respect Williamson over the past three years. Seemed like a smart guy. And not a supercilious prick like most of the senior management at Harmon Hall. Still, Andy had to look out for himself. The company had not been good to him. And Williamson *is* the company's top honcho. If Andy could only find some way to use this information — not necessarily to get revenge on the company — though that would certainly be enjoyable — but to advance his career... Yes, this time it would be more than vicarious. This time Andy would do more than dream. This time he'd take action. But what action? He couldn't afford to waste this opportunity. His career was suffering from terminal neglect and rapidly sliding into the sewer. Action was called for. All he needed was the right idea. God knows, he had the opportunity now. Whatever he did that involved Williamson, would not be personal. The man just happened to conveniently present himself as the ideal target for the as-yet-unborn scheme that Andy knew his fertile unconscious would concoct in the next day or so.

Andy could rationalize his scheming because of a conclusion he'd arrived at a long time ago. Having observed on far too many occasions that the company showed no loyalty to its employees, he'd reluctantly concluded that he owed no allegiance to the company—other than to do the work assigned to him each day.

The dinner Paul had prepared was, as usual, a masterpiece. He should have been a chef, thought, Andy. This was normally the highlight of Andy's day. A great meal, a chance to catch up on Paul's day. Andy didn't like to talk about his own work when he got home, but Paul did love to talk about his photography. Paul sat across the gleaming blond pine Ikea table, beaming. Andy could see that he was waiting for a compliment on the meal, a meal which they hadn't even eaten yet. Paul, aesthete that he was, believed that presentation was as important as the food.

"Well,?" said Paul expectantly, his thin frame leaning back in his chair, arms crossed confidently over his stomach. Paul was two years older than Andy, but didn't look it. He was not the Teutonic type that his thin, angular face and close-cropped sandy-brown hair might have suggested, though to call him gentle would have been to err to the other extreme. Paul was considerate and sensitive, but he was nobody's fool.

"Very pretty. What is it?"

"Pasta puttanesca. You want the English translation?"

"I know, I know. Whore's pasta. How nice. He then pointed to the salad, "And?"

"Four-green salad. New walnut-oil dressing I'm trying. It's got pomegranate juice in it. Bread's from Lombardi's," grinned Paul.

"And the wine? Where is it?"

"It's a barolo. It's in the fridge—to drop the

temp a bit. Should be served close to..."

"I know, 57 degrees for a heavy red. Everything looks great. Tell me about your shoot." He hoped Paul wouldn't have that much to talk about because tonight, for once, he felt like talking about his own work.

"Later, I can tell that you've got something on your mind. Mangia, Mangia," he beamed. "Eat and tell me."

For the first time all day, Andy lightened up. Paul always did this to him. He tasted the pasta and smiled.

"Another winner," he said. Then he turned more serious. "How'd you know I had something to say?"

"I know you."

"Yes, but I didn't do anything to indicate..."

"Don't know, but we've always had this thing between us, you know that, Andy. Anyway, since you've confirmed I'm right, tell me about it. I'm not psychic enough to know the whole story."

"Well you're right. Have I got a story for you."

Paul smiled, "A little less fanfare, please, and more substance."

"I was having lunch today at Canavan's. You know, that Irish joint over on First Avenue that I sometimes eat at."

"Yes, yes. Not such a bad place now since they fixed it up. Who were you with? Should I be jealous?"

Andy smiled confidently. He wasn't sure how Paul viewed his confident smile, but he enjoyed smiling it anyway. It buoyed him to think that his lover, even in jest, could talk about being jealous. Right at this moment, any little boost to his self-confidence was more than welcome.

"I ate alone," he said, a trace of annoyance in his voice. He'd been hoping Paul wouldn't ask. "Change of pace from the old routine. Anyway, it's not my lunch I want to tell you about. It's who I saw."

"Sorry," said Paul, ever the sensitive significant other and kicking himself for asking a question that so obviously embarrassed the man he cared most for in the world. "Tell me, tell me for God's sake. You've got me in suspense."

"Carson Williamson!" he announced dramatically.

"Name's vaguely familiar, can't place it though. Help me." Paul grimaced, knowing as he said it that Andy would be irritated by his failure to make the connection.

"You know who he is. I've mentioned his name before. Shit, half-dozen times at least." Andy felt himself rapidly becoming impatient —— a mood that for him usually augured increasing irritability. It was a side of himself he hated. He could sometimes avert it if he made a conscious effort, but it wasn't easy. Tonight he would make that effort. Calmly now, "He's the top dog at Harmon Hall—president and CEO of the company, and highly respected by everyone."

"You saw him at Canavan's? What's a guy like him doing in a place like that?"

"Exactly," smirked Andy. "Exactly."

"Well...you gonna tell me?"

"I'll tell you. I'll tell you. Just want to get the most out of this moment. He was cheating on his wife. Isn't that fantastic!"

"You know, sometimes I don't figure you at all. Are you saying you're glad he's cheating?"

"On a higher, cosmic level I find it just one more example of how disappointing human beings can be, and that's sad. But long ago I became a cynic, and I'm no longer surprised by anything. On a more pragmatic level, I see his indiscretion as a terrific career opportunity for me. Don't you see. I can use this!"

"I hate it when you talk like this. It's not like

you to want to capitalize on other people's weakness."

"Not the poor slob on the street, but Carson Williamson's a big boy. He can take care of himself."

"And what do you mean you can use this? What do you plan to do, blackmail him?" asked Paul sadly.

"No comment. Listen, this is the opportunity of a lifetime. I'm not letting it pass me by."

"You're nuts, you know that. You're nuts. How do you know he was cheating on his wife? Was he wearing a big A on his chest?"

"Cute. I have eyes. He was having lunch with one of the female lawyers I've seen around the building."

"So, it was a business lunch. That's cheating?"

"You could tell. You could tell by the way they were looking in each other's eyes. Hell, at one point he kissed her."

"Even that could be nothing more than an affectionate token. Are you sure you aren't reading too much into this?"    "Please, I'm not stupid."

"Yes, but you have a penchant for the conspiratorial."

"Trust me on this. It was no token kiss. Besides, a guy like that doesn't go to Canavan's if he cares whether he's going to be seen."

"You went there," said Paul unenthusiastically.

"Yes, I did, but I'm not the president of the company. I'm probably the only one from the company besides Williamson who's ever been to that joint. Believe me, those two are having an affair."

"Look, I don't give a shit if they are or they aren't, Andy. I just don't want to see you go off half-cocked on something that could end up hurting you. What are you planning?"

"I told you, I don't know yet. Something will come to me — soon."

"What kind of something? You gonna tell his

wife for Christ's sake? What would that get you — other than fired?"

"No, I'm not going to tell his wife, but you may just have given me an idea."

"I don't like that look in your eye, Andy."

That night Andy Mack lay in bed going over his options. Something was beginning to take shape. Paul was right. Telling Mrs. Williamson would indeed accomplish nothing but his own termination. But the *threat* of telling her could accomplish a great deal. Wait, if he and his wife were already on the outs, that threat alone might not be effective. But what if he also threatened to tell Howard Harmon. Harmon was a known dinosaur, a real straight arrow. They say he's fired people for the very thing that Andy'd caught Williamson doing red-handed. Yes, yes, this had possibilities. Good possibilities.

Could he do it, though? Did he have the guts to confront Williamson? Andy didn't think of himself as a courageous person. Most of his life he'd shrunk from confrontation. Definitely not a macho man. He smiled at this as he stared up at the ceiling in the dark bedroom. Christ, here I am plotting like Lee Harvey Oswald, mused Andy. No, there's a big difference, he thought. Oswald was a fucking whacko. Definitely not a rational guy. I, on the other hand, have a great deal to gain. Which is quite rational. And I'm not about to kill anybody either. No, all I'm going to do, if I have the guts, is go after what I deserve. If I can pull that off, nobody gets hurt. Big difference.

But did he have the guts to confront Williamson? What if he calls my fucking bluff and cans me on the spot? Sure, I could still tell his wife and Harmon, but what's the percentage. Everybody loses then. That's not what I'm after. Definitely not what I'm after. That would be more in the Oswald tradition. What I need is an insurance policy? What if, thought Andy, I had something in my hip pocket ——

just in case he calls my bluff? And because the gods were obviously looking favorably on Andy's new adventure in self-actualization, the idea came to him.

What if he had a story on reserve that he could call into play if Williamson didn't play ball? What if he could say that he was working on a manuscript of a book about blackmail? Then, as soon as Williamson exploded, Andy could hold up his hand and say, "Whoa. I'm sorry to upset you, sir. This has all been a little test of this manuscript I'm working on. Wanted to see if your reaction jibed with the reaction of the protagonist in the book. I know it was a little unorthodox, but I had to know. The book will be a better book for it." The gods must like the plan, thought Andy, because, as it so happened, he did have just such a manuscript about blackmail in his office. Maybe that's what planted the idea in his head in the first place. The idea was ordained in Heaven.

He'd enjoyed this awake time. He'd never needed much sleep anyway. Now that he'd worked out the broad strokes of his plan, he could fall asleep content. But no, sleep wasn't in the cards. That other nagging thought returned. What if Williamson and the lawyer were innocent. Very unlikely from where he stood, but what real evidence did he have? With what he was risking here, he'd best have more to go on. Ideally he should have some hard evidence to flash in front of Williamson to erase any doubt. With that though in mind, he settled upon a plan.

The next morning Andy sat in his office pondering his chances. Damn it! He was not going to lose interest in this just because it presented a few obstacles, not the least of which was how to get the hard evidence he felt he needed to insure success. Clearly he couldn't get it here in his office. He had to catch the two of them in the act. But when? And where? More easily said than done. Come on now, let's think this through like the intelligent guy you are.

You always say you're smarter than most of the creeps working here.

Okay, here's the chance to prove it. From what he'd seen yesterday, Williamson and the lawyer—her name was Ferrara, he knew that much—looked like they were pretty hot for each other. That means they must see each other often. Probably can't keep their paws off of each other. He smiled. Even presidents have their animal side. So if they see each other often, there's a good chance they'll see each other again in the next day or so. And since they can't see each other in the office — at least not in a compromising situation — it had to be either at lunch or after work. It'll be pretty easy to follow him at lunch, so that's no problem. But what about after work when the situation, whatever it is, is likely to be more compromising? How can he follow either one of them if he doesn't know where they're going? If they drive, he can't have his car conveniently ready to follow since he had no idea where they kept there cars. Actually, he knew Williamson usually was brought to work by a chauffeur. Quite unlikely he'd have his chauffeur take him to the place he was going to get laid by Ferrara. Not so easy is it Mack?

What if they take the train? They wouldn't be so foolish as to take it together. And if they did, how would he follow either of them when they got to the other end? Yes, yes. By eliminating what won't work you narrow the options down to what might. Coming into focus. Coming into focus ol' boy. Come on, come on. You're going to get it. That's it, find out where she lives. El presidente sure ain't going to bring the broad home with him, so it's got to be her place. So where does she live? That's your project for the morning, Andy boy, so get your ass in gear. You're going hunting tonight and tomorrow night and every night till you get what you want.

# FIVE

The small, upscale bedroom community of Larchmont in Westchester County is a great place to commute into New York from because of its proximity to the city — about thirty minutes by train. The streets are tree lined— enough green for all but the most bucolic in spirit. The residents are civilized— at least when it comes to their behavior on the streets. And culture is just a nine-iron shot away in any of the many country clubs that flourish in the suburbs just to the north of America's largest metropolis. Kate Ferrara's garden apartment was situated in an older section of the village, minutes only from the convenience of the Hutchinson River Parkway to the west and I-95 and Long Island Sound to the east. In short, Larchmont is an ideal suburb for busy executives and professionals. Kate's condo was a five-room unit in a two-story brick building that had been built in the early '50s. Solidly-constructed, the place was built to last. Originally it was part of a multi-structure complex of rental apartments. Now they were mostly condos. Upon making partner at Smythe, Goodstein and Blum, Kate had purchased the condo. It had been at the very depth of the real estate recession, so she'd gotten a real good deal on a well-cared-for unit on the ground floor— $550,000. A few years earlier the same condo would have gone for $650,000. And now, only a few years after she'd bought it, similar units were back up to $650,000. She'd reflected more than once that, as people so often observe, timing is everything in life. She'd bought at just the right time. Window of opportunity, said the previous owner. Kate had believed in windows of opportunity long before that, and the previous owner's words rang true. She'd not regretted her purchase for a minute. The truth was she loved the place.

Williamson, whose six-bedroom home in Rye, three stops further north on the New Haven line of the MetroNorth commuter line, was far larger and much more lavish, was nevertheless stunned the first time he visited Kate's place. She'd done a brilliant job of decorating. No distinguishable style that he could identify. Just a tastefully eclectic collection of things that appealed to her sensitivities. Somehow they all went together, accented and highlighted by the strategic use of contemporary lighting.

Kate had arrived home a half hour before Williamson was due to get there. She'd let her hair down, and after placing an assortment of disks on the CD player, had changed into a pair of form-fitting jeans and a complementary teal-and-purple rugby shirt. Harry Connick was playing one of his excellent renditions of Glenn Miller when the doorbell rang. As Kate went to the door she couldn't help thinking that this whole scene must have been repeated a few thousand times all over America in the last few months. That bothered her. But not because some people would say this was wrong. After all, I'm not married, she told herself, and he's a big boy. But what about her, his wife Laura? Should I feel guilty about her. She honestly didn't think so. Laura's a big girl, and from what Kate could tell, she didn't deserve Carr. Admittedly everything she knew about Laura she'd heard from Carr, but she had no reason to doubt what he said. His honesty is one of the qualities that appealed to her in the first place. No, what bothered Kate was that she was playing a role in a very common sociodrama — the tired late-20th-century phenomenon called "the affair". She loved being with Williamson, and she loved meeting with him the way they did. It all seemed so...exciting. But, she was not a starry-eyed kid. She really believed she loved him. What's not to love? But was their affair profound, or was it cheap and tawdry?

The bell rang again. Ferrara, she said to herself, you are too introspective for your own good. The man's good. You're good. One plus one equals very good. She opened the door.

# SIX

The traffic on I-95 was lighter than he'd expected. Good. Should be there in plenty of time. He'd left his office early in order to arrive in Larchmont before Williamson. He'd figured Ferrara would get there first. Give her a little time to fix herself up for Williamson, though from what he'd seen of her, Andy didn't think the legal dame needed much fixing up. Good looking woman. Anyway, it was fine with him if she got there first. That's what he wanted.

    He'd been tense on the drive up from Manhattan. Sort of the way he used to feel when he had to give a presentation in school. Keyed up, a kind of fluttery excitement in his throat. Form of stage fright. The old feeling had come back today. In fact he still felt that way. What he was about to experience was all he could think about. But what gave him the courage to go on was his memory of how he always used to feel after he'd given a presentation. Proud, confident, and ready for more. Face it, he was smart, and he'd been well prepared for those presentations. Just as he was today for today's little adventure.

    He was proud of the detective work he'd done this morning. He'd had no idea where the yuppie legal broad lived; yet through good solid reasoning and research he'd found out. His first ploy hadn't been successful, however. He'd called Ferrara at her law office and told her he was Eddie in personnel. That he was updating the Christmas card list, and would she please give him her current address to see if the Christmas card list was up-to-date. She'd said she'd be glad to. What did he have for her current address? That had stopped him in his tracks, and then she'd gotten suspicious. Bitch was smart, had to hand her that. Anyone else would have just given him the information.

Then he'd resorted to one of the proven techniques of police investigation—good old-fashioned leg work. Only he'd let his fingers do the walking. Starting in the East with Connecticut, he'd begun calling information for a Katherine or Kate Ferrara. He'd also tried Catherine. He'd started with Fairfield County, figuring that anything further east in the Nutmeg State would be too far to commute into New York. Next he'd called information for the 914 and 845 area codes, which included Westchester, Rockland, Dutchess, and Putnam Counties in New York State and had quickly struck pay dirt, learning that the only Catherine Ferrara listed in Westchester lived in Larchmont at the address he was now headed for. He'd called her number and gotten an answering machine with a young woman's voice that merely confirmed the number. This one sounded like a very good bet. To minimize the likelihood that there were several Kate Ferrara's he'd continued calling information for the suburban counties encircling New York. When he called information, the operator would ask him what city he wanted to check. Most of the time they didn't like it, but he persisted by saying he didn't know the city, but he was pretty sure Ms. Ferrara lived in such and such county. Since the phone companies kept their listings in giant computer databases, it really wasn't hard for them to check an entire county for the name. By calling back several times in each area code he was able to check each county. He'd struck out in New York's Putnam, Dutchess and Rockland Counties, as well as the Long Island counties of Nassau and Suffolk and continued to come up dry until he hit Morris County, New Jersey where he'd come upon another Catherine Ferrara. He'd called her number and gotten an elderly woman who said that she and her husband were both retired and hadn't worked in over 12 years.

He'd called the New York City area codes, 212, 646 and 718, and found no additional Catherine Ferrara who fitted the criteria, so he was reasonably confident that he'd found the right one up in Larchmont. Of course he could still be wrong. The woman he was looking for could have an unlisted number. Still, though Andy didn't think of himself as a gambler, he didn't view a drive up to Westchester that big a risk. If he turned out to be right, the drive would have been well worth the trouble. Of course, even if he were right, what's the guarantee that the horny prexy would be dropping in on the yuppie bitch tonight? Again, no guarantee, thought Andy, but if he was any judge of human nature, the chances were pretty good that there'd be at least one tryst tonight in Larchmont. And if not tonight, he'd come back every night until there was one. He knew he wouldn't have long to wait.

    He got off I-95 at the North Street exit in New Rochelle, just south of Larchmont. Larchmont was small, and he figured that if he approached it from the south on U.S. Route 1, the Boston Post Road, he wouldn't miss the intersection that would take him to Ferrara's condo. As he entered Larchmont in the fading light of mid-October, he couldn't fail to miss the smart boutiques and the look of casual affluence unconsciously radiated by the residents of the pleasant little town. Ms. Ferrara must be doing well to live in a place like this, thought Andy. Now that she's seeing Williamson she's most definitely doing well, he smirked inwardly. We'll see how long that lasts.

    He found the complex easily. Counted six buildings. Each appeared to house four condo units. Two on each floor. The style was sort of ersatz brick colonial. Not unattractive, thought Andy, but definitely not authentic. Her building was set well back from the street, behind some of the others. Perfect. He'd be less conspicuous that way. He parked three blocks down the street and started walking back toward the condos.  He was carrying a flexible over-the-shoulder canvas bag that contained everything he figured he could possibly need.

Now it felt as if someone were tickling the inside of his chest cavity with a feather.  He smiled in spite of his jitteryness.  How do you describe that feeling to someone else?  Well, he probably wouldn't try.  Christ did he feel uptight.  Nervous as hell.  His neck and ears felt flushed.  And his mouth was dry. *Remember how you'll feel afterward, he reminded himself. You'll look back on this and be proud.*  He knew that was true.

## SEVEN

"You look beat, my friend," said Kate empathetically. "Bad day?" She was perched on a blonde-oak kitchen stool preparing ingredients for a salad. Williamson stood a few feet away, leaning his tall athletic frame against the doorway. He held a chilled pilsner glass of Bass ale, Connick's arrangement of *Take the A-Train* drifting into his consciousness from speakers hidden somewhere in the adjoining living room.

"The usual. No, not quite true. Little worse than the usual." He paused a moment, "It's under control. I didn't think it showed."

"Yes, it shows. Sure it's only work?"

He smiled, "Yes, it's only work." He knew, of course, that it wasn't just his work that had him on edge. He knew, too, that she knew. A part of him admitted to another part of him that guilt played a not inconsequential role in his uneasiness. Guilt about what he'd been doing and guilt about what he was going to do.

In his mind's eye he saw a younger Laura, the one he'd met on a beautiful day in May on the Pont Royal in Paris 22 years ago. He was there on a business trip. Laura was still in college at the time. She was studying in Paris on a semester abroad. He'd been a junior exec, an international sales rep to be more accurate. Been sent to Paris because he spoke a better-than-passable French, a rarity in the American corporate structure at the time. A situation that, unfortunately, hasn't changed much since then, he thought wryly. It was Laura's junior year at Wellesley, and she was studying French literature. She'd been taking pictures from the bridge, and he'd offered to take hers. They'd hit it off instantly, and the furious week of activity together that followed had been the kind of cinematic romantic experience that most young people only dream of. They saw and did everything—

everything that Paris had to offer.

    The memory of that treasured romance was bittersweet for Williamson. He and Laura had been married 21 years. The electricity of that week in Paris and the early years of their marriage was gone. They'd been through a lot together since Paris, and she wasn't really guilty of anything, save perhaps not recognizing how he'd changed over the years. As a result, their relationship had changed. He'd grown, and therein lay the problem. But was it her fault? Probably not. If pressed, she'd probably blame his work.

    As far as he was concerned his work had never been a problem. He loved his work. Oh, his work had indeed had its share of difficulties and problems, hundreds of them. Some of them serious. Some of them would have been the undoing of people he knew. He never really thought of them as problems, though. They'd been challenges to overcome. Like some real-world Monopoly game. He'd always liked Monopoly as a kid, and just as he liked getting past GO on the famous board game, he liked attacking the real-life problems he faced daily at work. But to say his work was a problem would be getting it wrong. Work was his milieu, his métier. If one were to ask most people what their métier was, they'd say attorney, retailer, artist, baker, or whatever, because that was what they did best, or at least that was what they did for a living. He was different. He knew he was different. Always had been. Anything requiring organization and leadership had come easily to him from as far back as he could remember. What had been difficult for his classmates had been easy for him. What had been overwhelming for his colleagues on the way up had been little more than challenging exercises for him. When the problems were particularly tough he'd thought of them in a romantic sort of way as being challenges in an adult game, a game that he was good at.

He was damned good at work, any kind he'd ever attempted. Currently his work was heading up one of the three largest publishing companies in America. The numbers were bigger. The paychecks fatter. The players more important. At least they thought they were. And the decisions affected more people. But Carr didn't see the job as harder than any he'd done in the past. In some ways it was easier. He had more help, and the help he had was more talented. And he could delegate the detail stuff—the stuff that took a lot of time.

He was only the second non-family member to be CEO of Harmon Hall. He'd replaced the diminutive Parisian dynamo who'd come to the company from the French pharmaceutical industry six years earlier. Some had thought at the time that his dashing Gallic predecessor would stumble. No knowledge of the book business, they'd said. Not familiar with the American corporate culture. But Howard and the board had gambled and they'd won. The guy had been terrific. He seemed to possess energy inversely proportional to his stature. Within a year of assuming the helm he'd taken the vast family-owned business public after convincing the board that it would fade into the background of American publishing without an infusion of fresh capital. The decision had been the right one, and sales and profits had grown dramatically under his leadership. Then, three years ago, the little guy had told Howard that he'd been asked to head up a major rival. Howard, the board, and the entire company had been stunned. Just when the company was starting to really move, it was losing its prime mover. Worse, the mighty mite was taking his knowledge of Harmon Hall and its marketing strategies to one of the company's fiercest competitors.

Howard had felt that there was nobody in the company who could fill the shoes of the little Napoleon. Then a board member mentioned Williamson, who at the time was senior vice president of sales and marketing at still another major publishing house. One thing led to another, and Carr had negotiated a deal that would compensate him over $3,000,000 annually for the next three years. It was a sweetheart deal and the opportunity of a lifetime for Williamson. The rest, as they say, was history. Since then, Carr had more than justified the confidence the company had placed in him.

"Here, maybe this will make you feel better," said Kate. She'd just opened a bottle of white wine and was in the process of pouring him a glass.

He tasted it. Smiled weakly, "This is okay." He took another careful sip and melodramatically swished the light amber fluid in his mouth. "Better than okay."

"I would hope so. That's Montrachet you're drinking."

"You're kidding. That stuff is outrageously expensive. Must have run you a hundred plus."

"Not quite, but close. Got a friend at my local wine shop. Needless to say, I don't buy Montrachet everyday." she grinned. "But you're worth it."

He sipped from his wineglass, "It is good. What's the occasion?"

"I don't know, I'll think of something. Actually, one of my clients gave it to me. He was trying to impress me with his knowledge of wines."

"Well I'm impressed. It's great." He felt rotten.

"Good, I'm glad you like it. Are you all right now?"

"Yes, fine. Can I help you with something?" He'd pulled off his tie and rolled up the sleeves of his white business shirt.

"You can just sit there and relax. Here, have some more wine."

Recently he'd felt comfortable here. He shouldn't have. He knew that. The condo of a woman he shouldn't be with. To make matters worse, she was the attorney assigned to work with his company. The arrangement with Blythe, Goodstein and Blum did not provide for carnal assignations. He got up and walked over to the window. Until recently he'd honestly believed he could remain objective despite his relationship with Kate, even though he'd doubted whether Howard or the board would agree. Anyway, he had felt good here, though he didn't feel so great now, considering how he knew the evening would end.

His ability to relax with Kate, he was sure had been due to intellectual compatibility. When Kate asked him about work, it wasn't merely an indifferent gesture, which is what he felt at home when Laura asked. Kate really wanted to know. And she asked the right questions. Of course, he realized she had an advantage, being out in the real world. That, too, he supposed, was part of her appeal. Anyway he had felt comfortable here, but tonight he was not so comfortable.

Earlier they'd been talking about the repercussions of the company's decision to do the big dictionary. How this young editor, Andrew Mack, had stormed out of Tony Marcantonio's office because he hadn't been named to head up the project. Kate had asked if he thought that this Mack guy was so disappointed that he'd quit.

"I doubt it. He's a good editor, but known as a moody sort. Real loner. He'll probably brood for awhile, but I imagine he'll stay. Quite honestly, though, that's Stuart's opinion. I've never even met the guy."

They finished eating one of Kate's specialties, tarragon chicken with wild rice, and were both silent. Williamson leaned forward and started to talk.

"Kate, you're on the first floor here, and yet I notice that you always keep the curtains and blinds open at night. Somebody could easily see in."

"Not as easily as you might think, my hero. When you go outside you'll see that the building is constructed so that the first-floor windows are about eight feet above the ground. A peeping Tom would have to be mighty tall to see in. However, when I go to bed, and if you'll think back," she smiled at him conspiratorially, "when we go to bed, I always pull the curtains in the bedroom. Just in case somebody from another building has a telescope or something. Hey, I didn't think captains of industry feared anything. Are you worried someone will catch you in the sack with your corporate solicitor?"

He smiled appropriately, "I'm just thinking of you and the times we live in. Lots of crazies out there."

"Larchmont is not the big Apple. It's a nice town. Don't worry so much." She added an inch of Montrachet to his glass and turned suddenly. "Did you hear that?"

"What?"

"Thought I heard something at the window. Must be my imagination. You didn't hear anything?"

"Not really, what'd it sound like?"

"I don't know really. Maybe scraping. It was outside. God, you've got me jumpy now. Must be my imagination."

"I'll go out and look around."

"Don't be silly. It was nothing."

"Let me just take a quick look."

"Forget it. It's probably a branch from a tree. It's gotten a little windy out. Let's go into the bedroom, my horny honcho."

He hesitated before following her in. Kate was already taking off her rugby shirt. "Kate?"

She stood there in her bra—smiling, "Yeesss."

It was not the time to smile back. "Kate, I need to..." She unfastened her bra and let it fall to the floor. She stood there in front of him, the dim light from the lamp on her nightstand somehow making her full breasts seem even more nubile than he'd remembered from the last time he'd been in her bedroom. He had difficulty trying to stay in control.

"Yes, Carr?"

This was not going to be easy, "Listen, Kate..." she was removing her form-hugging jeans. He noticed that she wasn't wearing panties. He moved toward her and grabbed her hands in an effort to stop her. "Kate, there's something I have to say to you."

# EIGHT

Looking south from his vast office on the 30th floor of the Harmon Hall Building Williamson could see Midtown, lower Manhattan, and rising from the sun-dappled harbor still further in the distance, the majestic presence of the Statue of Liberty. To the west lay the West Side, the Hudson River, and New Jersey beyond. When he had a free minute, as he did now, he liked to look out at the breathtaking scape that only certain New Yorkers were privileged to see on a regular basis.

It was ten o'clock of the morning after. The worst part of the evening, as always when he visited Kate, had been the getting home late, hoping that Laura would be asleep so he wouldn't have to lie to her once again. Last night it was almost one a.m. Fortunately last night she'd been asleep.

He put his thoughts of last night aside and leaned back in his chair contentedly, hands clasped behind his head. A meeting planned for ten had been cancelled at the last minute because some idiot in accounting thought an essential report was needed tomorrow; not today. It was okay, though, he decided philosophically. Gave him a chance to catch up on correspondence.

Williamson was proud of his office. How could he not be? You could land a small plane on the surface of the huge teak desk. There was enough plush carpet on the floor of this one room to do a small home. He'd had the office decorated the way he wanted it. Used a trendy New York decorator who called himself Ivan. Pronounced Ee von'. No last name, of course. Pretentious, yes. Supercilious, you bet your ass. But the unctuous son-of-a-bitch knew what he was doing. The decor Ivan had come up with had grabbed Williamson immediately. Cost the company a goddam fortune. What the Hell, you only go around once.

The office definitely was striking. Everyone noticed it. Even if they didn't comment on it, they noticed it. He could tell by watching them. Williamson smiled in satisfaction. Then something caught his eye. He looked up and saw Betsy framed in the doorway.

"An editor named Andy Mack wants to see you, Mr. Williamson. He's been trying all morning. I think he's one of Mr. Marcantonio's people."

"What's it about?"

"He won't say. Just that it's extremely urgent, and that he must talk to you and no one else. Shall I show him in?"

"Yes, but tell him I can only give him ten minutes."

As soon as he saw Andy he recognized him. He'd seen him around the building a number of times. Had no idea who he was, though. Andy entered diffidently, a cautious expression on his round face. Williamson took in his average height and receding hairline in a glance. His hair was neither brunet nor blond, but rather indeterminate, reminding Williamson of a parched dirt road on a hot summer day. Probably not yet 30, he concluded. Body language suggested a lack of presence. Not at all sure of himself. Williamson had discovered as far back as college that he was usually pretty accurate at sizing up people. He tried to retain as much as he could about a person from the first meeting. Made it a point to remember the name. People were always impressed when, a year or even ten years after the briefest of meetings, you remembered their name. "Come in, come in," he said encouragingly to the hesitant young man. "Take a seat and tell me what's on your mind."

Andy sat in one of the comfortable chairs near Williamson's desk. He couldn't remember ever being this tense. He hoped that his words wouldn't come out an octave too high.

"Good morning sir," he said. *Good. Voice didn't squeak.*

"Good morning. Now what can I do for you?"

"Mr. Williamson, I don't want you to take what I'm going to say personally. As a matter of fact I have the highest regard for you."

"Okay, I won't take it personally, but you'd better get on with it because we only have a few minutes."

"Then I'll get right to the point. I would like to be promoted to managing editor of the reference division, with full responsibility for the unabridged dictionary project."

"Would you now?"

"Yes sir. Actually, I'd really like to be promoted to executive editor or even editorial director, but I'm not foolish. I know the staff would become suspicious."

"Is this some kind of a joke?"

"No, it's not a joke. Let me explain..."

"Well," interrupted Williamson, "I'm afraid it sounds pretty funny to me. Why in the world would I promote you to anything? I don't mean to sound insulting... Andy is it?... but I don't even know you. Nor do I know what you do." Had to put this clown in his place right from the start. It was coming back to him now. It was just yesterday that Stuart Markham had told him about this guy storming out of Tony Marcantonio's office the other day. Now this same guy comes waltzing into the president's office demanding to be promoted to managing editor and wanting to be put in charge of the biggest editorial project in the history of the company. Williamson was tempted to throw the little weirdo out of his office, but he hadn't gotten to where he was by being impulsive. Besides, in all his years in business, he'd never heard anything quite so audacious. He was curious to know where this kid was coming from, or if he was just so far out of touch with the real world that he shouldn't even be working at Harmon Hall. And if that were the case, which seemed likely, he'd have Stuart get rid of him fast.

"Sir, I know you're having an affair with Kate Ferrara." There, it was out. He'd said it. He waited for Williamson's reaction.

Williamson just stared at the nondescript young man seated across the desk from him. This couldn't be. How could this, this insignificant little bastard he'd never even heard of until yesterday know so much about his personal life. His normally lightning-fast mind raced for the appropriate comeback. Which he immediately realized was his first mistake. This wasn't witty repartee. This was his fucking life. He needed more than a snappy retort. His future depended on what he said and did in the next few minutes.

"Jesus, talk about chutzpa," he roared, figuring he'd use bluster at first to stall for time and to see where this guy was coming from. "You come in here demanding a promotion. Before I've even had a chance to respond to the absurdity of that one, you top it with an even more outrageous demand. You listen, and you listen good. I'm having an affair with nobody, and you're not getting any promotion. If you play your cards right, you may, just may be allowed to keep your job." He wanted to say, "Now get out of here," but he dared not let a loose cannon loose...not until he found out how much the little shit really knew.

"I figured you'd react that way," said Andy, gradually gaining confidence. After all, how much worse could it get? "I would, too, if I were in your shoes. But it's not going to work. You can't make me go away by huffing and puffing, because you and I both know it's true."

"I know nothing of the kind. What kind of nut are you anyway?"

"I'm no nut, Mr. Williamson. It would be better for you if I were," retorted Andy politely, but firmly, thinking as he did so how strange it was that he continued to address Williamson deferentially. He knew why, of course. Ironically, he still perceived Williamson as one of the most respected people in all of publishing. It was only because the opportunity had provided itself, that he, Andy Mack, had chosen to negotiate with the man at the top, and he honestly hoped that the negotiations would result in a win-win outcome for all concerned. Had chance given him some other high-ranking executive in the company, he would have made the same demands of that person. It was unfortunate for Williamson that he'd gotten caught playing hanky-panky, but, after all, Andy reflected, feeling pleased with himself, the guy made his own bed; now he can lie in it.

"Look, this is uncomfortable for me, too. Why don't I cut to the chase now so we can get this over with. The sooner we can resolve this, the sooner both of us can get back to making money for Harmon Hall." Williamson started to talk, but Andy cut in, "Wait, please let me finish. It won't take long, I promise you. I first became aware of your relationship with Ms. Ferrara when I saw the two of you eating lunch at Canavan's over on First Avenue."

"Ms. Ferrara and I were having a business lunch. I think your imagination got the best of you." Maybe this can be salvaged yet, thought Williamson.

"Great choice of restaurants for a CEO," said Andy with a sardonic smile. "I doubt it. Besides, the two of you were far too cozy for a business lunch."

"She's a charming young woman. In a way I'm like a mentor to her. Almost as if she were my own daughter. I can imagine how it might have looked, though. We chose Canavan's because I can't get any peace if I go to most of the mid-town restaurants. Unfortunately, I'm too well known."

"You are really smooth, sir. I can see how you got to be president. But I'm afraid I don't buy it. And that bit about your daughter. Talk about chutzpa. Are you banging your daughter, too?"

"Now wait just a fucking minute you little pant-load!"

"No, you wait a minute, sir." At that moment the phone buzzed. Williamson hesitated; then lifted the receiver.

"Yes, Betsy, what is it?"

"Is everything all right in there?"

"Yes, everything's fine. We're just having a little animated discussion. We'll be finished soon."

"All right. If you say so. By the way, Kate Ferrara just phoned. She's down in legal. Said she must see you. She'll be up in a few minutes. Shall I have her wait?"

"Yes, have her wait."

"All right. Uh... Mr. Williamson?"

"Yes, Betsy?"

"Nothing, nothing..." she said shaking her head as she hung up.

"That was good. We need a little more time, but how long is really up to you. I think you need a bit more convincing."

"You bet your ass I do."

With that, Andy was pretty sure he was home free. He could see that Williamson was already taking him seriously...that he obviously wasn't confident enough of his innocence to kick his unexpected visitor out the door. Sensing he was in the driver's seat, Andy proceeded. "To be honest, when I saw you and Ms. Ferrara acting so chummy at Canavan's I thought I was on to something. However, I also realized that my initial assessment was a serious indictment and that I'd better be sure of my facts."

"Damn right you had," Williamson barked, sounding more confident than he felt. "And I can tell you right now that you didn't find anything."

"Not true, not true. If it weren't for my upcoming good fortune, I'd be sorry to prove you wrong. But there's more, and you know it. Here, take a look at these," he handed his host three glossy black-and-white photos. Williamson blanched as he looked at the pictures.

"Where'd you get these?" His voice was little more than a whisper.

"Well that's really funny, sir. You know where I got them. I think you mean, how did I get them? That's a story in itself. I'm kinda proud of that, too. Took real detective work. To begin with I figured if I was right you'd be visiting Ms. Ferrara after work at least one night a week—probably more than that from what I could see at Canavan's. Can't blame you sir, she's pretty nice...for a lawyer that is," he chuckled. He was getting into it now. What a rush. A sense of power he'd never experienced before in his entire life. Williamson frowned, but remained silent.

"Anyway, you didn't disappoint me. Using a little investigative elbow grease...I won't bore you with the details...I discovered where Ms. Ferrara lived and then sort of camped out across the street. Surveillance the cops call it. Pretty cool huh? Well, as I said, you didn't disappoint me. Showed up the very first night. The operation was well planned, if I do say so myself. I had two cameras. One with fast black-and-white film; the other with infrared film. I wasn't going to waste this opportunity.

The first shot I got was of you going into her condo. If you look at one of those shots I gave you you'll see that I got the number of the condo in the picture. The next one was of the two of you in the kitchen. Nothing juicy, but compromising, nevertheless. That one and the next one were hard to get because those damn windows are so high off the ground. Had to hustle to find something to stand on.

Found an old lawn chair, but that still didn't get me up high enough. Finally, just in time, I might add, I found a wooden box that I stacked on the chair, and then it was fine. The last shot, you have a copy there. That was the clincher. Looks like you're undressing Ms. Ferrara, doesn't it? No doubt just before you hopped into the sack. Good shot of both of you don't you think?"

"Look, Andy, I know it sounds weak, but what you saw is not what you think you saw."

"You're right. It does sound weak. And I don't believe you."

Williamson shook his head in futility, realizing it was pointless to protest. Looking at the three pictures he held in his hand he realized he wouldn't be convinced, either if the tables were turned. "All right, you've made your point."

"I figured you'd say that. So...we're back to my original demand. Do I get the new job or don't I?" Andy was feeling smug and cocky now. Normally he hated this behavior in others, but he was due. For once in his life he'd be cocky.

"Look Andy, I'm curious. I'm not avoiding the issue, really I'm not. But I am curious..."

"About what?"

"About why you would want to get a job this way. What possible satisfaction can it bring you if you don't get it on your own merits?"

"I've been overlooked by this company long enough. Call me frustrated. Call me aggrieved. Call me pissed off. Call me all of the above. I've been at Harmon Hall long enough to know that I'll never get a fair shake here. I'm like the invisible man here, and all of a sudden I'm very visible. I can't be ignored anymore, and I won't be. Besides, I will be getting the job on my own merits. I'm using my brain and my initiative, wouldn't you say so?" He stared at Williamson defiantly.

"What made you think I'd promote you? Sure, this is embarrassing. Certainly I'd rather you didn't know about it, but why do you think I'd let you blackmail me for something that's done every day?" asked Williamson, trying to hold on. To what, he didn't know, but the need to survive forced people to desperation at times like this.

"From what I've been told, sir, you have an Ozzie-and-Harriet-kind of family. Or at least you did until recently. I doubt if you'd want your wife or your daughter to know about this. Why else would you be sneaking around the way you do? And if for some unknown reason you're not concerned about them, there's Howard Harmon. Word is he's pretty old fashioned about these kinds of things. Word is he's fired people for just what you're doing. Word is you like your job and would like to keep it."

"Okay, okay. So you're blackmailing me."

"I was hoping this conversation wouldn't go in that direction. I don't like that term. Let's just say I'm negotiating. Isn't that what you big executives do all the time?"

"We don't blackmail when we negotiate. There's a big difference, and you know it."

"Forgive me, but I don't see that much difference. You like to negotiate from strength, if I'm not mistaken?"

"Of course, but that's still not blackmail."

"Beg your pardon, but I don't see all that much difference. I'm just negotiating from strength. In this case, I happen to hold more aces than you do, but don't tell me you wouldn't use what I have if it would help you clinch a big business deal. Never mind, don't answer that now. I know you have other things on your busy schedule today besides me. We can philosophize another time at leisure. Let's not let semantics get in the way of concluding our deal."

"Look, supposing I agree to promote you. It's

not that simple, you know. There's only managing editor position in the reference division and that's filled, if I'm not mistaken."

"You're the president of the company. You can make it happen. Promote the present managing editor. Her name's Jacqui Dyer, by the way. Or transfer her. I'm sure you'll find a way.

"I can't just promote you out of the blue. I don't even know if you can do the job. If I did put you in the job and you dropped the ball, the board would be all over me in a New York minute for preempting Tony Marcantonio and Stuart Markham. They're responsible for editorial personnel. And rightly so. They're the ones closest to the staff. You must see that, Andy." It turned his stomach being so deferential, but he was afraid to provoke the blackmailer further. "Hell, they'd fire me for a stunt like that, and then where would you be?"

"I assure you I can do the job. You're just going to have to work this thing out, or you're going to have a bigger problem to deal with. I'm sure Tony Marcantonio and Mr. Markham will be happy to do a small favor for the president of the company. Don't make this sound more difficult than it is."

Suddenly Williamson was fighting for his very existence. How could this be? Twenty minutes ago he was king of the hill—luxuriating in his good fortune. Then, out of nowhere, appears this nobody threatening to destroy his life. There had to be an answer. He'd never been stumped before, and he wasn't going to be now. In the meantime, though, he had to placate Andy Mack.

"All right, Andy," he took a breath and plunged ahead, "We'll promote you in a week to managing editor of the reference division. People will raise their eyebrows, but I think I can make it stick..."

"Of course you can."

"Don't interrupt," said Williamson testily. Then, softening his tone, "Give me a few days, no more than a week, though, before the announcement. I'll need a little time to work this out. It won't be easy, but it's probably doable."

"Okay, sounds good. See, I'm reasonable. But I need insurance that I don't get screwed."

"Look, I'm not going to screw you, as you put it. Face it, you have me where you want me. I'd be a fool not to take care of you."

"You've got that right."

"All right, then, we have a deal. Now give me the negatives for the pictures."

"You know I can't do that. But, there's really no reason for you to worry, sir. After all, as you said, we have a deal, and it's in the best interests of both of us to stick to it. My understanding is that my promotion will be announced within one week and that I'll start as managing editor first thing the day after the announcement. Right?"

Williamson felt totally deflated. "Right."

"Good, then I'll let you get on with your day. No hard feelings."

# NINE

Carr Williamson walked slowly over to the end of the net where he'd left his towel. He wiped his brow and turned to his friend. "You're too good for me today, Herb. You played well."

Herb Wasserman grinned, "You must have let me win. I haven't beaten you in singles in over two years." Then he added more seriously, "You feeling all right? You really didn't play your game out there."

Williamson hesitated, as if not sure whether to proceed or not. Finally he said, "You got a few minutes? I've got something I'd like to bounce off you."

"Jeez, you look serious. Sure, sure. Let's go over to the clubhouse and talk."

The Harbor Club was not easy to get into. Money helped, of course, but money wasn't enough. Lots of people in Westchester had money, but they wouldn't all be accepted at the socially exclusive Harbor Club. The waiting list now was over three years long, and even if you waited, it was no guarantee the membership committee would accept you. The Williamsons had been members for the last four years. The Wassermans had been accepted two years ago. Ten years earlier, they wouldn't have been accepted at all. Williamson wiped his face again as he and Wasserman grabbed their tennis gear and walked across the elegantly landscaped grounds toward the rambling one-story white clubhouse which faced out onto Long Island Sound. Carr chose a table on the veranda, somewhat away from the flow of club members entering and leaving the dining room. A bronzed well-built young man came over and took their beer orders. College kid, thought Carr. Old man got him the job for the summer.

It was nearly noon on the last Saturday in August. The air was dry and silky smooth, and a coruscating radiance reflected off the choppy Sound. Sailboats dotted the sparkling surface as larger boats off in the distance moved silently toward the unseen Atlantic to the east, passing still other boats heading inexorably into New York Harbor to the west. Pleasure boats still at anchor, sails tightly furled, bobbed in the calm waters closer to shore. The view from the clubhouse was idyllic.

"Okay, my friend, why so serious?"

"I've gotten myself involved with another woman, Herb. You're the only one I've told. I didn't want to tell anyone, frankly, but you're my best friend, and the situation has gotten so complicated and become such a damn mess that I had to talk to someone."

"You want a reaction now, Carr. Or d'you want to tell me more?"

"No, let me fill you in first. Maybe you'll have some ideas." He paused, rubbing his eyes, "God, I hope so." He then proceeded to explain to his friend how he'd been seeing Kate for the past few weeks, how this bitter young editor at the company, against all odds, happened upon Kate and him at lunch, and how the guy wasn't satisfied with that and actually spied on him and Kate at her condo and took some very compromising pictures. Williamson went on to tell about the blackmail and about how he had had to make the most humiliatingly request of Stuart Markham, asking him to promote this young editor to a job he might not even be able to handle. Of course he couldn't give Markham a good reason other than to say, "trust me, Stuart."

"Is there more?"

"Yes. The night this guy spied on us at her condo, I went there to end the affair. Break it off for good. Ironic isn't it?"

"Ironic isn't the word for it. So did you?"

"Did I what?"

"End it."

"Yes, but who'd believe it?"

"Carr, I have to ask you ... If you broke it off, how did he get those compromising pictures?"

Carr shook his head disconsolately and proceeded to explain how Kate had begun to undress as he was trying to talk to her, to end it. He acknowledged how it would look to anyone seeing the pictures. How hard it would be to convince anyone that he did nothing improper that night. Besides, he added, he was there, wasn't he. And what's worse, he'd been there before, though he'd only slept with Kate twice.

"So there you have it. Pretty, isn't it?"

"Beautiful."

"Those are essentially the facts, but unfortunately there's more. The more is the turmoil that's tearing at my gut. You know, Herb, I've had it pretty easy so far. Fast track. Climbed the ladder and all that. Multimillion-dollar decisions. Dealt with heavy hitters. Never lost a night's sleep over any of it. But now...now my mind is churning. I'm afraid it'll affect my work, and all because I've got this little bastard in the wings waiting for me to make a mistake. Not to mention the mistakes he might make. I frankly have no reason to believe he can even do the damn job, and if he screws up I've got Markham and Marcantonio to deal with, and maybe even Howard himself. I honestly don't know if I'll be able to cover his tracks. I tell you Herb I feel like killing the son-of-a-bitch. All of a sudden my life has become so damn complicated. I feel like I've been living two lives."

"You have been ol' buddy, you have been," said Wasserman sympathetically.

"I'm really stressed out, Herb. Never thought I'd see the day when I couldn't handle something. That's almost the worst part of this. My feeling of infallibility, of invulnerability has been seriously shaken, and it's scary as hell."

"Well it's understandable with the freight you're carrying around. Face it, Carr, you're a very competent guy, but you were never invulnerable and never infallible. You've been riding a wave of success...a long string of successes, and it was natural to develop a mindset that assumed bad things happen to other people; not to you. But if you'll be honest, you'll admit that this didn't happen to you. You made it happen. Not the blackmail itself maybe, but you certainly opened the door to it. You made yourself vulnerable."

"You're right, of course. You don't think very much of me do you?"

"Oh for Christ's sake, I'm not judging you. Who can say what makes someone else do what they do? I don't know what goes on in your married life. Face it, as close as the four of us are, we don't see the other couple when they're home alone."

"Tell me what you think, though? I need another view from someone I can trust."

"Frankly, since you've asked, I don't understand how you could have rejected Laura. The Laura I know is a terrific gal. And from where I stand, admittedly from a distance, I think she's been a terrific wife to you. But what do I know?"

"Christ, Herb, don't you think I know Laura's been a good wife. If she hadn't been, this wouldn't be driving me out of my mind so. I wasn't seeing Kate because Laura's a bitch," said Carr emotionally. "Besides, I did come to my senses, admittedly a little late."

"Why were you seeing Kate? For the sex?"

Williamson sighed, then leaned forward, putting his face in his hands. "Oh God, I suppose that was part of it. It all sounds so cheap and dirty when you try to put it into words. Kate is no slut, Herb. She's a hell of a woman. She's bright, articulate, she understood me, and yes, she's attractive."

"And she likes to fuck..."

"You sure as hell don't mince words, do you pardner?"

"Did you want me to?"

"No, I guess not. I suppose I was secretly hoping you'd see it my way," said Williamson dejectedly.

"Like everyone who works for you, right? Face it, Carr, nobody ever tells the president things he doesn't want to hear. But back to what you just said. Do you really know what your way is? You sound awfully confused to me."

"I wish to hell I could say for sure that I did."

"Look, I'm gonna tell you something," said Wasserman. "I'll start with a small confession and then go on to my lecture. Are you up to it?"

Williamson smiled weakly, "Why not."

"To begin with, you've always been my idol. Here, I've always thought, is my best friend, and on top of that, the guy's one of the giants of American private industry. My friend. Son of a bitch. I'm a very fortunate guy to have such an important person as my friend."

"You're setting me up. I'm in no mood to be mocked."

"No, I'm fuckin' serious, Carr. I've always felt that way."

"Well you're no slouch yourself. Wall Street bond broker working the A-list. Hobnobbing with the crème de la crème up and down the East Coast."

"Lemme get back to my little speech. The point is, you know how I feel about you, so when I say what I'm going to say, you know it's from the heart. In my humble opinion you've got to take a long hard look at Laura and decide if you still love her," said Wasserman seriously. "If you still love her, I don't give a shit how great this other dame is, you gotta ask yourself why you rejected Laura."

"But I don't see it as rejecting Laura. At least I

didn't at the time. It was more that Kate and I were on the same wavelength. We were both out in the real world and talked the same language. She understood my needs better than Laura did."

"All this may be true. Only you know for sure, but you know what it sounds like from my side of the table?"

Williamson forced a weak grin, "Do I want to know?"

"Yeah, you do. You may not think you do, but you do. It sounds a lot like an attack of hot pants to me." Williamson started to protest, but Wasserman held up a hand, "No, wait, Carr. I can window dress it and call it a mid-life crisis, or one last fling, or proof of manhood, or even validation of your desirability. It's gotta fall in there somewhere, ol' buddy. Think about it for a minute. You're the president and CEO of one of the great publishing empires in this country. You're a success by anybody's standards. You could go out and get 100 women by the end of the week, for Chrissake. Why do you need validation? Can't be your ego is suffering. You didn't get to the top of the heap because of low self-esteem."

"I know, I know. Don't think I haven't been through all of the above scenarios a dozen times. Maybe you're right. Maybe. But at the time it seemed like more than that. Like being reborn. Like reawakening feelings you had as a kid."

"C'mon, Carr, you hit it. Kate reawakened feelings you had as a kid. Well you're not a kid anymore. Don't get me wrong, I could get aroused by some nubile young thing, too. At times it looks pretty good. But if you and Laura don't talk about anything interesting, who's fault is that?"

"Wait a minute, hold on now. Kate is not that young."

"How old is she?"

"Thirty-seven."

Wasserman grinned, "Ready for the rest home, huh?."

"Funny. Very funny."

"Okay, I shouldn't be so flip. Hell, I'd probably like her myself. Seriously, I know you wouldn't hang around with some bimbette, but the fact of the matter is you liked her because she's young, and because she's more adventuresome than Laura, more open to new ideas, and she thinks you're hot shit. Am I pretty close?"

"Close enough. But when you express it that way, the whole relationship sounds shallow. Believe me, Herb, it wasn't like that."

"Let me ask you the 64-thousand-dollar question. Do you still love Laura?"

"I knew you were going to ask that."

"Then of course you have an answer."

"Yes, I have an answer, and yes, I love Laura. I told you I broke it off with Kate."

"Then you've probably wrestled with this, too. Did you really love Kate, or did you merely find her exciting, or maybe the word is flattering? Flattering that this young attractive woman found you attractive? I'm sure it's crossed your mind that she found you attractive because you're president of Harmon Hall?"

"Of course I have, but she is no ga-ga-eyed groupie. She's a very competent attorney."

"How'd you meet her?"

"She's a partner in the firm we use to handle litigations. I know, I know. It's stupid. But it just sort of happened."

"Jesus, Carr, stupid isn't the half of it. No wonder you're stressed out. Does anyone else in the company or her law firm know?"

"No, or at least I'm almost certain they don't."

The tanned surfer type stopped at their table and asked if they wanted another beer. Wasserman looked up, "Yeah kid, bring us two more." He turned back to Williamson. "Okay, if you still love Laura, as you say you do, then breaking it off with this Kate was the right move. A little late, but at least a step in the right direction. There was no future in your relationship with Kate. Unfortunately for you bigamy is a crime in this country." Williamson frowned. "Sorry, bad joke. Seriously though, you had nothing but trouble ahead of you unless you made a choice. Even now it won't be easy. But looking at it from the standpoint of your mental health, you couldn't have gone on this way. Look, if I can be of any help at all, it's to reinforce the decision you made to break it off with this woman and to ask you if you don't share at least some of the blame for any dullness or lack of adventure that's overtaken your married life.

"I'm willing to bet that another element in this whole thing is that you've reached a point in your life where you suddenly realize that you probably can get other women, lots of them. And you think, no doubt unconsciously, that since there's a lot of fish in the sea, you should try a few different varieties. Hey, I'm not getting high and mighty on you. Don't think those thoughts haven't crossed my mind more than once. Over the course of a marriage we all come to times when we ask ourselves if we made the right choice. Usually it's when we're pissed off at our spouse for some dumb thing, but it can also be when we meet someone who's really nice, really sexy, and, most importantly, someone who pays a lot of attention to us. But I finally concluded that the differences are mostly superficial. I still love Estelle. I love her because of all that we've done together, and all that we've gone through together, and all those thousands of little experience, thoughts, and agonies we've shared—not to mention the great mother she's been to my kids. Sure, I'm not blind. Maybe she's not the best looker in the world. But she's not bad either, and there's always going to be someone better looking. Besides, I'm no prize myself. Anyway, Estelle's part of my life. In some ways the best part. She's the person I want to tell my good news to, as well as my problems. I won't lie to you, though, there are times when I'm tempted. Face it, some women look awfully good at times. So how do I deal with the temptation? I flirt a little, not much, but a little. Most of the time, though, I just sneak a look, and maybe fantasize.

"But here's the crux of it. I don't play around because at some point or other I realized that I could get another woman if I wanted to. When you view it that way you don't need further ego validation, or more to the point, validation that women still find you interesting. And, finally, there's the little matter of Estelle's feelings... and the kids'. Okay, I've said too much. The longest damned speech I've made in my life. Hope I didn't bore you, my friend."

"No, you didn't bore me. I appreciate your honesty. You know, Herb, even though I've ended my relationship with Kate, my problems aren't going to go away. Item number one: Do I tell Laura? And if I do, will she take me back? Item number two: This young editor can still get me fired if Howard and the board find out about this. The very fact that I got him promoted for the wrong reason could land my ass on the street. The best solution would be if this little creep just disappeared from the face of the Earth."

# TEN

Carmen's was the kind of place at which you could roll up your sleeves, relax, and not worry about how loud you were talking. The Williamsons and the Wassermans loved to come there. Tried to make it once a week unless something else came up. At Carmen's you didn't feel you were disturbing someone else, because they, too, were having the same kind of good time you were. Food was good, not great, but good. Mostly red sauce, and tasty, very tasty. And Carmen made you feel welcome. None of that phoney pretentious restaurateur stuff you encountered in so many of the more trendy restaurants in Westchester.

"So, guys, how did you two brave warriors do on the court today?" asked Laura with an impish grin.

"You don't wanna know," said Carr.

"Oh but we do," chimed in Estelle. "We do."

"Let's just say that I've had better days," said Carr. "Your husband whipped my butt. He played very well, unfortunately."

"Just to set the record straight," said Herb, "It's the first time I've beaten him in two years."

"Well, savor the moment. It'll be another two years before you beat me again. Can't let this winning stuff become a habit."

Carmen came over and hugged each of the four good friends. They made small talk for a couple of minutes,
punctuated by sincere laughter. Finally, Carmen asked what they'd like to drink. Herb said, "Carmen, you got any more of that great chianti we had last week?"

"Chianti classico?"

"Yeah, that's it."

"Yes, I gotta coupla bottles, You want?"

Herb looked at each of the others, and, getting

no objection, said, "Yeah, that sounds good."

The two couples chattered on for half an hour about tennis, the club, the latest outbreak of fighting in the Middle East, and Herb's new Lexus, which he said was, next to Estelle, the love of his life.

When Carmen came back to take their orders, Laura selected chicken with basil and white-wine sauce. Estelle said she'd have the same, and Carr took penne with Bolognese sauce, saying he knew meat sauce wasn't good for him, but he didn't cheat very often. No one noticed as Herb and Estelle exchange furtive glances. When it came to Herb, he chose shrimp marinara, and suggested that they get a couple of orders of stuffed clams as an appetizer they could all share.

"You seem pretty chipper, Carr," said Estelle. "Have a good week?" Herb looked at her, raising his eyebrows and slowly shaking his head a quarter of an inch back and forth.

"To be honest with you, Estelle," replied Carr, "I've had better weeks."

"I'm sorry to hear that, What's the problem?

"Just the usual business stuff. It'll all sort itself out."

"Gee, and here I always thought that no business problem was too big for you, Carr. I don't remember you ever having a bad week at the office. Must be a big problem." Herb gave her the Jewish malocchio and held his breath. Carr glared at her, wondering why all of a sudden this normally pleasant person was being such a royal pain in the ass. Then he looked over at Herb and knew from his friend's expression what the answer was.

"You didn't tell me you had a bad week, Carr," said Laura. "Anything serious?"

"No," he replied, trying to control his temper, "nothing serious. Don't worry. Don't worry."

"I know you've been terribly busy, but..."

"Laura, I said there's nothing wrong."

"Maybe he's just tired, Laura," said Estelle.

Carr gave her an angry look, Herb spoke up, "Look, Estelle, he doesn't want to talk about it."

"There's nothing to talk about, for Christ's sake," exploded Carr. "All I said was it wasn't the best week. Everybody has an occasional bad week at the office. If you don't have bad weeks, how do you recognize good ones?"

"Very astute," said Herb, forcing a smile. "Good folk wisdom. So how do you think the Giants will do this fall, Carr?"

Williamson knew he was being "handled," and he felt like expressing his resentment of the obvious patronization, but he knew also that the evening was resting on shaky ground and resisted the temptation to object. Instead, he excused himself, saying he was going to the men's room. Herb got up and followed him out of the dining room, intercepting him just before he reached the door to the rest room. "Carr, can we step outside for a second?"

"What's on your mind?" asked Williamson brusquely. The air in the parking lot was cool and dry, especially for late August. Herb could see Carr was annoyed, and hesitated before plunging ahead.

"Look, about Estelle..."

"You told her didn't you?"

"Well, yeah, but I had to."

"Bullshit, you had to. Jesus, I told you that in confidence, Herb. How could you do that to me?"

"She's my wife, for Christ's sake. You know how close we are. It won't go any further, I promise you."

"She practically let the cat out of the fuckin' bag in there just now. She can't wait to tell someone. She was baiting me, Herb, baiting me." Williamson never felt so out of control in his life. His closest friend had betrayed him. On top of that he had no idea how he'd be able to continue keeping his now defunct affair from his wife and daughter. And at Harmon Hall he no longer had the final say on personnel matters.

Herb reached out and held him by the shoulders, "It won't go any further, I promise you."

# ELEVEN

The mission Williamson had set out on was a risky one. It was Monday evening following the weekend in which he and Herb Wasserman had argued in the parking lot of Carmen's. In the wake of that unpleasant scene, Williamson was, if possible, even more on edge than he had been immediately after Andy Mack walked into his office that ill-fated day last week.

As Carson Williamson looked back over the past six months, he had to admit to himself that his nerves had become increasingly more frayed. This week had really brought things to a head, and he was no longer the self-assured captain of industry he'd fancied himself a week earlier. Strange how quickly the fortunes of love and war can change a person's life. He'd always thought of himself as a student of history, and the lessons of hubris had not escaped him. But the fall from contentment he was now so painfully experiencing had taken him completely by surprise.

It was now 7:30 p.m. He'd just gotten off the elevator at the 16th floor. No one to be seen. So far, so good. If memory served him right, the reference area was to his right. Hadn't been down here in quite awhile. He walked slowly, trying to appear casual in case he ran into someone. It didn't matter who he ran into because he, the president of the company, was not on his home turf. Not that anyone would deny him the right to be there. Not at all. It was just that they'd wonder *why* he was there. They wouldn't ask him, course. They'd ask the next person they saw, who would in turn ask the next person he or she saw, until it finally got back to Marcantonio and ultimately Markham. Even if such a chain of events occurred, it would not be a huge problem. Except that now, in his current state of vulnerability, he didn't need complications. No huge problem, that is, if he were merely seen in the corridor. There would definitely be a problem, however, if he were seen in Mack's office.

The lights were off in most of the offices. He'd counted on that. The majority of the office doors were open, too. The only office in the reference area that even had a lock was that of Tony Marcantonio, the editorial director. Williamson looked to his left; then to his right. He felt like a common second-story man must feel as he was about to break into a house. He pulled his carefully folded handkerchief from his pocket and wiped the beads of perspiration from his forehead. The building management turned the air off at six p.m., so it was becoming extremely uncomfortable in the building. *It's come to this. God, what have I done to myself?* Here he was, the CEO of the company, sneaking around, hoping to save his own skin. He shook his head. This was no time for self-indulgent pity.

Fortunately, the name of each editor was on the wall next to the door jamb. At last he came to A. Mack. The office was dark. It was a small office. Okay, nothing to be afraid of. Just dart in and quickly look around. If he could just find those photos and their negatives. The kid probably kept them at home in his apartment, but you never know. Be a shame not to look, just in case the obnoxious S.O.B. was so cocky that he kept them here. His problems would be over if he found them. Yes, it was worth the small risk. Besides, who's going to question the president if they did see him?

He had a story prepared, on the off chance that someone did come by. Kind of a lame story, but better than nothing. Still no one around. Then he had a vivid image of being caught in Mack's office. The humiliation would be unbearable. Maybe he should wait another hour, just to be sure. He remained standing in the corridor a few feet from the doorway, trying to look as if he were deep in thought in case someone came along. He looked both ways, as nonchalantly as he could. No one. Might as well get this over with.

Despite his nervousness, he had to admire the desk. It wasn't company issue Steelcase or whatever. No, Mack had somehow managed to wangle himself an antique mahogany masterpiece. Must have ten drawers. *Bastard has good taste, I'll give him that.*

He started with the middle drawer. It was amazingly clean. He moved quickly to the top side drawer. Very little there. Neat as a pin. *Tidy little bugger.* The next one down had a number of note pads, and three nine-by-12 manila envelopes, each sealed by its metal clasp. Behind these was a wooden file box. He quickly went through each of the manila envelopes. Parts of manuscripts in two of them and old expense reports in the third. He then turned to the file box. Business cards and scraps of paper with names and phone numbers on them. No pictures. He was about to turn to the next drawer when he noticed something strange about the bottom of the drawer. Nothing specific other than the fact that it didn't seem to match the sides of the drawer. And the drawer seemed a little shallower than it should be. Yes. It appeared to have a false bottom. Hardly noticeable at first glance. Finally he figured out how to pry it up. As he lifted it up, he came upon an assortment of papers and two more manila envelopes. Williamson quickly opened the first envelope. It contained what appeared to be the first few chapters of a book manuscript entitled **Blackmail**. Williamson didn't recognize the name of the author. He shook his head, *You son of a bitch.* He resealed the envelope and started on the second when he heard footsteps. Hurriedly he put everything back as he'd found it and started for the door. *Wait, better take a look first.* No one to the right...or to the left. As he stepped into the corridor a young man came around the corner toward him. "Oh, hi Mr. Williamson." He seemed startled. "Didn't expect to see you here."

"Hello there," recovered Williamson, feigning an air of authority that he didn't feel under the circumstances. "You're working late."

"Yeah, I get a lot done after the phone stops ringing."

"I know what you mean. Still, don't you think you've worked long enough for one day?"

"I suppose so. I'll be leaving soon. Good night."

As the young man left, Williamson pondered the advisability of going back into Andy Mack's office. That was a close call. Probably should leave well enough alone. But he was so close. He had to know what was in the other envelope. What if the young man came back? How far away was his office? Williamson followed the corridor the man had left by. About 10 or 12 doors away he saw a light. Must be him. Good, he's far enough away not to be a problem. He turned around and went back to Mack's office. As he opened the second envelope he could see it contained photographs. Yes, these were what he was looking for! They were all there. Not just the three Mack had shown him, but a couple dozen, the whole roll. But no negatives. Damn! Should he take these anyway? Mack would still have the negs. Then his cautious side advised him. Why provoke the little shit, if he couldn't get the negs, too. Can't tell what he'll do if you piss him off. Reluctantly he replaced the pictures in the envelope, and closed the drawer.

"Anything I can help you with, sir?"

Williamson jumped. "God, you startled me," he said as he looked up. The security guard, a gray haired man of about 65, was leaning into the office, left forearm on the door jamb.

"We don't have many people working in here at this hour, sir. This your office?"

# TWELVE

Jacqui Dyer sat quietly in the chair facing Andy Mack's desk. He'd called her in because he'd said he had something he wanted to go over with her. That was ten minutes ago, and Andy hadn't yet returned to his office. How long did he expect her to cool her heels? She ran a hand through her hair. She'd discovered a couple of gray hairs recently, but she doubted whether anyone else noticed. She'd be 39 in two months, so you'd expect a few gray hairs. Many people still considered her an unusually beautiful woman. The onset of 40 only seemed to enhance her appearance. Jacqui had always been ambitious. Still, she prided herself in never intentionally using her looks to further her career. Oh sure, she knew that, at times, it had been a distinct advantage. Couldn't help that. She certainly wasn't going to deliberately make herself appear plain. She was born with an asset, and she was thankful for it. By the same token, it clearly didn't cut any ice with Andy. Or Tony Marcantonio or Stuart Markham either, for that matter. Just Yesterday Tony had called her into his office to tell her that he was giving her project to Andy Mack. Some bullshit about how the division was being restructured. Andy was now going to be managing editor. Her talents could best be utilized in other ways. She'd have a lot more responsibility in the division in the months ahead. They had something important coming up soon that they wanted her to handle. Couldn't talk about it now, but he and Stuart didn't want her bogged down in one massive project. Hope she understood and saw how in the long run she'd be better off. She hadn't seen anything of the sort. As a matter of fact she'd created a minor scene until she finally got hold of herself. She couldn't believe what she'd heard from Tony. Andy was positively the least likely candidate for managing editor she could have imagined. And his people skills were something on the order of minus 10. How could they have put him in charge of the biggest project the company'd ever done? She shook her head in despair as she thought about it. She tried to put yesterday's devastating news behind her, but it was still too fresh, too raw. The anger was just below the surface.

She was just about to leave and come back later when Andy walked in and sat down.

"Jacqui," he began without apologizing for keeping her waiting. "I'm not at all pleased with the way you've organized the dictionary project. The more I get into it, the more I realize I'm going to have to make a number of changes."

She couldn't believe her ears. A week ago she'd looked upon Andy as a reclusive nerd. Sure, he appeared to be a competent line editor, as far as she could tell, but he'd never demonstrated any leadership ability. Now, this misanthropic pariah was demonstrating once again how insensitive he was. He could have at least said something about how he knew it must be tough on her losing her project. Instead he rubs salt in the wound — an extremely fresh wound at that — by telling her he doesn't like the way she's organized the project. She, who had managed numerous other, albeit smaller, projects successfully. What had he ever managed? Now this guy robs her of her big career opportunity. The project of a lifetime. It was all so Kafkaesque. She'd always considered herself a fairly easygoing person—at least until someone stepped on her toes. Andy Mack had stepped on both her toes with his entire weight. She wasn't going to knuckle under without a fight. "What's wrong with the project, Andy?"

"The schedule you've come up with, in my opinion, is all wrong..."

"Like what? Specifically?"

"Wait, I'm not finished." He ignored her glare, "I

think your approach to data gathering leaves a lot to be desired, and..."

"Andy, please, let me comment..."

"Wait until I'm through.  Then you'll have a chance to comment — though I don't see what good it'll do you.  I've made up my mind as to what must be done."

"Why are you doing this to me?  What have I ever done to you?"

"Don't be paranoid," he said patronizingly. "Nothing personal here. Don't worry, I'm not canning you.  You're a decent editor. But I'm sure you realize how important this project is."

"Golly gee, Andy, thanks for the news flash." She knew as soon as she'd said it that her smart aleck remark wasn't going to help her cause.

"Since you're able to treat this matter so lightly, I feel no compunction in telling you how relieved I am that I took over the project before things went too far off course. I really think this would have been too big for you, Jacqui."

For a moment she was speechless. Then, very deliberately she said, "I consider that insulting. I assure you this isn't finished."

"I'll have the final say.  I assure you,"

"Something strange is going on here, and I'm going to find out what."

"Not strange. Just logical. Senior management finally came to their senses. Tony appointed me managing editor, and put me in charge of the project. I hate to be blunt, but if you don't like it, find another job. Now I'm rather busy."

"You bastard! This is wrong, and you know it."

Andy Mack grinned contentedly, "I know nothing of the kind. Now I'd appreciate it if you'd go. I have things to do."

"I'm not letting this rest, Andy. You'll fry in hell before I accept this!"

\* \* \*

Up on the 31st floor, Tony Marcantonio stood glaring at Stuart Markham over the latter's immaculately clean desk. He took a moment to survey the room. Something was different. The furniture was the same, but the room looked substantially different from the way it had looked only a few days ago. It was the art, he realized. Expensive art and graphics. He had a couple of prints in his own office. Not originals. Nobody famous. Neither had cost him two hundred dollars with frame. Markham had upgraded the art in his office in just the past few days. And Tony could see at a glance that Markham's new acquisitions were inclined to be a bit pricier than what had been there before. As before, the pieces were contemporary work, but these new pieces were recognizable originals by famous artists. The Jackson Pollock on the far wall had to be worth a million or two by today's ridiculously inflated art standards. Not that Marcantonio liked Pollock. He could never quite understand how people could drip paint on a canvas and have the art world fawn all over them as if they were the second coming of Da Vinci. And was that a Rauschenberg? Holy shit! Where did Stuart get his money? These two pictures alone had to be worth at least a couple of million. He turned back to Markham.

"You've changed the art work, Stuart. These are big league."

Markham beamed proudly. His weakness, he knew, "I have good friends in the art world, Tony. Believe me, I bought them for a lot less than their current value. Decided to bring them in from home. I still have one or two rather good canvases at home, too. But, I'm sure you didn't drop by so unexpectedly to discuss art. What can I do for you?"

Marcantonio got right to the point, "Stuart, what the hell have you unleashed on me?"

"Tony, Tony. Sit down. Stop hovering."

Marcantonio dropped into a chair and continued excitedly, "Stuart, you forced this guy on me against my will. For whatever reason. Okay, you're the boss. But I have to tell you, it was a mistake. The guy's in the new job two days and already he's alienated half the staff."

Markham examined his immaculately manicured fingernails. "Why don't you tell me all about it. As dispassionately as you can, if you don't mind."

*You're such a snob, Stuart. Such a pompous pain in the ass.* "I'll start at the beginning," said Marcantonio, trying to control his emotions. "First thing he does, within two hours of taking over his new office, is start to rearrange the editorial assignments in the department. That's not part of the managing editor's job description for Christ's sake. And get this, he tells me about what he's doing, after it's a fait accompli. Doesn't consult me first. Just goes ahead and does it. Who the hell's he think he is, Stuart? I never saw such balls! It was almost as if he didn't care what I thought. I'm his boss, damn it. Nobody in his right mind goes into a new managerial position and does that."

"All right, so he's a little hasty and a little rough around the edges. Besides his bad manners, though, did he make any really inappropriate personnel moves?"

"They were all inappropriate, if you consider that he didn't take any time to consider them. That is unless you informed him of his promotion a long time ago, Stuart. In which case I have to go on record as saying that I would consider that a real slap in the face. Frankly, either way, I'm not too happy about your not giving me the courtesy of at least talking to me about it before you went ahead and did it."

"I want you to believe me, Tony, when I say that this was not planned in advance. Let's just say that there were political reasons for promoting young Mack. I must ask you to indulge me on this one. Please don't ask for any more explanation than that. It's extremely uncomfortable for me to have to handle it this way, but I think you understand that in a company this big there are many forces to contend with."

"Okay, okay. Pretty mysterious. I'll play the game. Probably Howard or Williamson putting on the squeeze. Kid must be somebody's relative. You don't have to answer that."

"Thank you, Tony, for being so understanding," said Markham almost humbly, for him an unfamiliar emotion.

"I'm trying, but you should be aware that golden boy's emergence has been particularly hard on Jacqui Dyer.

"Yes, of course. I'm sure it has."

"He's not only grabbed her project, but apparently he's been adding insult to injury by telling her how badly she organized it. Shows absolutely no compassion or understanding. Instead of trying to boost her morale, he's undermining it to the point where I don't know what she'll do. This guy is trouble, Stuart. I'm tellin' you. To be honest, I'm not sure how I should handle him. I'll tell you one thing I am sure of, though, I think the kid is unstable as hell. Another reason why I never would have dreamed of giving him this responsibility."

"You've already made your point about the dubious qualifications of your new managing editor," said Markham, frustration showing on his face. "We're both going to have to be a little patient here, something that neither of us is particularly good at. Believe me, I do understand."

"All right, I'll put this to the test tomorrow. I'm going to give Mack a little reminder that he works for me."

"Yes, you do that, Tony, but remember, we do

have a political situation here so try to avoid all-out warfare."

"You mean I can't offend this guy or someone from above will descend upon me and have my job? Is that what you mean, Stuart? If that's the case, so be it. I'm sorry, I can't function as editorial director if I know that my key manager is gonna go running to some higher up just because I disagree with him."

"Look, all I'm saying is try not to let this thing get out of control. Reason with the young man and we'll all be better off."

"Look, Stuart, it's not just my sensitivities at stake here. It's a multimillion-dollar project. This could be a disaster for the company, if he seriously messes things up."

Markham inhaled deeply. After a few seconds, he exhaled slowly, a despondent expressing suffusing his patrician features. "Good God, Tony, don't you think I know that?"

\* \* \*

Down the hall, relaxing during a momentary hiatus in his hectic schedule, Carson Williamson reflected on the previous evening. What a disaster. Well, maybe not a disaster, but not good. Not good at all. The damn security guard did his job proud. How many security guards do anything but take up space? He had to run into one who took his work seriously. When he'd told the guard that he was the president of the company and that he, the guard, was doing a fine job, the guard had said, "That's kind of you to say, sir. May I see some identification?" Christ, he, the president of an international giant, with nearly 4,000 employees worldwide and with offices in London, Sydney, Auckland, and Toronto as well as here in New York, he, Carson Williamson, was reduced to the status of some petty break-and-entry man. The indignity of it made him cringe every time he thought of the embarrassing incident. Fortunately he'd had a couple of his business cards in his wallet. He shuddered to think what would have happened if he hadn't had them with him. Nothing else in his wallet said he was president of Harmon Hall. Not his driver's license, not his credit cards. Nothing. And the security guard clearly didn't recognize his name. *Not as big a deal as you think you are, Williamson.* If he hadn't found those business cards the guard would have had to call the security office or walk him to his own office so he could show the old guy his name on the door. Another lesson in hubris, learned the hard way.

Still, the guard would remember the incident, and no doubt report it to Birchfield, that manipulating former FBI agent who'd been head of security for Harmon Hall for the past ten years. Okay, his story would probably satisfy Birchfield. He'd told the guard that they were thinking of doing something with the space the reference division was in, and he was just looking it over when it was quiet so as not to disturb anyone. He pledged the guard to secrecy, saying, "You know how the rumors would fly if people thought they were going to move." The guard had said not to worry. The secret was safe with him. *Sure it is. For about five minutes.* Another complication, but easier to handle than, "Did you hear that Carson Williamson was caught going through someone's office last night. Like a common thief."

He'd handled the lousy situation as well as he could have. It could have been a lot worse. What if the old guy had caught him going through Mack's drawer? That would have been a helluva lot harder to finesse. He wasn't out of the woods yet, but thank God it wasn't worse.

# THIRTEEN

It was 7:15 a.m., and Andy Mack had already been in his office a quarter of an hour. Until last week he'd never gotten in before 8:45. Usually closer to 9:30. But since being promoted to managing editor he'd discovered energy and enthusiasm he hadn't felt in years...maybe never. It was a good feeling. *Frankly, my boy, you're amazing. You've come a long way, Andy.* Okay, so he wasn't the most popular manager in the company. But what was it people said about the need to break a few eggs if you wanted to make an omelet? He had to let his staff know who was boss right from the start.

He wasn't interested in winning popularity contests, anyway. He was interested in respect, something that had been sorely lacking in the first 29 years of his life. He'd always resented Tony Marcantonio's ignoring him while coddling the rest of the editors in the department. He smiled with satisfaction at how suddenly the tables had been turned. He knew that virtually every move he made now was pissing off Marcantonio. And there was very little Tony could do about it. *It didn't get any better than this.* What was Tony going to do, fire him? Fat chance. God, what a beautiful situation. This is the kind of situation that employees fantasize about, and he was living it. Who would have believed it. And all because he'd had the balls to stop wishing and actually do something about his life. Of course, being given the opportunity was great good luck, but how many people would have had the courage to act on it? He thought about all the whiners he knew who would merely consider the Williamson affair nothing more than a juicy piece of gossip instead of the mother lode. Yes, that's not bad, the mother lode. It was a testimony to both his imagination and his initiative that he did more than just gossip about what had so serendipitously dropped into his lap a little over a week ago. And he wasn't going to lose any sleep over whether or not it was morally acceptable behavior. Was the company's treatment of Andy Mack so morally equitable? Was Williamson's behavior so virtuous? Hardly. No, it was clear for anyone but a fool to see that it was the individual — in this case himself — against the giant corporation, a corporation, like all corporations, without a soul and without a conscience. Getting ahead at Harmon Hall was a survival skill. Morality had nothing to do with it. Fortunately for him, it was a skill that he was finally learning to master.

What he was doing might cause a little inconvenience to Williamson. His girlfriend might not be too happy either. Tough. Not to mention Marcantonio and his boss, that stuffed shirt, Markham, both of whom had to be fuming about having their hands tied. And that bitch Jacqui Dyer seemed about ready to explode over losing her project. He smiled in satisfaction. Finally, after eight years of being pushed around, or worse yet, ignored, he was in the driver's seat. And it was about time. If the others were unhappy, so be it. It's about time they felt a fraction of the frustration he'd put up with ever since he'd joined the company. Every one of them should suffer a little.

He felt the presence of someone in the doorway. He looked up and recognized his visitor. He was a little taken back, but quickly recovered. "To what do I owe the honor of this visit?" he asked smugly.

His visitor smiled and stepped into Andy's office, closing the door quietly in the process. "Andy, please don't consider it an honor. You've caused me and several other people a lot of trouble. Frankly, I don't see the problem going away. As things stand, I see my future being ruined by you. I can't have that, Andy.

With you around, nothing is right. With you out of the way, everything will be right."

"I don't think you have any choice," grinned Andy wickedly.

"Oh but I do, I do." With that, the visitor pulled out a small handgun with a silencer attached, took careful aim, and shot Mack twice in the chest. For a brief moment Andrew Mack didn't move. His smug expression didn't change. Then the full realization of what had happened to him showed in his dying eyes as he fell forward onto the paper-strewn desk. "Say goodbye, Andy," said the visitor, who then turned, looked both ways, and casually walked from the office and out of the reference department.

When the intercom buzzed, Williamson glanced at his Rolex. Exactly eight a.m. "Yes, Betsy, what is it?"

"It's Walter Birchfield, Mr. Williamson. Says it's urgent."

"What could be so damned urgent at eight o'clock in the morning?"

"He wouldn't tell me."

"Never mind. Just thinking out loud. Put him on."

"Mr. Williamson? You there?" asked the gruff voice of Harmon Hall's chief of security.

"Yes, Walter, what's so important?"

"Someone's been shot down on sixteen, sir."

"Oh my God, who?"

"One of your editors. Guy named Mack."

"Is he...?"

"Yeah, 'fraid so, sir. Shot twice through the chest. Must have been instantaneous. Poor bastard."

Carr's mind had been racing all morning. He had to concentrate on what he said to Birchfield. Birchfield had the reputation of being a wheeler-dealer, always looking for an angle. Word was he was never a great field agent for the F.B.I. Yet somehow he'd been able to persuade Williamson's predecessor to hire him as chief of security for Harmon Hall. Williamson had never been able to find out much more than that, but he sensed that Birchfield's reputation for being a little sleazy was well deserved. Still, he'd never had any reason to fire him. Despite his reputation, and despite his unkempt, overstuffed appearance, he was efficient and clearly intelligent, in an unconventional, redneck sort of way.

The most annoying thing about Walter Birchfield, thought Williamson, was his blue-collar practice of peppering his conversation with sir. Williamson wasn't sure whether this fawning behavior reflected a perceived class distinction on the part of Birchfield or whether the overweight security chief was simply an inveterate ass kisser. One thing Williamson did know was that he couldn't afford to treat the man lightly. The guy had more connections than a sewer pipe.

"Where are you calling from, Walter?"

"I'm at the scene of the crime, sir. The office next to his. Felt you should know right away. But I gotta call the police now."

"Of course, I'll be right down, Walter."

As he approached Andy Mack's office, Williamson could see that a small crowd had formed in the immediate area. He excused himself as he pushed through to where Birchfield and three of his security guards stood talking in front of Andy Mack's office.

"Oh hi, Mr. Williamson," said Birchfield. "He's in there, just the way we found him."

Williamson pushed open the door and looked in at the body of Andy Mack slumped over his desk. No blood to be seen. Looked as if the poor son-of-a-bitch were taking a nap. "Who found him?" he asked.

"Young woman in the office directly opposite.

Name's Fern Mallory."

"How long ago?"

"About 7:45. She was dropping something off and found him like that. Scared the hell out of her. She's over there, with some of the other editors. She called me right away. Lucky she got me. I'm usually not in till eight or a little after."

"Does Stuart Markham or Tony Marcantonio know about this?"

"Not yet, sir. I understand they both get here about 8:30 or so. Didn't see any point in calling their homes since both of them are probably on their way in."

"Right. Good thinking," he said absent-mindedly. He was thinking ahead — to how the whole thing would shake out after the dust had settled. One thing was certain, the little prick was really dead. "Do you have any idea who could have done this, Walter?"

"Right now we haven't got a clue. We've asked everyone here to stay put until the police come and say they can leave. I've also positioned men at each entrance to the building. No one's to leave until the police come and give the okay," said Birchfield proudly. He was convinced he'd handled things professionally and competently.

"Can your men keep people from leaving, Walter? I mean, if someone wants to leave, what are your people going to do?"

"If anyone refuses to stay, we're asking them to show identification. We'll at least know who left and at what time. If they refuse I.D., each of the men has a camera and will snap their picture. Little trick I picked up years ago."

"Sounds like you're on top of things. I wish the police would get here so we could get the body out. This place will be a circus until we do. Does he have a wife, by the way?"

"Someone said he's gay. Lives with another

guy. We called the deceased's apartment, and got a machine. Recording mentioned Andy and a Paul. Paul must be at work somewhere."

"Probably," said Williamson. He'd drifted off again with his own thoughts. Andy Mack was dead. Not just shot and wounded, but dead. He'd seen it with his own eyes. He could relax now. Sure, there'd be all kinds of inquiries and bad press for the company, but in the end he'd be in the clear. God, what a relief.

# Part 2

# FOURTEEN

Gwen Pappas joined the New York City Police force five years ago at the age of 19. She'd attended Queensborough Community College her first year out of high school. Gwen did well at Queensborough, but she'd always wanted to be a cop. Her father was a cop. Without telling her parents she applied to the police department. When she was accepted, she made the decision to put off finishing college until some later date. During her first four years on the force she achieved an outstanding performance record. Then she was promoted to homicide detective. This was the first time in her four years on the force that she had any doubts at all about her chosen career. She wasn't too sure that she wanted homicide, but as time went on she discovered that, despite the often disgusting circumstances and the nearly always sickening sight of corpses — she still hadn't gotten used to that — she had to admit that she was actually a very good homicide detective. Gwen's father, who never rose above detective first grade in his 23 years on the force, was now living vicariously through her. He'd retired only three months before she made detective, and he was convinced she'd be the first woman police commissioner in the City of New York.

Euripides (Rip) Pappas had been in homicide for the better part of his career with the New York City Police Department. His parents, originally from the Isle of Rhodes, loved the theater and loved the classics. They'd named their first-born after the Greek tragedian who lived from 484B.C. to 406B.C. Detective Pappas had been good at his work, nobody ever denied that, but he manifested what department shrinks had eventually called a "personality disorder," a problem that kept him from otherwise well-deserved promotions throughout his career. Pappas was moody and unpredictable. On more than one occasion he'd been known to give inexperienced assistants the worst kind of verbal tongue lashings, regardless of who else was present. He'd repeatedly justified these tirades by maintaining that he had no tolerance for stupidity or sloppy work. Claimed that he had a right to expect the same level of dedication to the job that he'd given to his work for the entire 23 years.

Pappas never hid his disappointment when someone failed to measure up to his standards. Very few ever did. As the years went by, and he failed to earn promotions, he became cynical and petty. He seemed to take pleasure when others failed to live up to "his" standards. His infamous short fuse made him an unfortunate legend in his own time, and guaranteed he'd never rise above detective second grade.

Clearly Pappas wasn't the most popular cop in the precinct. He might have been the least popular. His last partner summed it up by saying Pappas was not exactly a barrel of laughs on the job. Still, even his harshest critics, if pressed, would admit that, if you could stand the abuse, you could always learn something from Rip Pappas. Hell, if you were assigned to duty with Pappas, you might even get the perp. The smartest of the young cops who served their stints with Rip Pappas endured it with a strong case of mixed emotions. They knew they'd learn something, so they figured they'd put up with his crap for awhile. But they couldn't wait to move on to another partner. Any other partner. To Gwen, however, Rip Pappas was a hero. He was her idol. As long as she could remember she had hoped to be half as good a cop as her dad was — not realizing that, in many ways, she was already better. She was only vaguely aware of his flaws, because he'd seldom exhibited his "impatience" with her, the apple of his eye.

Today Gwen was working with Dawson Flynn, an experienced, and savvy detective who'd seen it all.

Getting assigned to work with Flynn she considered a stroke of great good luck — a consideration not shared by all of her fellow detectives. They told her she was naive if she considered herself lucky to work with Flynn. Oh his detractors admitted Flynn knew his stuff, but that didn't make him any easier to work with. In their view he was irritable, impatient, and not the most tactful colleague in the precinct. He liked to do things his way. On top of that he was a bit odd. That was putting it nicely. The more outspoken of his colleagues considered him a royal pain in the ass. Flynn and Pappas had only been working together for a few weeks now, and Gwen had begun to understand what her fellow officers were talking about. Flynn wasn't the easiest man to work with. But it hadn't been as bad as they'd led her to expect either.

A uniformed cop named Sweeney accompanied the two detectives. As the three policemen arrived at the scene, Flynn flashed his badge and shouted, "Police! Who's in charge of security here?"

"Right here. Walter Birchfield, chief of security. And this is Mr. Williamson, president of the company."

Flynn shook their hands indifferently and addressed Birchfield, "Right now you're the one I want to speak to." He turned to Gwen and said, "Get a list of these people and see that nobody leaves until I say so. Okay, Birchfield, let's see the body."

Two minutes later Flynn and Birchfield emerged from Andy Mack's office, and Flynn said, "Okay everybody, as soon as we get your name, position, or address, and a quick statement you can go back to your jobs. A forensic team will be here in a few minutes. You cooperate with them and with the officers here, and this won't take too long. Mr. Williamson, you and I better talk now."

# FIFTEEN

The forensic team had done its work. The photographer took a bunch of shots, shooting the body and the crime scene from every possible angle. Specialists dusted the area for prints, and examined everything in the office that could conceivably be examined. The job had been thorough. Flynn and Pappas had conducted brief interviews with the people at the scene of the crime and finally the body had been removed from the office. The office was now sealed with yellow tape, with a uniformed officer guarding the crime scene. Thus, a shaky semblance of order had been restored to the reference department at Harmon Hall.

  Back in his own office Flynn sipped black coffee cautiously from a mug that was still too hot to drink. He looked across his dented metal desk at his partner. "So whaddya' think Gwen?" Gwen looked a bit surprised at the question. It was high praise when Flynn asked for an opinion from an assistant. Or was he testing her?

  "You've seen a lot more than I have, Dawson, but..." she stopped herself. "I know that sounds patronizing, but the fact of the matter is, you have. Anyway, this one seems real strange to me. Not a robbery. Didn't touch his wallet. Doesn't look like a crime of passion either. That kind of killing usually happens in the home, or in a bar. And it doesn't look like the work of some nut gone berserk either, so I doubt if it's a random killing. Besides, random killings are more public. Lots of people around." She paused for a second; then said, "That leaves someone inside the company...with a motive. But what? And why in the building?"

  "Good questions, Gwen." Flynn looked appreciatively at his junior partner of the past month.

She was bright, conscientious, and easy to work with. And he couldn't help feel an involuntary attraction to her. Actually, her mouth was a little too large, and her nose was far from perfect, but even given the defeminizing way she gathered her long auburn hair on her head, she was an attractive woman.

Who was he kidding? Why should she be interested in him. He was 17 years her senior, and way past his prime. He knew he'd let himself go in recent years. Didn't seem to care so much about personal appearance as he used to. Those extra inches around the waist didn't help either. Hell, he'd always had bad luck with women anyway. Why should Gwen be any different? He shook his head imperceptibly and returned his attention to Gwen, "All good questions. Let's look at what we have so far. This Mack guy was managing editor of the reference division. Just promoted last week according to Fern Mallory, the editor in the office across from his his. And not too well liked, if you can believe her."

"I think you can. Several of the editors I spoke with said he was a real S.O.B. Some pretty strong language from some of them — considering the guy just bought the farm. How do you figure it, Dawson? Mack is in his new job one week, and already he's despised. I mean, even the worst prick takes longer than that to cause so much animosity."

Flynn winced, "I never heard you say that before."

"Sorry if I shocked you. Guess I'm not man enough to talk like one of the boys."

"Do you want to be one of the boys?"

"Well, yes, I suppose I do, on the job that is."

"You're doin' fine. Be yourself. Anyway, you've got a point. Mack must've been a regular Dale Carnegie. Okay, so this guy was not Mr. Nice Guy. Is that a motive for murder? If it is, half the bosses in this town would be dead." A wry grin crossed his face,

"For that matter, so would I. There has to be more to it than that. You with me on this?"

"Yes. I agree. This thing was too neat, too clean to be the work of some employee who suddenly lost control. My guess is it was carefully planned by someone with a better reason than 'I hate your guts, Andy.'"

"There's going to be a lot of pressure from above to solve this one. People don't get shot in office buildings. Not good for business. Not good for the city's image. The mayor'll be all over the commissioner, and right on down the line. We gotta find this guy."

"What makes you think it's a guy?"

"Nothing. Could be a woman. Christ, the place was crawlin' with 'em over there. Point is we don't stop until we find the perp. Think out loud for a minute. What do we know, and what don't we know?"

"We can assume that whoever did this was no stranger to Mack. First of all, why would a perfect stranger come into the building and shoot another stranger. Good chance he'd be noticed, if he did try it."

Flynn grinned, "What makes you think it's a man?"

She smiled sheepishly, "Touché. Whatever. Anyway, if for some strange reason a whacko came into the building, there's a good chance someone would have noticed that he, or she, didn't belong."

"Maybe not at seven a.m. Don't forget, there weren't many people around the building at that hour. I'm more inclined to think the perp did it at that hour—seven in the morning—so he..." Flynn quickly recovered, "or she, wouldn't be seen."

"I agree. But I still think it's unlikely a stranger would come into the building to make a random hit. They'd consider it too risky. Feel too conspicuous. I think it's someone Mack knew, someone who could find Mack in that building without asking anyone for directions. Which, to my way of thinking, means there's a good chance it was someone who works at Harmon Hall."

"Good chance, but don't eliminate friends and relatives."

"True, but I'd lean toward colleagues, Dawson."

"So would I. Okay, let's get on with it."

"Where do we start?"

"Let's look at your list."

"I suppose the A-list has to include all the editors in the reference division," said Gwen. "As we talk to people there, we may find somebody with a more specific motive than 'I hated his guts.'— someone whose toes got stepped on hard."

"Yeah, who else you got?"

"You got Birchfield, the head of security, and his people. Unlikely candidates, but you've got to put them on the A-list — if only because of proximity. Then you have Williamson, the president of the company. Not very likely, either, but he was in the building."

"So were fifty other people, from what I can tell. What about Mack's roommate? What do we know about him?"

"Nothing now. Apparently he's at work. Don't know where. We should get somebody over to the apartment tonight."

"What about the two editorial honchos that Williamson mentioned? We haven't seen them yet?"

"You mean Markham, the editor in chief, and Marcantonio, the editorial director of the division. Can't put them on the A-list since neither of them had come in by the time we left. We should talk to both of them, though, to see what they thought about the guy they just promoted."

"Okay, Gwen, you and I will take the key players. We'll get someone else on some of the less likely candidates. You and I are going to find ourselves a motive."

"What are our chances?"

"I think they're pretty good."

* * *

Herb Wasserman's assistant had gone down the hall for a minute so he answered his own phone.

"Hi, it's me," said Estelle. "You busy?"

"I always have time for you, my sweet." He truly did enjoy hearing from her in the middle of the day. They'd been married 24 years, and as far as he was concerned, each year had gotten better. At the moment he was free and could lean back and enjoy talking with his "best friend." Carr Williamson was his best friend outside of Estelle, but there was no one on earth he'd rather be with than her. They both realized that they enjoyed a rare marriage if you considered current standards. His oak-paneled office was one of those Manhattan paradoxes. It looked as if it belonged in some steeped-in-tradition British gentleman's club. The truth was that it occupied a large piece of real estate on the 44th floor of one of the newer office towers on Wall Street. The bond business had been good to Herb, and he considered himself lucky. Because of the business he enjoyed a lifestyle that only people in the top one percent income bracket could enjoy. He really didn't have a financial care in the world. And he was thankful every day of his life for his good fortune.

"I just got a call from Laura Williamson, and thought you might want to call Carr." Herb smiled. Estelle had this elliptical way of speaking that frequently left him totally in the dark. This was one of those times.

"Look, I know that you women have ESP or some sort of linguistic sixth sense that enables you to communicate without saying all the words, but I'm not of your gender...in case you hadn't noticed. I haven't a clue as to what you're talking about. Why would I want to call Carr?"

She laughed, "I guess I didn't give you all the details." Then, seriously, "There's been a shooting in the Harmon Hall Building. Someone was killed there this morning. My God, it's terrible."

"Who got killed?"

"Some editor. I think his name was Mack. That's his last name. Right in his office. My God what's happening to this country when a person's not even safe in their own office."

"Do they know who did it?"

"I don't think so. Who could have done such a thing, Herb? And why?

Why indeed? wondered Wasserman.


After he'd hung up, Wasserman couldn't get the call out of his mind. Carr had told him about being blackmailed by this young editor at Harmon Hall. He'd gone on at length about how the blackmail had made life miserable for him, how he'd been put in a position that forced him to make humiliating requests of other senior executives at the company, and how he had to virtually grovel at the feet of this junior-level editor if he didn't want news of his affair to leak out to Laura, the company, and to Howard Harmon. What bothered Wasserman most was Carr's statement, no doubt made in the depths of frustration, that he'd like to kill the young editor.

His friend Carr could never kill anyone. He was sure of it. But the murder of this Mack guy was an awful coincidence. Mack's death certainly solved a lot of Carr's problems. Still, it must be one of those horrible coincidences that do happen from time to time. Suddenly Wasserman found himself wrestling with a terrible ethical dilemma. Should he tell the police about his friend's statement at the club? What kind of friend would he be if he did that? But if, God forbid, Carr had killed the editor, what kind of a person would he be if he held back important evidence?

# SIXTEEN

It was three o'clock in the afternoon. Mack had been dead eight hours. Dawson Flynn and Gwen Pappas had spent their noon hour at the precinct on 54th Street in order to brief Lieutenant Farrell and to grab a sandwich while they planned their next moves. Now, back in the Harmon Hall Building, they were about to interview the young woman who'd discovered the body of Andy Mack. She sat quietly behind her desk, nervously folding and unfolding a piece of paper. Flynn and Pappas sat in front of the desk, facing Mallory.

Fern Mallory was a slight, barely five-foot tall wisp of a woman. Not an outdoor person, she preferred her books, and her extensive collection of baroque CDs. Her pale white skin had seldom experienced more than a fleeting exposure to sun. Her severe, close-cut hair and fragile frame gave her a boyish appearance.

"Sorry to make you relive this, Ms. Mallory," said Gwen, "but I'm sure you understand that it's important that we learn as much as we can while the incident is fresh in your mind."

"I understand," she said, her voice deeper and more resonant than the two policemen expected from such a small person. "God knows, it was a shock. I'm still shaking a little. But please go on. I'm okay."

"Would you tell us exactly what happened this morning?"

Mallory leaned back, putting her hands to her face and sighing as she did so, as if the physical act of touching her forehead would help her remember. Slowly she leaned forward, letting her hands fall to her lap. "I was dropping off a manuscript. He'd asked for it the day before, but I'd been working on it at home, and I'd left it there. He said he needed it first thing in the morning. Well he'd only been in his new job a few days, but word was already out that he'd begun coming in early. I mean real early. Like around seven o'clock. He never used to come in early. Anyway, Andy and I had never hit it off too well. That's putting it mildly." She seemed nervous, "One time he....."

"He what?" interjected Flynn.

"Nothing. Nothing really. Anyway, since he was now my boss, I thought I'd get off to a good start and get the manuscript to him shortly after seven. Score a few points early on, and they stand you in good stead later on," she smiled weakly. "I guess you'd call it sucking up."

"What was the manuscript about?" asked Flynn.

"Nothing very exciting. It was the first few letters of the alphabet of a new pocket dictionary we're doing. Andy had never seen any of it. I think he just wanted to know what it looked like."

"Was there anything unusual about this dictionary, anything new or out of the ordinary?" queried Pappas.

"Not really. If you're wondering if it might have had something to do with his murder, I can't imagine why it would."

"You mentioned that you and Mack didn't get along too well." Pappas looked her straight in the eyes. "Tell us about that."

"Jesus! You think I did it?"

"We don't think anything yet," said Flynn. "These are the kinds of questions we have to ask a lot of people. I'm sure you can understand that."

"I shouldn't have limited it to me. Though as far as I'm concerned I don't mind telling you that I'm not sorry he's gone. He really was a miserable excuse for a human being."

"What did he ever do to you to cause you to feel this way?" asked Gwen.

"Look, I told you. He had trouble with most people. Not just me."

"Yeah," said Flynn, "but a minute ago you started to say that one time he did something. You didn't finish. What was that all about?"

"I, I really don't know what I was thinking. There's nothing really. Other than what I've already told you."

It was becoming clear to Flynn and Pappas that Fern Mallory could see that by airing whatever it was she'd started to say she might be airing a motive for murder. She continued cautiously, "Look, he had trouble with most people. He was the kind of person who, when he was at the Xerox machine making copies of twenty different pages, wouldn't let you in to make one copy. I know that doesn't sound like much," said Mallory. Then adding, as more came to her, "He used to play music too loudly in his office. People would ask him to lower it, and he'd just say something like 'You'll get used to it.' And when we chipped in for birthdays and gifts for people who were leaving, he'd never contribute. You'd never ask a favor of him because he'd always say no. He wasn't a very nice person, and he wasn't a very nice boss. But he was worse as a boss because he had power over you. No, I doubt if there was anyone on the staff who liked him."

Pappas looked at her soberly, "Would anyone have hated him enough to kill him?"

"Oh my God. I've heard that question in the movies. But this is real. God. I don't think so. If we killed everybody who wasn't nice..." she trailed off.

"Who had the most to lose when Mack was appointed to his new job?"

"We all lost, but I know what you mean. Let me think," she closed her eyes for a moment, and then spoke, "You know, this puts me in a very awkward position. Most of these people are my friends."

"And you don't want to even suggest that one of

your friends might be a killer. Of course, we understand." empathized Pappas. Look, this is serious. It's not business as usual. Any information we use will be used with discretion. If a person is innocent, that will come out, and they won't get hurt. If they're guilty, well.... It's your obligation to share with us anything that might have the remotest connection with our investigation."

"I know, I know. Of course you're right. I suppose Jacqui Dyer got hurt as much as anyone."

"How's that?" asked Flynn.

"Well she'd just been given this big new project. An unabridged dictionary. I know, it sounds dull, but this is a big deal. The budget runs into the millions. Then Andy entered the picture and took the project away from her. An awful slap in the face. But I can't believe she'd kill him. Besides, I assume Andy had the blessing of Tony Marcantonio and probably even Stuart Markham. If that's true, it wasn't entirely Andy's fault, though I know he was unbelievably obnoxious about it when he took over. Jacqui's tough, but she's fair, and I think, a pretty decent person. I don't believe she'd kill — even for something like this."

"Can you think of anyone else?" asked Flynn.

"No, and as I said, I don't think Jacqui'd do anything like that no matter how pissed she was. Editorial people are not violent."


Tony Marcantonio took his feet off his desk and closed the sports section of the *Times* where he'd been reading about the Giants chances for their season opener. Miraculously they'd won all of their preseason games so, being a confirmed contrarian, he was convinced they'd have a losing regular season. He came around to the front of his desk to greet Flynn and Pappas.

"Officers, please make yourselves comfortable. Just reading about the Giants. You follow football?"

"They could be a decent team this year," opined Flynn.

"Maybe. But I'm nervous. Can't go by preseason."

"I know what you mean, but they've looked good so far," continued Flynn.

"Hope you're right. Still, look who they've played..." countered the editorial director, unwilling to let optimism rule the day.

"Look, Mr. Marcantonio," interposed Gwen sharply, "we're investigating a murder here. Can we put the football on hold?"

Marcantonio's face reddened. "Excuse me detective. By all means have the floor," he snapped.

Flynn interjected, as calmly as he could, "Sorry, sir, but we're a little tense. We wanna catch whoever did this." He gave Gwen a look of disapproval.

Marcantonio struggled to control his anger at the impertinence of the young female cop. Finally, he regained his composure. He allowed his curly black hair to grow longer than he would have otherwise preferred because it tended to cover the growing bald spot on the crown of his head. He was proud of his body. Just under six feet and a solid 185. Muscle, not fat. He worked out five or six days a week. Weight training for muscle development and tone; racquetball for aerobics and fun. In the warm months he played softball in the publishers league. For 43 he was in pretty damn good shape. If it weren't for that bald spot...It was an obsession and it drove him nuts.

Gwen tried again, trying to sound less severe, "We understand that this Mack guy wasn't the most popular person in your department. We were wondering, then, why you would have promoted him to manager?"

Marcantonio kept his gaze on Gwen. She was waiting for his answer. He chose his words carefully.

"For the record, it was managing editor. I'm

sure you know that you don't chose a manager on the basis of popularity." Flynn looked as if he were going to interrupt, and Marcantonio held up his right hand, "Wait, I know what you're going to say. This guy was more than just a little unpopular. True. Very, very true. He was not well liked."

"So I assume he had some redeeming qualities that convinced you to promote him," offered Pappas.

Marcantonio looked uncomfortable. His eyes turned upward, and his face effected an awkward smile. "Not exactly. Look, this is a real strange situation. I feel a little funny talking about it."

"Don't follow you," said Flynn. "Just tell us what happened."

"Look, it wasn't my idea. I got pressure from above. This has never happened to me before. I frankly didn't know how to handle it. I would never have promoted Mack. As a matter of fact I'd been looking for an excuse to can the guy. Promoting him was the last thing I wanted to do."

"Who pressured you?" asked Flynn.

Marcantonio drew in a deep breath. He expelled it slowly. "My boss, Stuart Markham. You're not going to tell him about this conversation are you?"

"Not if we don't have to. We're not here to bust your chops, but this *is* a murder investigation. Still, we don't say anymore than we have to. So what did Markham say about promoting Mack?"

"Frankly, he seemed uncomfortable about asking me to promote him. And if you know Stuart, he doesn't show discomfort often. He was a little vague. Told me he knew it was unconventional, knew it was putting me in a tough spot. But he said he wouldn't have asked me if it weren't important. Stuart's a proud man, and something had made him very uncomfortable, or he wouldn't have come to me like that."

Pappas turned to Marcantonio, "How did you

react at the time?"

"I got pretty heated up. As I said, I wanted to get rid of Mack, and then my boss asks me to promote him to the second most important job in the division. C'mon. I was livid. But Stuart finally calmed me down. As Stuart said, it's the first time he ever asked me to do anything like that. So I went along with it for the sake of corporate harmony. Ha! Where's the fucking harmony now? Excuse me. Incidentally, as much as it annoyed me, I didn't tell anyone why Mack was promoted. I took a lot of heat from my staff and other people in the company because of it, but sometimes you just have to play the game. I don't undercut my boss. God knows it's not always easy, but I don't operate that way. That's why I hope you don't have to mention this to Stuart."

Flynn shifted his weight in his chair, "As I said, we'll try. Now tell us why you think Markham pressured you into promoting Mack."

Marcantonio laughed nervously. "I wish I knew. Maybe Mack was a relative. Or maybe Stuart owed him some humongous favor. Maybe he was blackmailing him or something. Christ, I don't know. I'm just guessing." Suddenly he stopped, as if an idea had just struck him. "You know, at one point in that conversation I sorta got the idea that he was being pressured by someone else. Like *his* boss, or the board, or a member of the board."

Pappas studied him, "Do you remember exactly what gave you that idea?" .

"No. It was nothing that obvious, just an impression I had. I'm not even sure if I read it right.

"We understand that Mack took this new dictionary project away from one of your editors," observed Gwen. "How'd she react to that?"

"You mean Jacqui Dyer. You people work fast. Well, as you can imagine, she was beside herself. One week she has the biggest project of her life.

Responsible for a budget of $18 million, and the next week she has it taken away. Yeah, she was not a happy camper. Wait a minute, guys! Jacqui is no murderer."

"Nobody said she was," said Pappas. "By the way, who's idea was it to take the project away from her — Mack himself, or you?" Gwen allowed a pregnant pause before continuing, "Or was it Markham or someone else?"

"God this is embarrassing. That, too, came from Stuart. I honestly don't know if it was his idea or the idea of someone above him. It certainly wasn't my idea. I told you...I wanted to can him."

Flynn cleared his throat, "Let's talk about you for a minute. Other than what you've already told us, how were you affected by Mack's promotion?"

"I'm no killer, either. How was I affected? Well, it put me in a very bad position. My staff assumed it was my decision to promote him. As a result I'm sure their respect for me took a nose dive. I certainly resented being in that position. Even if I'd wanted to blame someone else, it still took away a lot of my authority. Face it, it weakened my position. On top of that, Mack seemed to know that I couldn't touch him. He went around here like some cocky bantam rooster. Flaunting it in my face. He knew I didn't like him. I'm sure he felt the same about me. So all in all it was a lousy situation that kept getting worse."

Flynn looked him straight in the eye, "So Mack's death put an end to all your troubles?"

"Now there you go," said Marcantonio sharply. "I told you, I didn't kill the guy."

"I know you said that," parried Flynn provocatively, "but you have to admit, it did solve a lot of problems for you."

"Or for someone else," countered Marcantonio.

At about the same time Flynn and Pappas were meeting with Tony Marcantonio, Carr Williamson was on the phone with his wife, Laura. "Okay, so you'll meet me here in my office—about six-thirty, quarter to seven. John will drive us over to the hotel and wait there." John Dubcek had worked as a driver for Harmon Hall for almost 12 years. Williamson was the third CEO Dubcek had driven for. When Williamson didn't feel like taking the train or driving himself, Dubcek would meet him with a company car and allow Carr to sleep or do work in the back seat. John always drove Williamson to and from the airport and often to functions in and around Manhattan. Having a company car and driver at his disposal was one of the many presidential perks that Williamson enjoyed.

Williamson wanted his wife to be at certain functions. She enjoyed most of these events anyway, and besides, it was good for his image. Tonight they'd be visiting the enemy camp, so to speak. Tandem Publishing was celebrating its 60th anniversary and had invited key people from the industry and from other media as well. It promised to be a gala event. Timing wasn't so great, though, with this murder and everything. How could he relax? Last night he'd almost gone back to Mack's office to get the photos, but he'd changed his mind at the last moment. No doubt now the cops had them. Still, maybe they weren't so smart. There was always the chance they'd miss them or not even know what they had. In the meantime he'd enjoy tonight's gala as much as he could. He knew there'd be questions about the murder. Not only from the press, but from others in the industry. And no doubt from Howard Harmon who was bound to be there.

\* \* \*

His corner office on 16 was fourteen floors below Williamson's, and somewhat smaller. Certainly not small, though. A handsome office. One he was proud of. Around the room he'd placed mementos of the many high points of his celebrated career. They were highly visible, but tasteful. There were the three photos of himself, each taken with a different President of the United States. There were numerous other photos taken with world-famous authors. There were framed letters of thanks from internationally celebrated dignitaries. By any professional standard Markham would be considered a success.

"We've just finished speaking with Mr. Marcantonio, and we'd like to ask you a few questions now if you don't mind. Shouldn't take too long." Flynn had just squeezed into Markham's office ahead of the two people waiting in the outer reception area. He'd explained to Cathy, Markham's assistant, that it was official police business.

Markham looked at his watch. About four fifteen. He had the two people waiting, plus another visitor after them. Then there was the Tandem function in the evening. Still, he knew the police wouldn't wait. Best not to annoy them anyway. Not that he had anything to fear. There was no way they could connect him to Mack's death.

He'd made a career of hobnobbing with the social and monied elite, yet he felt uncomfortable with those of lesser station. He wasn't quite sure how such people thought or what their values were. He'd never been able to fathom the notion that some of them claimed not to want power or fame or even money. He was convinced that such people were merely rationalizing away their own incompetence. The two police officers sitting in front of him fell into that vast unknown realm of society which included foreigners — especially third-world types — Martians, poor people, small towners, and blue-collar workers. They were all hard to read as far as he was concerned. He never knew what to say to them. Experience had taught him that what he thought witty or charming either went right over their heads or seemed somehow to annoy them. "Yes, of course. Please do come in," he said. "Dreadful business, dreadful. How can I be of help, officer? I'm at your service." *Hope I'm not coming on too strong.*

"Can you think of anyone who'd want to kill Mr. Mack?"

"You get right to the point don't you officer."

"It's detective. Detective Flynn".

"Yes, yes, of course, *pathetic little title for a wretched little job.* How careless of me, uh...detective."

"Mack, sir. Who'd want to kill him?" continued Flynn.

"Well, he wasn't a very popular young man, but I can't imagine someone wanting to kill him. I was hoping you people in the constabulary..." he smiled. Getting no reaction, he continued. "...you people in the police department would have some idea who did this dreadful thing. I'm sure you can appreciate the effect it's having on morale here. Don't you have any clues or something?"

"We're working on it," said Gwen. "Can you think of anyone here who might have had it in for Mack?"

"Well, in his brief tenure as managing editor he'd managed to alienate most of his staff. But as I said, I don't see any of them killing him. It's a big leap from dislike to murder."

"How about this Jacqui Dyer?" prompted Gwen.

"Ah, you've heard about her. Well, yes, certainly she was more than a little miffed when our recently deceased managing editor took away her project. Can't say I blame her. But again I say to you, she's not a killer."

"Excuse me for being blunt Mr. Markham," said Flynn. "But if you say you didn't blame her for being annoyed, why did you allow Mack to take her project away?"

Markham's eyes turned cold. He struggled to control his temper. He wasn't used to being challenged, especially by low-ranking civil servants. "Frankly, neither Mr. Marcantonio nor myself had anything to say about his getting the project."

"Isn't that a bit unusual...I mean for a new manager to make such a big decision without even running it past his boss?" pressed Flynn.

This...detective, whatever he was, was getting annoying. "Yes, it was, detective. But you misunderstood my answer. I said neither Mr. Marcantonio nor I had anything to do with Mr. Mack getting the dictionary project. I didn't mean that young Mack made the decision." Markham sighed before continuing, "Unfortunately, the decision was passed down from above. I then told Mr. Marcantonio to implement it. I can assure you that neither Mr. Marcantonio nor I were happy about it." This is the sort of thing that embarrassed Markham almost beyond tolerance. He didn't like it when anyone knew that he hadn't made certain decisions. He was extremely uncomfortable when he was not in control, and this situation was exacerbated by the fact that he was admitting it to the two detectives. Yet claiming credit for the decision would have made him look stupid. So he had to deny it. The whole business was impossible.

Flynn was one of those annoying people who looked you right in the eye when he spoke. Markham knew what was coming next.

"Can you be specific?"

Damn, this cop was really getting to him. "I'm not sure I follow you, detective," lied Markham.

Flynn continued to look directly at him, "If neither you nor Mr. Marcantonio made the decision, who did?"

While protecting Williamson was the last thing

he cared about, he did resent being grilled like this, "If you must know, it was Carson Williamson. He's the president of the company."

"We know who he is," said Gwen. "I assume that having such a decision foisted upon you from above was sort of a bitter pill to swallow?"

Markham glared at her, "You might say that."

"Do you know why Williamson did that?" asked Flynn.

"No, he asked me to do it as a favor. Said he didn't ask such favors very often, and that he appreciated my co-operation. What choice did I have?"

"I can see how this could have created a lot of personnel problems for you."

"A few."

"But the murder of Mack sort of solved those problems for you didn't it?" said Flynn, returning Markham's steely stare.

"Well, yes, I suppose it did, but you're not suggesting...?"

"I'm not suggesting anything, but since you seem to be suggesting it yourself, you could have had a motive."

"That's preposterous, and you know it."

"Not so preposterous from my point of view," prodded Flynn. "The way I see it Mack somehow got Mr. Williamson to reverse a major decision you and Mr. Marcantonio had previously made. Williamson's decision to put Andrew Mack in charge of the big dictionary project was a serious challenge to your authority. A real embarrassment because it suggested, if word got out, that you're not running your own show. On the other hand, if you took the blame, you got blamed for a really bad decision and looked foolish. You don't seem like the type of man who'd enjoy looking foolish in front of his employees. Still, in the end you decided to live with the lesser of two evils and took the heat rather than let your staff think you weren't in control. Your staff believed the unpopular decision was yours. Mack then made things worse with his grating managerial style. This was seen as a further reflection on your judgment in appointing him. It looks to me like his death has put an end to all your problems, Mr. Markham."

"Now wait a minute, I'll speak to the commissioner before I'll let you bully me with your gestapo-like tactics."

"Sir, you can speak to whoever you want," said Gwen. "My partner didn't accuse you of anything. He merely pointed out that you had as much motive as anyone."

This wasn't going the way Markham had expected it to go. He seldom found himself in a tug of war with his emotions. His wife used to accuse him of having ice water in his veins. Perhaps he did, but why, then, did he let these two-bit flatfoots get to him? He had to get control of himself and the situation.

"Of course, off...er detectives, you're right. We're all a bit on edge here. I'm sure you can understand. And yes, you're right. Young Mack's death did eliminate a few problems. But I hope you don't think that that's how I solve my problems," he laughed nervously. "I've encountered many problems in my time, and I've always been able to deal with them by making sound business decisions. I'm not a violent person."

"You're not the first person here to say that," said Gwen.

# SEVENTEEN

Howard Harmon hardly noticed the elegant majesty of the Shoreham Hotel ballroom. One of the city's celebrated citizens, he attended galas like this all the time. Long ago they'd become tiresome obligations. Tonight, the bouncy beat of the fashionable society orchestra at the other end of the room went right over his head. Nor did he take particular notice of the yuppiesque claques of eager young men and women in their smart business suits clustered around smaller groups of captains and lieutenants of industry. The captains of industry — celebrities in their own right in the tight, but influential world of publishing — tended to do most of the talking while the younger people hung on their every word, hopeful of catching at least one quotable tidbit they could spread around the office in the morning.

Harmon stood just inside the entrance to the ballroom, surveying as much of the vast room as he could from that location. He was looking for Carr Williamson. Carr had phoned him in the morning after the body of Andy Mack had been discovered. Now, hours later, Harmon wanted to be brought up-to-date, and as soon as possible. He knew he'd be questioned ad nauseum tonight, and he didn't like to be caught off balance by people who thought they knew more than he did about his own business. Being well informed, after all, had made him the billionaire he was.

There, he saw him. Talking with that tiresome Stuart Markham. Harmon moved his not insignificant frame toward the small group. Close to six-three and pushing 250, Harmon was not a man easily ignored. He had the kind of bearing that people — admirers and detractors alike — called presence. He approached Williamson and Markham, and noticed a woman standing with them. He recognized her as Williamson's wife, Laura. As Harmon neared the group, Williamson turned to him, "Howard, good to see you." He sounded more enthusiastic than he felt, "Betty with you?"

"Hello, Carr, Stuart. Laura, you look lovely as usual. Betty's tied up with one of her charities tonight." Then, his eye caught the attention of another woman standing in a small group thirty feet away. The woman instantly recognized him. He motioned to her to come over. At first she seemed reluctant to leave her group. Harmon motioned to her again. She made her excuses to the people she was with and came over and joined Harmon and the others. "And here's your hotshot corporate lawyer, Carr," boomed Harmon. "Forgive me young lady, but we met some months ago, and I'm embarrassed to say that I don't remember your name. I know you're with Blythe, Goodstein and Blum? If I'm not mistaken, you're a partner."

"That's right, Mr. Harmon, I'm Kate Ferrara."

"Of course, you handle the litigation for Harmon Hall. I hope we haven't been keeping you too busy," said Harmon with a chuckle.

"Busy, but not too busy, sir," said Kate with a smile, stealing a quick look in the direction of Carr. Markham caught the glance, though he doubted anyone else did. Carr proceeded to introduce Kate to Laura, feeling like a Judas as he did so.

Harmon then turned to Markham. "Stuart, this is a terrible thing that's happened to your young editor. I couldn't believe it when Carr called me this morning. Do the police have any idea yet who did it?"

"I'm afraid not, Howard. If they do, they haven't told me. Must have been someone from off the street."

"Now why would you say that?"

"I simply don't believe anyone in the editorial area is capable of such a thing."

"Well, Stuart, I have to say both options sound highly implausible. I'm flabbergasted by the whole thing. Carr, I'd like to speak to you alone for a minute, if you don't mind. Would you folks excuse us?" With that he drew Carr aside, well out of earshot of the others.

"Carr, what the hell happened over there? My God, Harmon Hall is already all over the news. Radio, TV, and the Post. The rest of the papers'll have it by morning. Do you have any idea who killed this guy...and why?"

"Howard, I have no idea. It doesn't make sense. I've been thinking about it, naturally, all day. I agree with Stuart. I can't see any of his editors doing such a thing. And why would any other employee do it? But you hit the nail on the head a minute ago. It's totally implausible that someone from the street would just walk in and fire away. Hell, if it were some lunatic you'd think he'd just fire at the first person he came to; not go to an office, shoot someone and slip away. A nut usually wants to attract attention."

"Okay, okay. So you know nothing. Look, Carr, there's something funny here. Right now we need damage control. First thing tomorrow get together with your security guy, and tighten up security at all entrances. Then make an announcement over the PA to that effect. When the press calls, that's all you tell them. The company's tightened up security. The police are working on the case. I don't think we should offer any theories. The press'll have a field day with whatever we come up with."

"I've already met with Birchfield about tighter security. It's already in effect. I've also issued a memo stating that all requests from the press should be channeled through my office."

"Fine. Keep me informed at least once a day until this business is settled. We'd better rejoin the group."

\* \* \*

The five-story brownstone on West 75th Street, just

west of West End Avenue, was exquisite. The late afternoon sun highlighted the recently sandblasted red-brick and granite exterior. A gentrified building in a gentrified neighborhood, thought Pappas. A flight of eight stone-and-concrete stairs led up to a stone-and-concrete stoop. Smart varnished double-oak doors reflected the setting sunlight. The doors looked solid and heavy. And like the doors to all New York homes, they were locked. Flynn scanned the list of residents just to the right of the entrance. There it was: Three-A, **Mack and Manwaring**. He pressed the buzzer. Hopefully Mack's roommate would be home, and they could get some answers. He tried the buzzer again. After a minute or two he stopped. "Let's try a neighbor," he said without looking at Gwen. He pushed the button next to Three-B, Carlino. A woman's voice, surprisingly clear, came over the small speaker: "Yes?"

"Police, ma'am. We'd like to speak to you for just a minute."

"The police?"

"Yes, ma'am. Doesn't involve you. Just need a minute of your time. May we come up."

"You have ID?"

"Yes ma'am."

"Come up."

Not finding an elevator, they walked the two flights up to the third floor. Flynn knocked on three-B. The two officers stood patiently as an eye was pressed to the inside of the door's peephole. Then, slowly they heard a lock turning and a bolt being removed. The door opened a few inches, but the chain remained attached. A woman peered through the narrow opening.

"Could I see the ID please?"

"Of course." Flynn flipped open his wallet and held it a few seconds so she could see it.

"Can you tell me what this is about?" asked the

woman.

"It's about your neighbor. May we come in?"

The door closed and they heard the chain rattle. The door reopened, and a woman of about seventy stood aside, inviting them to step in. She wore a pale blue housedress that buttoned up the front. Her deep intelligent eyes revealed the concern she was feeling at having two policemen drop in on her unannounced.

"What's this about my neighbors, officers?"

"It's about your neighbors in three-A," said Flynn. "Do you know them?"

"Not well. We exchange a few words in the hall now and then. But that's it. Two young men. They're actually rather friendly. Gay I suppose, but never any trouble. Good neighbors. Why? Why do you want to know about them?

"Then you haven't heard?"

"Heard what?"

"One of them was murdered this morning?"

Mrs. Carlino's hand flew to her mouth. "Here? I can't believe it."

"No ma'am. At his place of business. In his office."

"Oh my goodness. Which one was it?"

"Mr. Mack."

"Oh dear. Oh, that's terrible. Terrible. He was such a nice young man. They both were. Who would ever do such a thing?"

"We don't know yet. We were hoping you might be able to help us. Have you ever heard the two of them argue or fight?"

She hesitated a moment, "Maybe once or twice. They do raise their voices rather a lot, and they sometimes play their stereo too loud, but these walls are pretty thick. You don't hear much."

"Have you heard them argue recently?" asked Pappas.

"I think I did a few evenings ago. Can't be sure just what night. You don't mean to say that you think Paul Manwaring would kill his roommate just because they had an argument?"

"Not necessarily, though it might depend on what they were arguing about. Have you seen Paul Manwaring in the past day or so?" asked Flynn.

"Well, no, now that you mention it, I supposed I haven't. I think he's been away. Seems like he mentioned something to that effect when I saw him last week."

"Did he say when he'd be back?" asked Pappas.

"No, I don't think so. Just said he'd be away for a few days."

"Okay Mrs. Carlino, would you give us a call at this number when he returns?" Flynn gave her his card.

"If I notice, I certainly will."

"We need to go into that apartment now, even though he's not home. They didn't by any chance leave a key with you, did they?"

"No, you'll have to see Mr. Amino. He's the super. In One-A"

"Thanks, Mrs. Carlino. Don't forget to call us when he comes back. And make sure you don't tell him you're calling."

"Land sakes, what do you take me for, officer?"

Amino reluctantly let them into the apartment, but followed the two detectives around as they made a quick, but careful tour around the extremely neat and tastefully appointed apartment. This brief look-around failed to turn up anything revealing.

"We gotta stay on top of this, Gwen," said Flynn. "Better get someone in plain clothes over here to keep a watch on the place until this guy shows up. Wouldn't count on Mrs. Carlino. She might not hear him come in."

\* \* \*

"Hello,"

Thank God she was home so he could talk about it. He'd thought of nothing else all day. Had to get her take on it because he had to make a decision soon. "I'm glad you're home, Estelle. Look, this thing with Carr and the shooting is driving me up a wall. You know ... what Carr said when we were playing tennis."

"You mean that he felt like killing some young editor. But, Herb, you don't even know if the one who got shot is the one Carr was talking about. This is a quantum leap you're taking."

"Maybe you're right. Maybe not. I just have this funny feeling. I mean you weren't there. You should have heard Carr. At that moment I really believe he could have killed that editor."

"What editor? What editor?'

"I know, I know. How can I be sure it's the one who got shot? I can't, but I just have this feeling."

"Herb, Carr is your best friend. Do you really believe him capable of such a thing?"

"Normally, no, of course not. But this editor could ruin his career and ruin his life."

"Sounds like he did a pretty good job of that himself. It wasn't the editor who cheated on his wife."

"Look, don't get off on that, okay. Right now we're talking about murder."

"Yes, Herb, but I know he's guilty of having an affair. I don't know if he's a murderer. As bad as his infidelity to Laura was, you can't believe your best friend is a murderer?" She looked at him questioningly.

"I know. Your logic is impeccable, as usual. But what if they don't find the murderer, and I'm sitting here next week knowing what I know? Don't you think I should go to the police?"

"But what do you really know? You don't know if this was the same editor Carr was referring to, and you don't know if Carr was only lashing out in frustration when he said that to you."

"I don't know, but I think I'm obligated as a citizen to say something if no one else turns out to be the killer. After all, I don't know that I'm wrong either," said Wasserman disconsolately.

"No you don't," she agreed soberly. "I understand what you're saying. God forbid that you read his comment right. I guess I have to agree that if this goes on for very long and the police don't find the killer, you should probably tell them what you heard. Hopefully it won't come to that, and the police will find the killer soon. And you and Carr will still be friends, though I don't know if I can handle him after this."

Wasserman held the phone in front of him and and rolled his eyes. *Leave it alone, Estelle. Leave it alone.* Okay, then, I'll give it a week. If no one turns up, I go to the police and lose a friend."

"If your fears are correct, you won't want him as a friend."

# EIGHTEEN

"So who do you pick in the Giants game, Dawson?"

"I didn't know you were interested in football. You just makin' conversation?"

"C'mon, Dawson, can't a woman be interested in sports?"

"Yeah, sure, I just didn't know you were, that's all."

"You're just like every other man. You carry your prejudices on your sleeve."

"Get off it, Gwen. Don't give me that feminist crap. All I said was I didn't know you were interested in football. Look how impatient you were when Marcantonio wanted to talk about the Giants. You practically took his head off. Hell, in the few weeks we've worked together you've never so much as mentioned football."

"Okay, okay. So I'm not a fanatic. Just because I can't rattle off standings, doesn't mean I don't like football. Sorry I asked. Let's get a bite to eat."

They were cruising up First Avenue, approaching 35th Street. Traffic was moderate to heavy — normal for mid-day in Manhattan.

"Not hot dogs again, okay?" moaned Flynn.

"What's wrong with hot dogs?"

"Three days in a row?"

"How 'bout a pizza?"

"The woman's a gourmet. Don't you eat anything but junk food?"

"I like junk food."

"I know, so do I. In moderation. Don't you know that stuff'll kill ya?"

"So what do you want, Dawson? A salad?"


They sat in a window booth. The coffee shop was clean. Nothing special, but clean. Flynn sat with a half-eaten turkey sandwich in front of him. "So what do you do when you're not workin', Gwen?" Then he added with a grin, "I mean besides follow sports?"

"Jesus, what a smart-ass. I said I like sports okay. I even go to one or two Knicks games every year. But when I'm home I read a lot and listen to music. And believe it or not, I like to cook. Being an arch feminist, I don't usually let that out."

"Being an arch junk food lover, just what do you cook? Hot dogs?"

"No. When I'm home I cook better stuff, because I like better stuff, too. I'm kind of a split personality when it comes to food. I like to experiment with pasta, chicken. Once in awhile a little seafood."

"You cook like this for yourself?"

She smiled, "Not always."

"You seeing someone?"

"You asked me that the first week we worked together?"

"And you said, no, not really. Whatever that meant. Anyway, a few weeks have passed, so I thought I'd ask again."

"Why, do you care?"

"Why would I care? I'm just making conversation, to quote you. You know I'm seein' Melissa anyway. So, are you?"

"Not now. The reason for the 'not really' was because we had some problems. Well, they turned out to be, as they say, unreconcilable, so we're not seeing each other anymore."

"I'm sorry. Guy can't be too smart," said Flynn, pushing back a few strands of his thinning sandy hair and not feeling too smart himself for saying it.

"Don't be, but thanks. It's better this way."

"Look, Just so you'll know, I'm not that much of a sports freak myself. I was just giving you a hard time."

"Well, you had me fooled. So what does grab

you then?"

"I'm afraid it's nothing very exciting. Some other time, okay? Let's talk about the case."

"You're not gonna to leave it there, Dawson. What is it?"

He sucked in a deep breath, "I grow roses. Not exactly the image you associate with a cop, is it?"

"Hey, I think that's neat. You gotta show me your garden."

"I read everything on the subject I can get my hands on. Exhibit at flower shows when I get the chance. Even won a couple of first prizes. Weird, huh?"

"Maybe unusual for a cop, but certainly not weird at all. I think it's kind of nice, Dawson. A side of you I never would have guessed in a million years. Hey, you're ashamed of it."

His face began to take on the hue of one of his prize-winning roses, "Maybe I am. I've never told anybody else at work, and I'd app..."

"C'mon, Dawson, what do you take me for? I won't tell." Then she smiled, "Unless you give me a hard time."

"Thanks, but can we talk about Harmon Hall?"

"You're right. Are we going anywhere with this thing?"

"Not yet we aren't. But I got a feeling it's gonna break soon."

"What makes you say that?"

"Got to. The whole thing is so damn bizarre when you think about it. Somebody there has to know something about this."

"Maybe, but how do we find out who?"

"We keep the pressure on. Those kinda people don't have the nerves for this sort of thing. Someone'll let somethin' out... and soon, if we keep the heat on." He took a noisy slurp from his coffee mug.

"Sounds good."

He feigned a look of annoyance. Then, as if he'd

thought of something he said, "I better go outside and call in. Be right back."

Gwen nodded and took a bite of her sandwich.

Three minutes later, Flynn swung back into the booth, "Mack's roommate just got home. Our guy's still watching the place. Let's get over there before this guy takes off again."

As they parked on West 75th Street, a young black man got out of a car halfway down the block. He was wearing a pair of worn jeans and a yellow golf shirt. Approaching Flynn and Pappas, he quickly identified himself as the plainclothesman who'd been watching the apartment. "Guy's still up there."

"Thanks," said Flynn. "Wait here until we come out. Shouldn't be more than 45 minutes I'd guess." He and Gwen approached the front of the now familiar five-story building. Flynn glanced at Gwen and then rang the buzzer next to the names Mack and Manwaring. The voice on the intercom was that of a man. "Yes, who is it?"

"Police, we'd like to come up and see you for a minute."

"Yes, yes. Of course. Come right up."

At the top of the landing the door to 3A opened, and a thin man stood holding the knob, inviting them to come in. Gwen figured him at about 28. Maybe younger. He was wiry, but not frail. Dressed in a black T-shirt and jeans. His haircut reminded Flynn of the style worn by the ancient Romans. At least the way they looked in the old movies he'd seen on TV.

"Come in officers. I've been expecting you."

"Then you must know why we're here," said Flynn.

"I assume it's because of Andy."

"Do you mind if we sit down, Mr. Manwaring?"

"No, no forgive me for being so rude. Please,

please." He motioned them toward the couch in the living room. As they walked from the front door into the room, Flynn and Pappas found themselves once again admiring the tastefully decorated apartment.

"Nice place," said Flynn sincerely. You do this yourselves or have it done?"

Paul Manwaring smiled for the first time. "Actually I did most of it. Andy was preoccupied with other things."

"Sounds like he didn't pull his own weight," suggested Gwen, hoping to provoke a response.

"No, that's not it at all. Decorating just wasn't his thing."

"Did you and Mack get along well?" asked Gwen.

"For the most part, yes. Oh we had our differences from time to time, but generally we got along quite well. Why else would we have lived together?"

"Well I'm sure you know that a lot of people who live together don't get along too well, Mr. Manwaring," explained Gwen.

"Yes, I see your point. Well we did anyway."

"You never argued or fought?"

"Oh I wouldn't say that. I wouldn't say that. Just a few days ago we had a beaut. Still, it was over fast."

"Can you tell us what it was about?"

"In light of what's happened I feel I should. Frankly, it's been troubling me ever since Andy told me about it, and now... You know, I still can't believe he's dead. That he's not coming home tonight," Paul Manwaring wiped his eye with the back of his hand.

"Sorry. It's going to take a little getting used to. What I wanted to tell you was...was that I think Andy was blackmailing the president of his company."

# NINETEEN

Paul Manwaring got up and straightened a tilting Miro print on the opposite wall. As he assumed his seat once again, he continued talking without missing a beat. "Andy didn't actually say he was going to blackmail the president. When I asked him directly if that's what he planned to do, he was evasive. Said something like, 'No comment.' Then he said that this was a great career opportunity for him...he was definitely going to exploit his discovery. He said, and I quote, 'I can use this, Paul.' And when I said, 'Andy, it's not like you to capitalize on other people's weaknesses,' he said, 'the president of Harmon Hall is a big boy. He can take care of himself.' Knowing Andy, when he talked like that he definitely intended to do something. I'm just assuming it was some kind of blackmail. Anyway, I told him he was crazy. Aside from the fact that it was wrong, I told him he could get hurt doing something like that."

"And what did he say then?" asked Flynn.

"He just said, Paul, trust me on this."

"Did he say who the president was?" Gwen knew the president was Williamson, but she wanted to be sure Manwaring was talking about the same man.

"Carson Williamson."

"What did Andy say he had on this Williamson?"

"Andy claimed Williamson was having an affair with some young female lawyer who works at Harmon Hall. He said he'd seen them at a restaurant called Canavan's—in Manhattan—behaving in a very compromising way. When I asked him if he could have been mistaken, he claimed there was no mistaking it."

"Can you tell us where you were yesterday between seven and eight a.m.?" asked Flynn.

"No, officer, I didn't do it. I was right here in

this apartment."

"I don't suppose anyone can verify that," said Flynn.

"You're right, detective, no one saw me here in my own apartment at that time. And I don't suppose anyone saw me leave at around eight-thirty. I didn't get up until about seven. By then Andy had already left. Since his new promotion he'd been going to work early. He'd become a fanatic about the job. Lot of good it did him."

\* \* \*

Flynn and Gwen could sense the stares of employees as they made their way through the corridors of the reference division of Harmon Hall. After getting directions from a middle-aged woman they found the office they were looking for. A strikingly attractive woman was sitting behind a desk, talking with a young man sitting across from her. Dawson felt his face flush as he looked at one of the most stunning woman he'd ever seen. He glanced over at an impassive Gwen. The woman looked up and noticed them. "Yes, can I help you?"

Flynn thought of a thousand clichés, but fought down the impulse to make a fool of himself. "Jacqui Dyer?"

"Yes, what is it? I'm in a meeting right now."

"Police, ma'am," said Gwen, "We need to speak with you for a few minutes."

Her face registered a moue of annoyance. She appeared to be considering what to do next. Finally she said, "I'll be right with you, officers." She and the young man went back to their discussion. It seemed like no more than a minute or two before the scraping of chairs signaled the break-up of the meeting, and the young man came out of the office and left.

"All right, I'm free now," said Dyer, motioning

them in. "I was going to say, 'Now what's this all about?' but I think I can guess. You're here about Andy aren't you?"

"Yes ma'am. I'm detective Flynn, and this is detective Pappas.

"Well I'm not sure I can tell you anymore than you've probably already heard."

"We understand that you were one of the people who lost the most turf, so to speak, when Andy Mack was promoted." As she said that, Gwen studied Dyer's face carefully. Flynn studied her, too, though not for the same reason his partner did.

"I suppose you could say his promotion was my loss. That doesn't mean I killed him, though."

"No one's saying you did, Ms. Dyer," countered Gwen. "I'm sure you understand we have to ask these questions. Anyway, we hear that he actually took this big dictionary project away from you. Is that right?"

This time it was Dyer's turn to flush. Flynn observed a reddening of her neck rising upward toward her ears and into her cheeks. She was obviously having trouble dealing with the question. Finally, she responded.

"Yes. And it was totally wrong. I know he's dead. That's terrible, but he was completely, totally wrong in that decision. And not just because I'm the one who suffered. Everyone here thought the same thing. It didn't make any sense." She was getting more emotional with each sentence. "As a result of what he did the project is so screwed up it'll take a month to get it back on track."

"Now that Mack is dead, will the changes he set in motion continue?" asked Flynn.

"I hope not. Stuart Markham and Tony, that's Tony Marcantonio, my immediate boss, came by this morning and tried to calm me down. They implied that they would probably reverse Andy's decision in the next couple of days. I hope so."

"Do you think it's likely?"

"Tony's got his problems, but he's not a bullshitter. I doubt that he'd lead somebody on if he didn't mean it. I trust him."

"Meaning you don't trust Markham?"

"I didn't say that. It's just that Tony has this reputation for being a straight shooter."

"And Markham doesn't?"

"I don't know Markham as well. Look, just between us, no, he doesn't. Though he's never done anything to me, at least not that I know of."

"So Markham has a reputation for being a little less than a straight shooter?" Flynn waited for her answer.

"Look, are you going to tell him what I say?"

"No, ma'am. Just gettin a little background." assured Gwen.

"Well, he's considered by people who know him better than I do, as smug and arrogant. Someone who just tolerates the little people. Meaning most of the people in the world. But he's smart and ambitious. Word is he wanted the job of CEO, and Williamson came in and took it right out from under him. More likely, though, the board saw through him. I think I've said enough. Probably too much."

"You said a minute ago that Marcantonio has his problems. What did you mean by that?"

"You people....." She looked exasperated. "It's just that he has a temper. But, he's still a straight shooter. You just have to understand him. At least he has principles."

"Can you tell us where you were and what you were doing between seven and eight a.m. yesterday?" asked Gwen.

Jacqui Dyer shook her head in disgust. "My God. Because I took the brunt of Andy's inept managerial judgment, you suspect *me*? Forgive the histrionics, but there really is no justice in this world.

For the record, I was home in bed. At least until about quarter to eight. After that I was on the subway riding to work. I didn't get in here until maybe eight thirty. When I saw the crowd and the police was when I first found out about Andy. And as you may have guessed, I'm not sorry he's gone. I didn't kill him, though I sure wanted to. But killing's really not my style."

"Can anyone testify to the fact that you were home in bed?"

"Yes, detective, I live with my boyfriend. He was still there when I left."

"What's his name?" asked Flynn.

"Jack Phillips. He works on Wall Street. I'll give you his phone number. Is there anything else?"

"No, not now anyway. Thank you for your time."

# TWENTY

"I tell you, Gwen, even if she is guilty, I'm willing to give her a little slack. What a contrast to the rest of the women in that department. I was beginning to think that one of the requirements for working on dictionaries was that you had to look like a man."

"God, you men are all alike. Okay, she's attractive..."

"Attractive, she's gorgeous!"

"Dawson, she's got a boyfriend. And he works on Wall Street. You better stick to Melissa."

"Melissa and I aren't doin' so well right now, if you must know."

"Since when? I thought you were seeing her pretty regularly."

"Yeah, well, we were. But...ah forget it."

She was about to pursue it, but thought better of it. She started to get up from her desk, "Want some coffee?" They'd only gotten back to the precinct squad room 20 minutes ago and were planning to catch up on some of the paperwork that never seemed to go away. Flynn was about to see the lieutenant to fill him in on their progress...or lack thereof.

"Can't hear ya, Gwen. Wha'd ya say?"

The noise was deafening, even for this normally busy squad room. A baldheaded officer was trying to explain to a distraught woman why the police could do nothing about her husband's use of foul language, no matter how excessive it might be, since foul language is not a crime—no matter how offensive. Several phones were ringing at once. A young woman officer, trying to be heard on the phone, was patiently explaining to someone on the other end that it would be best to talk calmly to the boy who practiced his trumpet at any hour, day or night, in the apartment above. Two uniformed cops struggled to bring in a young black who cursed and resisted every step of the way. Still another officer was coaxing and cajoling a shabby homeless man who seemed oblivious to his surroundings and any urgency about moving in a forward direction. No doubt a lethargy brought upon himself by the large bottle of cheap wine he'd nearly finished consuming when the officer observed him exposing himself at the entrance to a neighborhood liquor store.

"I said do you want some coffee?"

"Yeah, thanks. Regular. Hey, I'm trying to get in to see his nibs. Bring 'im up to date. Wanna join me?"

"Not unless you want me."

"Might be good if he heard it from both of us."

"Okay. Let me get the coffee. Just be a sec." She stepped to her left to avoid a collision with the reeling homeless man. The man looked at her and smiled. "Good evening, miss," he slurred cheerfully.

"Good evening to you, my friend," said Gwen as she exited the squad room.

Lieutenant William Farrell was a trim, well-groomed man in his late forties. He was as meticulous with details of the job as he was with his own appearance. Farrell lived and breathed police work, and had no patience with cops who didn't. People who knew him said that during the recent police scandal, when bad cops were turned up in several precincts around the city, he was mortified everywhere he went, carrying the scandal on his back as if it were his own personal disgrace. No one had ever heard Bill Farrell tell a joke. No one had ever heard him laugh at one, for that matter. Lieutenant Farrell was a serious cop.

Gwen was returning with the coffee when Farrell opened his office door and motioned for Flynn and Gwen to come in. Gwen pulled Dawson aside and whispered, "I just found some very interesting pictures.

Very interesting. Take a quick look before we go in. Flynn took the photos and looked quickly at each of them, whistling as he did so.

"Yeah, the plot thickens. Where'd you get 'em?"

"I'm embarrassed to tell you."

"Detectives!" bellowed Farrell from across the room. "If you don't mind. I have a meeting in five minutes."

As Flynn and Gwen stood facing him, Farrell addressed Flynn, the more senior officer, "All right detective, what do you have on this Harmon Hall business?"

"Well, sir, I'm not sure.

"Would you mind explaining that?"

"Well it's a very strange case. Doesn't seem to fit any of the classic homicide patterns. For one thing, it's unlikely the perp is a close relative. That kind of killing usually goes down in the home or in some kind of family location. Why would a relative go to the guy's office where he'd attract attention because he obviously didn't belong there? It's also unlikely to be a random killing. These guys usually look for crowded places. A McDonald's restaurant. A post office. Places like that. Guys who do that attract a lot of attention. They want attention. And I doubt if it's a contract killing. We can't find any mob contacts for this Mack guy. No known shady connections at all. Fact is, he didn't have many friends of any kind. The guy was weird, but squeaky clean. At least as far as a record is concerned. The most logical bet would be someone he works with, but that doesn't play out too well either 'cause those people don't seem like the killer type."

"And just what is the killer type, detective?"

"I know. I know, lieutenant. But these people really don't fit any of the usual stereotypes. Sure, a lot of 'em were pissed at Mack for how he ran the department. He was definitely not Mr. Popularity. But the one with the best motive has a solid alibi."

"Who's that?"

"A Jacqui Dyer. She's the editor who had her project taken away by Mack."

"What's her alibi?"

"She was home in bed when the killing went down. Her live-in boyfriend swears to it. Wall Street type."

"He could be lying."

"He could be, captain," interjected Gwen, "but I doubt it.
Besides, we may have a better suspect."

Farrell looked at his watch. "I only have a minute. Who?"

"Carson Williamson."

# TWENYTY-ONE

"The president of Harmon Hall Publishing Company?," snorted Farrell incredulously. "You're not serious, detective?"

Gwen took a deep breath and bit her lower lip, "I'm afraid I am, sir. Look at these."

With a skeptical sneer on his face, Farrell grabbed the photos. Slowly the sneer melted away, and his expression became serious. "Jesus," he said.

"These are devastating. Where the hell did you get them?"

"They were mislaid in the property room, lieutenant. Frankly, we should have seen them sooner, but somehow they got tucked under some stuff. What can I say? Someone screwed up. Maybe it was me. I honestly don't know."

"All right, all right. Get on with it. Where were they found... originally I mean?"

"They were in one of the drawers in Mack's desk at work. Where he got them I can only speculate," said Gwen, recovering her composure.

"Yes, so can I," said Farrell. "And I don't like where it takes me. I don't like this at all. So you think maybe Mack discovered Williamson having an affair and decided to blackmail him? And Williamson decided to put an end to it?"

"We only saw these pictures a couple of minutes before we came in here, lieutenant," said Gwen. Flynn looked at her as she continued. "Haven't had time to consider the possibilities, but what you just said seems like a good bet."

"Well," said Farrell, soberly, "we've got ourselves a motive. It's not enough, though. And besides, with the computer software available these days, people who know how can fiddle with pictures. These might not hold up in court, but they do give us a starting point. You both should go see this Williamson. But be gentle, detectives. Be gentle. Williamson has friends in high places. For starters, he's a buddy of the mayor. Which, just between you and me, may not be such a great recommendation, but the point is, he's got juice. We either need him to make a mistake or we need more evidence. See what you can get from him." He shook his head in disbelief. That's all detectives. Keep me informed."

"So where the hell were those pictures, Gwen...that they just show up now?" Flynn and Pappas were back in the squad room and Dawson was struggling to control his temper. "Christ, we looked like the goddam Keystone Kops in there."

"I know, I know. Truth is they were there all along—with the other stuff we got out of the desk. There were several manila envelopes, and I guess we just thought we looked through all of them. We obviously didn't. Stupid. Anyway, we've got them now, and suddenly we've got ourselves a real hot suspect."

"Don't count your chickens. It's one thing this Williams guy..."

"Williamson,"

"Whatever. It's one thing this guy is fooling around. It's a big jump, though, to say he's a killer."

"What do you honestly think, Dawson?"

"He could be. He could be. But let's not assume too much till we talk to him."

"You've got to admit that this is one helluva motive. Guy in Williamson's position can't afford any bad press. Hell, if his wife didn't divorce him, the company would. At least this company would, from what I hear of Howard Harmon."

"I agree it's motive, Gwen. But motive is not guilt. We already know other people had reason to want Mack out of the way. Look at Jacqui Dyer."

"Okay. Let's go see Williamson."

Williamson had skipped lunch today. He'd eaten a container of yogurt in his office and told Betsy he was going for a walk. He'd felt like being alone for awhile. From time to time he enjoyed walking the streets of New York at mid-day. It gave him a chance to think, to sort things out. Today he had a lot to sort out. The heat wave had broken, and walking was pleasant, though he hardly noticed. He walked north on Third Avenue and took a left onto 53rd Street, passing the monolith of the CitiCorp Building as he approached Lexington Avenue. No one recognized him. He was glad of that. Right now he didn't feel like talking with anyone. Carr Williamson was not normally taken to melodramatic interpretations of life's difficulties. The ones that couldn't be controlled he viewed as the tax one had to pay in order to enjoy the many high points in life. He didn't usually stew over problems that were out of his hands. A waste of time. And those difficulties that people brought on themselves he saw as object lessons that smart people learned from in order to avoid repeating them in the future.

It had been easy for Carr Williamson to form these mechanistic interpretations of life's struggles, no doubt because he'd encountered so few problems in his own life. He'd led the legendary charmed life, and until now, he'd never given much thought to it. To him it had been normal. Now, suddenly, he was faced with a problem that he couldn't easily take care of. It was a problem of his own making, and one that forced him to take stock of himself in a way he'd never experienced before.

He supposed, because he was inherently a decent man, that it was good for him to be taken down a peg, but why did he have to be taken down as far as he now feared he could fall. He'd created his own problem, certainly, amplified many times over by young

Mack, but nevertheless he himself had set it all in motion. The tragedy was that this was one problem from which he might never recover.

He couldn't help but think of a Greek tragedy. Comparing his situation with the dramatic tragedies of ancient Greece wasn't all that ludicrous, he thought, for he could clearly foresee that his own downfall could easily be as complete as those of the ancient protagonists. He could lose his wife, his daughter, and his job. Not to mention his freedom. The whiz kid Carson Williamson would be nothing more than a bitter memory.

The only ray of hope was for the photos not to show up. Like a fool, he'd left them there when he'd had the chance to take them. He felt for the first time in his life the kind of desperation the vast majority of other human beings felt every day of their lives, the *If-I-only-won-the-lottery* kind of desperation he'd pitied in others. If somehow the photos didn't materialize, he had a chance. But he knew it was long shot. Still, why hadn't they turned up by now?

He sidestepped a young couple, too much in love to even notice the near collision. Then, like an epiphany, it came to him. The one thing he could do and should do. More to the point, he wanted to do. He'd have to tell Laura about the affair before she saw something about it in the press, or was contacted by the police. He'd speak with her tonight. That's the least he could do, though God knows it wasn't much. And maybe...just maybe. That decided, he was ready to get back to his office.

He was still on Lex, approaching 34th Street. He looked west towards the Empire State Building, once again the tallest building in New York, and now rapidly becoming the tallest outmoded office building in the city. Still, it was occupied and functioning, and it continued to host tens of thousands of tourists from all over the world. Over three-quarters of a century old, a little shopworn, but still standing tall and stately. He envied the proud old building. He looked at his watch and started back. It still had its dignity.

* * *

"Officers, please come in," said Williamson graciously, skillfully hiding his dread of what might follow. It was now two fifteen. He'd been back in his office for less than thirty minutes. "Here, please sit down."

Flynn and Gwen took the two chairs facing the couch in the conversation corner of Williamson's spacious office.

"Now, what can I do for you?" asked the CEO of one of the world's great publishing houses.

Gwen began, "Well, sir. We hate to bother you again, but we've come across some very disturbing evidence that we thought you might be able to tell us about."

*This is it,* thought Williamson "Yes, detective, what evidence is that?"

"Well, I'm a little uncomfortable even showing you these, but I can't think of any easier way to do this. Here, it's these pictures. We know that woman is not your wife?"

Carr shook his head sadly, "No, detective. It's not my wife. Where did you get these? Not that it matters, I suppose."

"We think it does matter, Mr. Williamson," said Flynn. "We found them in a drawer in Andrew Mack's desk. We're assuming he took them."

"Uh huh, and you think I killed him for the pictures?"

"Well, yes, Mr. Williamson," said Gwen, "it did cross our minds."

"If I killed him for the pictures, why would I leave them behind?"

"Good question. Maybe you knew he had the

pictures, but didn't know where they were. You figured if you killed him, they wouldn't show up."

"I see your point, detective." *Why am I fencing with them? I haven't even denied killing the little twit. God, they're more convinced now than when they came in here.* "Detective...Pappas is it?"

"Yessir."

"I didn't kill Andy Mack."

"You admit having an affair with Ms Ferrara?"

"Well I haven't admitted any such thing, but I guess, given these pictures, there's no point in denying that I've been seeing her. That doesn't mean I killed Mack, though."

"It would seem," interjected Flynn, "that you had a good motive."

"Yes, I guess I did. But, I didn't kill him."

"If you didn't, do you have any idea who might have?" probed Flynn.

"I wish I could say I did. I know he wasn't too popular down there, especially since his promotion. But I can't imagine someone in our editorial department killing their boss just because he made unpopular decisions. Hell, I would have been dead a long time ago."

"Why was Mack promoted if he was so unpopular?" pressed Gwen.

"First of all, you don't promote people because they're popular, you promote them because they can do the job."

"From our inquiries," pressed Gwen, "we haven't found anyone who believed he could do the job. As a matter of fact, we have reason to believe his promotion came about because of pressure from a senior officer in the company—someone higher up than Mr. Marcantonio or even Mr. Markham. Could you comment on that?"

He looked at the two detectives who sat patiently waiting for his answer. They appeared to be in no hurry. Why should they be? In their minds they knew they had him. They weren't rich. They weren't famous. They probably weren't known outside of their own precinct. But they had that self-assured look of people who know they can face tomorrow with no fear of losing their jobs, their families, their reputations... even their lives.

"Sir?" prodded Gwen as gently as she could.

How long could he stonewall, and would it really matter in the end? Eventually he'd have to tell them about the Andy Mack's extortion demands."

"Okay," he said, almost in a whisper. "You may as well know. A couple of weeks ago Mack came to my office and threatened to expose my affair with Kate Ferrara. He claimed to have seen the two of us in compromising situations.

I said it was nonsense. Told him to get the hell out of my office. Then he pulled out these pictures."

"What did he want from you?" asked Flynn.

"Said he wanted to be promoted — immediately. He also wanted to be put in charge of this new unabridged dictionary project we're doing. I have to tell you he floored me with that one. I told him it was ridiculous. He wasn't the least bit qualified. He reminded me of the pictures. I won't bore you with the details, but I finally acceded. I agreed to promote him to managing editor of the reference division. I also told him I'd find a way to put him in charge of the new project. I had no choice. It was that or my own ruination. Of course I still had to sell my senior editorial executives on putting Mack into the managing editor spot and the project directorship. God knows it wasn't easy to do that. I lost more than a little credibility with that one. Anyway, I admit that whoever dispatched young Mack did me a favor. Or at least I thought he did when I first heard about it. I couldn't believe how lucky I'd gotten. Now I'm not so sure. I suppose I'm your top suspect now?"

"I'm afraid you're right up there," confirmed Flynn. "Can you tell us where you were at the time of the murder?"

"You'll have to tell me what time that was, detective. I mean I know Mack was found Wednesday morning, but I don't know exactly when he was killed."

"We're saying it was sometime between six-thirty and seven-forty-five in the morning. Can you account for your whereabouts in that time frame?"

"Well, yes, I think I can. I was on my way in on the train from Rye. Took the 7:03. I walked from Grand Central. Got here about quarter to eight. Don't remember exactly."

"Did anyone see you who could verify that?" asked Gwen.

"Only a few thousand people on the street, but no one's going to remember seeing me. Oh my God, I can't believe this. Wait, wait. I gave some money to a homeless man with his little daughter. Such a sad case. What future does that little girl have? Anyway, he might remember."

"Why do you think he'd remember?" asked Flynn. "People must give him money all the time."

"I gave him ten dollars. My guess is most people give him change or a dollar at most. Maybe I'm wrong. But he might remember."

"Tell us where you saw him." Flynn continued.

"Up against the building on the corner of Park and 46th or 47th. No, 46th. I'm sure it was 46th. On the east side. He's not there all the time. He wasn't there Thursday, for instance. He's there a lot, but then you won't see him for a few weeks. I suppose he finds another location..."

"Did he say anything when you gave him the ten dollars?" asked Gwen.

"No, I don't think so. He just looked at me and nodded. Then he gave the money to his little girl, and she put it carefully in her pocket. But the father didn't say anything. I don't think he's all there, frankly."

"Well, sir, you better hope we can find them," said Flynn. "They're your only alibi. Give us a description and we'll check it out, but I wouldn't count too much on it."

## TWENTY-TWO

"Flynn," the sergeant yelled across the room. "There's a guy on the phone says he wants to talk to someone about the Mack homicide. Says he might have some information."

"Got it Vito. What's his name?"

"Wasserman. Line three."

Flynn picked up the receiver. "Detective Flynn. What can I do for you?"

"Detective, my name is Herb Wasserman. I'm a friend of Carson Williamson, and what I want to talk about is a little delicate."

"How's that?"

"I might have something that could possibly, and I emphasize possibly, incriminate him."

"Williamson?"

"Yes."

"You said he's your friend?"

"Yes officer. That's why it's delicate. I mean I'm not even sure I should be calling you."

"Okay, Mr. Wasserman. Why don't you just tell me about it. First, could I have your telephone number? In case we get disconnected." Wasserman nervously gave his number. At the same time Flynn motioned to Gwen to get on the line. Flynn continued.

"All right, can you tell me how you happen to know Mr. Williamson?"

"We've known each other for years. Play tennis together. In the same club. Get together with the wives on a regular basis. As I say he's my friend. Until now I'd say he's been my best friend."

"Why do you say 'until now'?"

"You'll know when I tell you?"

"I've got a suggestion, Mr. Wasserman. Why don't we come and see you. Might be better." Flynn knew that whatever it was Wasserman had to say, he and Gwen would understand it better if they met face-to-face. Much easier to tell where this Wasserman was coming from if you talked to him in person. Body language, eyes and all that. Not to mention the fact that they had no proof that Wasserman really was who he said he was. Anyone could phone in so-called incriminating evidence. This was too important a case to take evidence the easy way. "What's your address?"

Wasserman gave his Wall Street address; then hesitated. At last he said, "Perhaps I should come to see you."

"Flynn could tell that Wasserman wasn't eager to have the police make an appearance at his Wall Street office.

"I think it would be better if we go to you. We'll play it pretty low key, and," he added, "we'll be in business clothes."

The address on Wall Street was in one of the prestigious new all-glass towers. As they were shown into Wasserman's office it quickly became apparent that their new source was a very high roller. The office was only slightly less impressive than Williamson's vast quarters uptown in the Harmon Hall Building. They'd introduced themselves to Wasserman's secretary as Gwen Pappas and Dawson Flynn, saying, "He's expecting us." Wasserman had obviously been listening, for he carried out his end of the charade smoothly, "Hey, c'mon in. Good to see you."

Flynn glanced at Gwen and smiled, *The flip side of police brutality: police sensitivity.*

As they sat down, Wasserman went over and closed the door. "Thanks, I appreciate that. I admit I'm a little nervous about having police in my office." He smiled weakly, "Nothing personal. I'm sure you understand."

"We understand," said Gwen.

"Okay," continued Flynn. "Now why don't you fill us in."

"Yes, yes. I will. First let me ask you if you have any other suspects. You can see where I'm coming from. If you're hot on the trail of somebody else, maybe I don't have to tell you what I know."

"Sir, I hate to pull procedure on you," said Flynn, because I do understand where you're coming from, but we're not at liberty to tell you that kind of information. And even if we do have other suspects, you're obligated to tell us what you know anyway. It still might have a bearing on the case."

"I guess I knew the answer before I asked it. Officers, I have never, and believe me, I'm not prone to be melodramatic, but I have never found myself in a worse dilemma than this. I'm afraid that I will truly be damned if I do, and damned if don't tell you what I know. I sincerely hope I'm wrong about this because if I'm right, it means my best friend is a murderer."

"Why don't you just tell us. Maybe it will come to nothing, and you'll be able to forget about it," said Flynn.

"That would be nice, but I don't think this is going to have a happy ending." Wasserman got up and went to the nearest window and stared out. The two detectives looked at each other, but remained silent. After what seemed like a painfully long pause, Wasserman turned and came back to his seat. "On the Saturday before this young editor was killed, Carr and I played our usual tennis match. I remember the match well because I beat him for the first time in two years. He's a better player than I am, but that day he was terrible. I asked him after the match what was wrong, and he suggested we sit down and have a beer. He told me he was having an affair with another woman. That in itself was a shock. Then he told me that one of his employees knew about it and was blackmailing him."

"So far you haven't told us anything we don't already know, Mr. Wasserman," said Flynn. "Is there more?"

"I'm afraid there is," said Wasserman disconsolately. "Carr went on to tell me how this guy was screwing up his whole life. At one point he sounded so desperate that he said, 'I feel like killing the son-of-a-bitch!' At another point he said something like, 'the best thing would be for this creep to simply disappear.'" I didn't think much about any of this until I heard about the murder. Even then I pooh-poohed the idea that Carr could be responsible. I talked it over with my wife and we agreed that I'd wait one week from the day of the killing. Then, if no one had been arrested, I'd speak up. God, how I wish you'd found somebody!" He sighed, Gwen noticed that his eyes were red. He looked like hell, she thought. Then Wasserman added dejectedly, "Well, there you have it. I did the right thing. I ratted on my best friend."

Gwen looked at him compassionately, "Yessir, you really did do the right thing."

## TWENTY-THREE

Armed with a supportive, if not enthusiastic, "go ahead" from Lieutenant Farrell, Flynn and Gwen found themselves in the cluttered office of Maggie Muñoz, one of the many overworked assistant D.A.s in the Borough of Manhattan. In her early thirties, Muñoz somehow managed not to look harried, despite the inhuman caseload she handled. She wasn't their first choice, but she was available.

"You want me to what?" she exclaimed, brushing her auburn hair back from her forehead.

"We want you to issue a warrant for the arrest of Carson Williamson," said Gwen.

"Is that who I think it is?"

"If you mean president of Harmon Hall, the answer is yes."

"Hey guys, c'mon. Your job isn't tough enough? Can't come up with the killer, so you go for self immolation. This man's a pillar of the community. The commissioner will have your asses—not to mention mine." Getting no response from the two detectives in front of her, Muñoz lowered her decibel level and continued, "Okay, okay, what have you got?"

"Item one," said Flynn. "Williamson was being blackmailed by Mack." Muñoz looked surprised. Flynn continued. "We've got some pretty compromising pictures that Williamson was aware of—taken by Mack and used by him to extort a big promotion."

Muñoz said nothing, but it was clear that she was listening.

"Item two," chimed in Gwen. "Williamson's best friend, a Herb Wasserman, heard him say he felt like killing the little S.O.B. Wasserman also claims to have heard Williamson say that the best solution to his problems would be for the editor to disappear from the face of the Earth."

"Anything else?"

"Yes," continued Gwen. "A security guard saw Williamson in Mack's office two nights before the shooting. Says Williamson was acting suspiciously."

"What's that mean?"

"He was coming out of Mack's office, with a guilty look on his face—as if he'd just been going through the desk."

"As if...! As if...! As if, my friends, is not evidence. As if is one man's opinion. What else you got?"

"That's it," said Flynn. Then remembering, "Well, we do have Williamson's admission that he was having an affair, and that Mack was blackmailing him.

"Okay, so you have motive. But just how strong a motive is it? Look, maybe Williamson didn't want his wife to know about his affair. Still, she'd eventually find out anyway. So why would he kill Mack for something he'd probably tell her himself when he was good and ready?"

"You'd have a point, Maggie, if his wife were his only concern." Flynn paused to be sure Muñoz was following him. "We have reason to believe, though, that he didn't want his boss, Howard Harmon, to know about it. Harmon's chairman of the parent company, and apparently he's some kind of stickler about marital infidelity and the scandals that go with them. They say he once fired an executive for having an affair. Word is, Williamson was up for the presidency of the parent company. If word of his affair reached old man Harmon, his chances for the big job would have been nil. More than likely he'd have been fired from his present job, which incidentally pays him over five mil a year. Imagine what the presidency of the parent company would pay. I'd say that's motive enough."

Maggie Muñoz nodded, indicating agreement.

"Do we have any really hard evidence?"

"If you mean an eyewitness, no, we don't. But motive and opportunity ain't bad Maggie," said Flynn.

"Hell, the motive's terrific. And don't forget his best friend's testimony."

"Some best friend," countered the prosecutor. "With friends like that..."

"Yeah, I know," agreed Flynn. "Still, it's gotta count for something. What's the guy got to gain by puttin the screws to his friend?"

"You tell me, detective. Maybe he's got some kind of ax to grind, and this is his chance to get even. Or maybe he has some kind of agenda of his own, and this is his way of furthering it. Stranger things have happened."

"Maybe, but he seemed pretty broken up about telling us. Didn't read him as a phoney."

"Okay, maybe you're right, maybe you're not. If you're wrong, though, my ass is in a sling. So's yours. I can't afford to lose a case like this, my friends. My upwardly mobile yuppie career would nosedive faster than a disabled space shuttle."

"We understand, Maggie, but the only way we'll know for sure is if we put some heat on him. We've gotta arrest him," pressed Flynn. "Everything we have points to him. Besides, if we're right, think what that will do for your career."

"You both feel pretty certain about this?"

"Yes," said Gwen. "We do." Flynn nodded his affirmation.

"Look, with something this big I need to confer with my boss. I'm inclined to agree with you, but this is too hot to go solo on. Give me a call in a couple of hours. I'll have an answer for you."

On the way out Gwen turned to Flynn, "Think she'll come through?"

"I hope so. I really want to nail this guy."

"No doubts, Dawson?"

"No. Do you? I thought we were in agreement."

"We are. It's just that I..."

"Have doubts, or maybe you feel sorry for the guy."

"Maybe a little of both. C'mon, Dawson, if we're wrong, Williamson will be ruined."

"We're not wrong. Look, just because the guy wears thousand dollar suits and went to a fancy college doesn't give him any special right to do in some guy who's puttin' the screws to him."

"Who's saying he should get special treatment? I just want to be sure."

"Christ, Gwen, I'd think being a woman you'd be hot to see him fry—just for his affair with that woman lawyer."

"Of course that bothers me, but that doesn't make him a killer. Look, I know the evidence that we have points to him. We don't have any choice. It's just that I won't get as much pleasure out of taking him in as you apparently will."

Flynn shook his head, "You're a hard woman to understand, Gwen.

"I know, my dad tells me that all the time."

"How is your dad, by the way?"

"As a matter of fact, he's not feeling so hot. Said it's probably indigestion, but with the weight he's carrying I'm kinda worried. Gonna stop over and see him after work tonight. Thanks for asking. Let's eat. Then we can check back with Maggie.

# TWENTY-FOUR

As they emerged from the elevator on the fortieth floor, Flynn and Gwen exchanged looks, hoping to get from each other an unspoken last-minute confirmation that they were in fact doing the right thing. They were both aware of the magnitude of what they were about to do. Maggie Muñoz had given them the green light less than an hour earlier. They'd already picked up the warrant and were about to make the arrest. Could there be anything more embarrassing, anything more personally humiliating than being arrested in one's own place of business? Throw in the fact that the one being arrested was president of the company. What would happen to the man's career? His distinguished reputation in the community? His family? Imagine his children. In this case there was just one—a teenaged girl named Jennifer. If they were wrong about Williamson... They tried not to think about it. But if they were right, and they were ninety-nine percent certain they were, they'd have a bloodthirsty killer in custody. All of the bad that would ensue from the arrest would be of his own making.

Betsy Conway greeted them warily. Years of experience and a hard life had made her wary. Her shrink had called it hyper-vigilant; her enemies called it paranoid. "Yes, detectives, I assume you want to see Mr. Williamson?"

"Yes, ma'am," said Flynn.

"He's on the phone right now. He has a meeting in five minutes."

"This will only take a minute," said Gwen.

"Oh, I think he's off the phone now," said Conway as she buzzed Williamson. "Mr. Williamson, those two detectives are here again to see you." She looked up at the two visitors, her face sad with concern. "He said to go right in."

The inside of Williamson's office seemed darker than last time. He looked up as they entered. "Good afternoon, detectives. I hope this won't take long. I have a meeting in a couple of minutes."

"It won't take long, sir. But you're going to have to postpone that meeting." Flynn hesitated for a second. He could see from the dejection in Williamson's intelligent eyes that the man knew what was happening. "Carson Williamson, you're under arrest for the murder of Andrew Mack. You have the right to remain silent, you..."

As Flynn droned on Williamson remained seated behind his desk. He didn't want to move. This couldn't be happening. Just last night he'd told Laura everything. She'd been devastated. He knew she was still in shock. And now this... He looked up again at the two detectives. Is this what it feels like those fleeting seconds before you die? Only it wasn't his past life passing in front of him. It was his future. Scenes flashed by in his head: The upcoming meeting. A vacant chair where he should have been sitting. Managers speculating about how they'd feel if it had been they. Speculating about how they'd be affected by his absence, his arrest, his demise...his humiliation. Then a tearful Laura...how he'd hurt Laura...How he'd brought disaster and humiliation to the woman who'd given him the best years of her life. And his adoring daughter, Jennifer. Where was the pedestal now? Would she ever respect him again? And Kate. Then Howard Harmon, his boss. The frames moved on like an old-fashioned slide show—to his friends, especially Herb. What would Herb think? And what about his job? And the position with the parent company? It all seemed like fiction. After all, he was Carson Williamson, president and CEO of Harmon Hall, one of the world's biggest publishing companies.

And the prison cell. Or worse.

"If you'll come with us, sir," said Gwen.

"I have a meeting," Williamson's voice was barely audible. "What do I do? I can't just leave without a word."

"Tell your secretary something quickly. Tell her you'll be in touch. We have to take you in now. I'm sorry," said Flynn. "Use your phone to do it."

Zombielike, Williamson picked up the phone and buzzed his assistant. "Betsy, make my excuses to Mike Clancy and the others. I..." he hesitated as long as he could, "I've just been arrested. It's all a mistake, of course. It'll all be straightened out soon. Oh, and call Kate Ferrara and tell her. Tell her I'll need someone from the firm to handle my case. Oh yes...," Williamson sucked in a deep breath before he proceeded, "call my wife and tell her, and call Howard and tell him. Tell them I'll be in touch as soon as I can...Thank you, Betsy. I appreciate that. Yes, yes. I'll be okay. Now stop that. Everything will be all right. No, I can't talk anymore. The long arm of the law is waiting. Just take care of those calls for me. Oh, call my wife first. That's the least I can do." He put the receiver back in its cradle and slowly got up.

"I'm going to have to put these on you, Mr. Williamson. Sorry." Gwen held up the pair of handcuffs.

Williamson wilted visibly, "Are they really necessary, detective?"

"I'm afraid so, sir."

## TWENTY-FIVE

It was a typical corporate board room. Perhaps a bit brighter than most. Certainly more cheerful, thanks to the pastel decor. Ironically, almost three years ago to the day, Evelyn Ravenswood, noted up and down the East Coast for her interior designs, had been commissioned by Williamson to redo the room. He'd considered the room depressing and off-putting. Not the kind of place where America's most forward-looking publishing company should be launching his new plans for the twenty-first century.

Howard Harmon, chairman of Harman Hall as well as of the parent company, Harmon Communications, wearing a dark blue, almost black Armani suit, was seated at the head of the long, massive, inlaid-teak table. "People," he said. He spoke only slightly more forcefully than his usual conversational voice. That was enough, for his normally stentorian utterances were more than adequate for getting people's attention. "People, I think we'd better get started."

The room became quiet almost immediately, each board member recognizing the seriousness of the meeting that was about to begin. Harmon surveyed the room, making eye contact with each person before he resumed speaking, "I've called this unscheduled meeting on very short notice because Harmon Hall is faced with a situation of extreme gravity. I think by now each of you is aware of what I'm talking about.
"For the record," He looked at Harriet Stahl who was secretary of the board and who would be taking minutes. Why did it suddenly come to him that she might resent it that the board had selected her, a woman, to serve as secretary? "I'm talking about the arrest yesterday of Carson Williamson, president and chief executive officer of Harmon Hall Publishing

Company. I would like to dispense with the reading of the minutes from our last meeting. You all have a copy of them. And I'd like to turn immediately to the question of how we deal with Carr Williamson's arrest.

"Before you offer up any ideas, I'd like to take a minute or two to say that I don't know very much about this. All I really know is that he was arrested for the alleged murder of one of the company's young editors, one Andrew Mack. I want to emphasize the word alleged. Knowing Carr as I think I do, I have to believe that this is all some sort of terrible mistake on the part of New York's finest. An attorney from our outside law firm of Blyth, Goodstein, and Blum is handling the case. I hope to ..."

"I'm not so sure that it's a good idea for B.G. and B. to be involved here, Howard," interrupted Warner Phillips, Harmon Hall's chief corporate counsel. Phillips was a gray haired, somewhat dispassionate man with an aristocratic manner and features to match. He had Choate and Yale written all over him. "I'm not sure Harmon Hall should be providing legal representation on this kind of a case. It's clearly not a business matter."

"I'm sure you're right, Warner," said Harmon. "I'm sure you're right. I believe Carr requested them as he was literally going out the door with the police officers. At least that's the way I got it from Betsy, his assistant. I don't want it to appear that we're not supporting Carr, but you're right, this is not something the company should be footing. Would you take care of this Warner. Maybe you can suggest a good criminal lawyer to Carr. See to it yourself, though, don't send someone else. All right now, how are we going to handle this?"

"Do we have any idea how long this is likely to take? No, that was a stupid question." All eyes turned to the stunning, fortyish woman at the other end of the table. It was Martha Cartwright, head of the trendy chic ad agency, Cartwright, Inc. "Let me phrase it differently. If we think Carr will be released by the police soon, whether because of bail, insufficient evidence, whatever, what should we do while he's still in custody, and what should we do when he's out? It seems to me we must consider both situations, and we should decide what actions we're going to take—before we leave this meeting."

"Look," interjected John Attenborough, executive director of the Metropolitan Museum of Art and the newest member of the board, "I personally like Carr a lot. He's a good guy, and he's been good for this company. I don't believe he's capable of doing what he's been accused of. I doubt if any of us believes that. Nevertheless, I think we must proceed on the basis that he'll be absent from the business for an indefinite period of time. We simply don't know how long. And Harmon Hall can't function without a leader. We're going to have to provide some way for the company to be managed in his absence. And we need someone now." Several people started to speak. Attenborough held up his hand. "No, wait, hear me out. I know. Some of you'll point out that if Carr went on vacation we wouldn't appoint a replacement. True. But this is clearly not a vacation." No one chuckled at this. "If he were on vacation and there were a business emergency, Carr could be reached. I have no doubt that when he goes away he keeps in touch. That's not going to happen here. But far more important than that is what I fear could become a crisis of leadership—a sense here at Harmon Hall that nobody is in charge. That there is no one to turn to for direction. Even if Carr can be reached now, his leadership has been seriously impeached."

As Attenborough spoke, Stuart Markham allowed the slightest trace of a smile to show on his face. Nothing that the casual observer would think twice about. Inwardly, however, he beamed. "No," continued Attenborough, "I truly regret that until this awful situation is cleared up, Carr is going to be a liability around here. I say this with a sad heart, for I somehow feel that this is all a terrible mistake."

*This is terrific!* Markham leaned back in his comfortable board room chair. He'd never in his six years on the board enjoyed a board meeting so much.

"I suppose it was inevitable—that it would come to this." All eyes turned back to Howard Harmon. "I was one of the most enthusiastic supporters of Carr when we brought him in here three years ago. Until this unfortunate turn of events I've never had reason to doubt my support or the board's decision. But today... I have to tell you I've never enjoyed anything less in all my years in business. Still, I'm afraid I must agree with John. Somebody has to be in charge here. Do I hear any suggestions or nominations for acting president?"

Arthur Levinson, president and CEO of New York Merchants Bank leaned forward, "I nominate Stuart Markham for the position of acting president of Harmon Hall Publishing Company. I further stipulate that he hold the position until such time as the board deems Carr Williamson fit and capable of resuming his position at no liability to the company, or he is deemed unable to assume his former duties, in which case the board will reconvene and decide on a permanent replacement."

"Seconds?" prompted Harmon.

"I second it," said Martha Cartwright.

"Any discussion?" asked Harmon.

"I'd suggest that at this point Stuart excuse himself while the motion is being discussed," advised Warner Phillips in his most august courtroom manner.

"Of course," said Markham getting up to leave, trying not to smirk. He knew he should have made the suggestion himself, but he'd been too caught up in the upward spiral of his own fate to think of it.

When Markham had left the room, Harmon looked about the room. Seeing that he had everyone's attention, he proceeded, "Let's have discussion of the motion on the floor."

Mike Clancy, director of sales and marketing and senior vice president of Harmon Hall, cleared his throat, "Ladies, gentlemen. I agree that we need someone in charge here. What I have to say may look like sour grapes or jealousy. I want to state from the outset that that is not the case. You'll have to take that on faith." Several board members shifted in their seats in anticipation of what was about to be said. "I have a great deal of respect for the professional abilities of my colleague, Stuart Markham. He's done a great deal for this company. He's brought us some of the best authors in the industry. He's given us an extremely competitive product line. He's put together an incomparable team of editors. And he's done a lot, lot more. Now having said that, I'm going to suggest that you nominate another person for the position of acting president. I say this with the best interests of this company in mind. I hope by saying this that I don't live to regret it."

Directly across the table from Clancy, R. Thompson Roehrer, former president of Mobil Oil Company and member of half dozen corporate boards, smiled broadly as he began speaking. "Mr. Clancy, I don't think you can make a speech like that without giving us some sort of explanation. You've just given Stuart the strongest kind of endorsement, yet you tell us to pick another person. I think we need to hear a little more."

"Yes, I agree, said Harmon. I think you'd better tell us what's on your mind, Mike."

"I'd hoped I wouldn't have to get into specifics. I'd sort of assumed that many of you knew Stuart well enough to know what I'm talking about, so that it wouldn't be necessary to say any more." Clancy scanned the room, looking for signs of support. A couple of people winked, but no one moved to speak. Reluctantly, he continued, "Stuart has some personality traits that turn a lot of people off. He..." As he looked frantically about the table for support, he met nothing but stony silence. In two or three instances cold unfriendly eyes staring back at him like lasers. The winkers had now gone completely blank. "Then there's the incident in Stuart's third year at Harmon Hall. I'm sure most of you have heard about it." Clancy looked around the room, desperate for a sign of support. A salesman by instinct and a self-taught political animal, Clancy had never felt so alone, so alienated. He'd clearly misjudged his audience, and he didn't make that mistake often. "Look, I don't want to get involved with character assassination or..."

"I should hope not!" snapped Arthur Levinson.

"Look, I certainly didn't mean..." Clancy's cause, if it ever had a chance, had nose-dived precipitously.

Harriet Stahl, director of human resources at Harmon Hall and someone who knew Markham well, gestured for the floor. She knew exactly what Mike was trying to get across. She'd been with Harmon Hall back when Markham, in his third year with the company, had, according to some fairly reliable reports at the time, engineered the undermining and dismissal of Willard Campion, the man who was his boss at the time. With an ingenious smear campaign and some allegedly forged documents that had made the hapless Campion appear both inept and dishonest, Markham had underhandedly arranged his own first big move up the corporate ladder. No proof had ever materialized, but most old-timers in the company, to this day, believed something had happened. Stuart seemed the type.

Harriet Stahl, like Clancy, was a political animal. And on this occasion, a better reader of the collective Zeitgeist of the board. It was clear now which way the wind was blowing, and she was not about to make an enemy of the editor-in-chief, and very likely the new CEO. "Perhaps Stuart has personality traits that bother some people. I'm sure we all have traits that annoy some people. That in no way negates his contribution to this company. You, yourself, Mike, acknowledged some of his accomplishments. Everyone has his or her own style. Stuart has his, and it's clearly been effective over the years."

"Anything else, Harriet?" asked Harmon.

"No, I've said what I wanted to say."

Harmon continued, "Does anybody else want to add something...or put up another name?" No one attempted to speak. "There being no further discussion, we'll proceed with the voting." Warner Phillips suggested a secret ballot. Within three minutes Harmon stood up, "Ladies and gentleman, Stuart Markham has been elected acting president and CEO of Harmon Hall by a vote of six to three."

## TWENTY-SIX

He hadn't moved into Carr's office yet. After all, the board had just acted this morning. Wouldn't look good if he appeared too eager. He took a moment to reflect on what had just happened and how he'd gotten there. He realized that he'd allowed his moral standards to slip gradually over the years—all in the name of pragmatism. He'd never been what the common vernacular referred to as a boy scout. Even as a child he'd recognized that good guys finish last. He certainly hadn't gotten any more virtuous lately. Still, he hadn't allowed his good taste to slide. And rushing into Williamson's office too quickly would definitely be in poor taste. More than a little tacky. That could wait. He could make the move in a couple of weeks. No hurry. People would know who was in charge. They'd just think more highly of him for not grabbing the office right away. He chuckled. God, how predictable people were.
    And Clancy. He always knew the lowbrow son-of-a-bitch hated him. Nothing but a salesman who'd gotten lucky anyway. When Arthur Levinson told him after the meeting that Clancy had spoken out against him, he wasn't surprised. But that was okay. Markham's mind saw opportunity in even the most unlikely situations. He could already see how he could use Clancy's indiscretion to his advantage. Undoubtedly Clancy would fear that word of his treachery would get back to him. Stuart could play on Clancy's fear like a cheap violin. Who knows, the moralistic moron might even feel a little guilt along with his fear. That would make him even easier to manipulate. Markham was always comfortable with his own thoughts. Perhaps that was why he found himself resenting the interruption of the buzzer on his

intercom.

"Yes, Cathy. What is it?" He'd decided to retain his assistant of ten years. He'd keep Betsy Conway around, too—for awhile—she knew where things were and what Williamson was working on. Cathy could pick her brains for a few weeks; then he'd let the pushy bitch go.

"Walter Birchfield is waiting outside," said Cathy. "Said he needs to see you."

Markham considered for a moment whether he should force Birchfield to make an appointment and come back later, or see him now. In his twenty-plus years at Harmon Hall, Markham had come to know Birchfield as an unpleasant and unsavory character. He really didn't want to see him, but his instincts told him he'd better.

"Tell him to come in, Cathy."

A huge hulk of a man, Birchfield was wearing a cheap brown suit that appeared to be one size too small—especially around his more than ample stomach. He was tall, over six feet, but the overall impression was more of bulk, than height. He smiled broadly as he entered Markham's office.

"Hello, Walter, what can I do for you?" Markham hoped he sounded friendly.

"It's what I can do for you," said the big man smugly.

"Oh, how's that?" Markham looked at the still-smiling face and the disheveled suit and wondered what indeed this loutish oaf could do for him.

"Since you're in charge now, I thought you should know...Oh, by the way, congratulations, sir. Anyway, I thought you should know what one of my men saw a coupla nights before that editor got himself killed."

At this, Markham grew tense. What did this overgrown bumpkin know? Had his man seen him near Mack's office? He narrowed his gaze. "Yes, of course, Walter. Go ahead. What did he see?"

"Well he was making is usual rounds. He was in the reference division area...where the editors are, and he heard this noise coming from a dark office. As he got closer he could see from the nameplate that it was Andrew Mack's office."

"Yeeess..." said Markham cautiously, holding his breath. *What did this caricature of a small-town southern sheriff know?*

"Well, he goes to look in, and out comes Mr. Williamson, looking kinda guilty, if you know what I mean. 'Course my man doesn't know it's Williamson until the guy shows him his business card. He didn't just take Williamson's word for it that he was president. Guy's real conscientious. We're lucky to have him..."

"Yes, yes, Walter, that's good. Get on with it."

"Anyway, my man says it looks as if Williamson had been messing around in the desk, though he can't be sure. It all happened so fast."

"Anything else?" Markham kept his fingers crossed.

"No. That's about it. Just thought you should know."

"You did the right thing. By the way, keep me informed of anything, anything at all that you think I might find interesting...or useful. Do you follow me?"

"Yes, sir, I believe I do," smiled the security chief. "I believe I do."

"Oh, and Walter, Let's work together closely, shall we. I'm sure we can find ways to make your job more rewarding in the future. I want to take good care of you. Let's give some thought to that. Why don't we plan to meet here in my office next Monday and discuss your situation. Say eleven o'clock. Will that be convenient with you?"

"Yessir, that will be just fine. I look forward to having you run things around here."

## TWENTY-SEVEN

Birchfield leaned back in his overstuffed leather swivel chair. He always felt more confident in his own office. For the last half hour he'd been going over in his mind what Markham had said to him. The possibilities were pleasantly intriguing. It looked like now, finally, he'd be treated with a little respect around the company. And more than likely he'd see a little improvement in the ol' bank account.

There wasn't much about Markham that he liked, but he did understand the man. They both marched to the same drummer, only Markham did his marching on Park Avenue, and he did his in Jackson Heights, Queens. One thing he did like about the acting president was that you could work with him. It was obvious now that they both realized they could help each other. He smiled. Talk about strange bedfellows. Really strange the more he thought about it. Markham was a snob, but he was a practical one. Williamson, on the other hand, seemed more like a regular guy, but he went by the book. You couldn't work any deals with him, not like you could with some of the brass around the company. On the surface, Williamson was a real straight arrow; yet apparently he wasn't as clean as he appeared to be. Didn't he kill this Mack guy? God knows why, but he obviously had some reason. Strange indeed. Birchfield threw up his hands. How do you figure?

He was about to make a phone call when he noticed that a young man had appeared in the doorway. "You looking for me?" he said gruffly.

"Yes, if you're Mr. Birchfield."

"That's me. C'mon in. What's on your mind?"

The young man looked unsure of himself. "I may know something about the Mack killing. I feel I should tell someone, but I'm not sure who I should talk to. I thought I should start with you. Maybe you can advise me."

"Why don't you begin by telling me who you are." said Birchfield abruptly, always one to take advantage of someone he perceived as being weak or diffident..

"Oh, sorry. Tad Szczepanski." I'm an editor upstairs. On sixteen. Reference division."

"You better spell that name for me."

"Sure. T-A-D...."

Birchfield rolled his eyes upward, "Not your first name. Your last name."

"Right, sure. S-Z-C-Z-E-P-A-N-S-K-I. It's Polish."

"I kinda figured," said Birchfield, shaking his head. "Okay, so tell me what you know about the Mack killing."

"It was on the Monday night before the killing. I think it was Monday. Yes, it was definitely Monday. I was working late on this project. I was the only one left in the department. At least I think I was. Anyway, I'd been at my computer so long I was getting stiff, so I got up to stretch my legs. Went out in the hall to walk. As I approached Andy Mack's office I thought I heard somebody opening and closing drawers—probably desk drawers—though from where I was standing in the hall I couldn't tell for sure. Look, should I be telling you this, or someone else? Maybe the police?"

"Finish your story first. Then we'll decide how to handle it."

"Okay," said the young editor, grateful for any kind of affirmation that he was doing the right thing.

"Anyway, as I rounded the bend in the corridor, there was Mr. Williamson, looking kinda guilty. Like he'd just been in Andy's office and didn't want me to know it. Now I can't prove that he was in there, but that's the impression I had at the time."

"Well, okay Spanski, but..."

"Szczepanski."

"Right. As I was saying, that's interesting, but it doesn't tell me anything I don't already know. Ya see, one of my men saw Williamson there the same night. But thanks any..."

"Wait. There's more."

"Oh?"

"Well, after I saw him, I went back to my office. Not long after that, your security guard came by. That's probably how you know Williamson was there."

"Yeah, go on, kid. Finish your story."

"Well, about an hour later, give or take a few minutes, I got up again to stretch. Took another walk, and as I neared Andy's office I heard somebody in there again. Now, I'm thinking, this is weird. Seems like everybody but Andy uses his office. My curiosity is aroused so I figure I'll just saunter on by and catch a glimpse of whoever's in there."

"Well, who was it?" demanded Birchfield impatiently. "Who'd ya see, kid?" By now Birchfield was more than a little curious himself.

"I'm still not sure I should have come here. I'm really uncomfortable about this. I can't afford to jeopardize my job."

"Look, Spanski. This is a serious matter. You need to tell me what you know." Szczepanski winced as the chief of security once again murdered his name. Birchfield pressed his point, "Homicide's a felony. You can't hold back evidence." Birchfield neglected to mention that Szczepanski was obliged to tell the police; not him. Seeing that the diffident young man needed a little more reassurance, he added, "Look, as head of security I hear a lot. If I blabbed everything I heard, I'd be out on my ass. Just tell me who you saw. Then you and I can decide how to handle it."

"Well, okay. I still hope this doesn't come back to haunt me. But I'm assuming when I tell you you'll act appropriately."

"Count on it. Now who'd you see?"

# TWENTY-EIGHT

"You sure of this, Spanski?"

"Absolutely."

"Very interesting," Birchfield's wheels were churning now. "You're right. This is a delicate matter. Let me think about how to handle this so we don't get you involved if we don't have to. After all, you gotta work here. Right?" Tad Szczepanski nodded, appreciative of Birchfield's sensitivity. Birchfield continued, "Give me a day or two. Have you told anyone else about this?"

"Nobody. As I said, I've been wrestling with it for days. No, you're the first person I've spoken to."

"Good. As I said, give me a day or two. One or two more days won't make any difference. I want to be sure we do the right thing. So you don't get hurt. I'll let you know what I decide. In the meantime, don't mention this to anyone. I know you won't. You did the right thing, kid."

When Szczepanski left, Birchfield picked up the phone and called Markham's office. Cathy said her boss was just finishing up with someone. Would he hold? After a two-minute wait, Markham came on the line, sounding at the same time both unctuous and impatient, "Yes, Walter, what is it?"

"Something important, Stuart. I need to see you now."

"Can it wait?"

"No, Stuart, it can't. I'll be right up." He hung up without waiting for Markham's response.

On his way to Markham's office, Birchfield couldn't help but see the humor in the situation. This would be his second visit to Markham's office in all the years he'd been with Harmon Hall. And both visits were on the same day. All of a sudden Markham needed him. Funny how that made all the difference in the world. If he was right, and a lifelong cynical view of his fellow man convinced him he was, Markham needed him a lot. As he entered the outer office, Cathy motioned for him to go on in. Markham was just getting off the phone. "Sit down, Walter, sit down. I don't have much time, but you made it sound so important on the phone that I moved a couple of things back a bit."

*Bet your ass you did.* Birchfield settled his bulk into a chair and waited for Markham to continue. He didn't have long to wait.

"So what is it Walter?" asked Markham indulgently, trying to contain his curiosity.

"About an hour ago, sir, I got a visit from one of your young editors." *Damn!* He'd have to stop sirring Markham...now that they were more or less equal partners.

Markham's eyes narrowed, "And who might that have been?"

"Kid named Tad...he's got this Polack name. Here, I wrote it down. Damnedest spelling." He slowly spelled the name, "S-Z-C-Z-E-P-A-N-S-K-I."

Markham smiled smugly. The man was a brute, "Szczepanski, Walter. Tad Szczepanski. Yes, it's Polish. So what did this young *Polack* want?"

*Go ahead and mock me all you want you Park Avenue prick. You'll show a little more respect in a minute.* "Well, he told me he'd seen Mr. Williamson coming out of Andy Mack's office two days before he was killed—at night, when everybody else was gone. Apparently Williamson was rummaging around in there...looking for something."

"Interesting. Did he have any idea what Williamson was looking for?"

"No, he didn't actually see Williamson in the office...he was just coming out. Said he had this feeling that Williamson was looking for something."

"Well, Walter, that is interesting. No doubt it had something to do with the killing. Maybe young

Mack was holding something over Williamson's head. Some sort of threat or something. I think, Walter, that you'd better tell the police what Szczepanski told you."

Birchfield was enjoying this now. He'd hated the stuffed shirt sitting across from him for years. Now he was going to make him squirm. "I haven't told you everything Spanski said..."

"Szczepanski."

"Whatever." *What a pain in the ass!* Anyway, seems like there was quite a bit of activity in Mack's office that night." Birchfield grinned conspiratorially before he proceeded to tell Markham what Szczepanski had described to him earlier in his office. As he finished, he folded his arms over his ample gut and leaned back contentedly in his chair, stretching his legs out in front of him. A trace of the smirk remained on his jowly face, as he waited for his boss's reaction.

Markham fixed Birchfield with a steady gaze. He had to decide how to play this, and he had to decide now. Had to maintain his presidential mien; yet he didn't want to destroy the artificial, but perfectly functional rapport he'd established with the man earlier in the day. It was a rapport based on a shared intrigue and founded on mutual self interest, if not respect. They didn't have to love each other. All they had to do was work together. And as long as Birchfield perceived it to be an arrangement in his own best interests, they'd both be better off. If, however, Birchfield's animosity toward him exceeded his greed, well.... He didn't want to think about that. Markham couldn't help but think that if his wife were still alive, he probably wouldn't have gotten himself into this. She'd been the superego in the family from the start. Sort of the way the police kept society from complete disintegration. She'd policed their relationship, and, as it turned out more than once, his behavior. Now that she was gone, he usually gave in to his baser instincts. Well, too much water under the bridge to worry about that now. He looked over the top of his neat desk at the sprawled figure of the chief of security. At least he didn't have to socialize with him. Better get this over with.

"Walter, I could use your help on this."

# TWENTY-NINE

From his studio apartment on the 14th floor of the near-luxury high-rise Renaissance Towers in Fort Lee, New Jersey, Tad Szczepanski could see across the Hudson to the west side of Manhattan. He'd opted for living in Fort Lee rather than Manhattan because it was easily accessible to New York without all of the problems, not that it didn't have problems. Any place this close to New York was bound to have its share of urban aggravation. But as bad as things were on the Jersey side, they were worse in Manhattan. While it was only a studio, the place he now called home was still expensive. At least for him. Fifteen hundred bucks a month. He was a second-year assistant editor making $36,500 a year, and there was no way he could afford that kind of rent. But his parents wanted him to live in a decent place so they subsidized him to the tune of $500 a month. Even with the subsidy he barely got by. But it was worth it to be able to pursue a career in publishing. He was young. He could handle it. Things would get better. He wasn't worried.

It was Szczepanski's third year out of Bucknell, and he was generally pleased with the way his life and career were going. He'd taken the summer after graduation off to hike around Europe with his best friend from college. Then he'd gotten a job at Harmon Hall as an editorial assistant. Lousy pay, but he'd been a quick study and a year-and-a-half later he'd been promoted to assistant editor. Six months later he got another raise. Still lousy pay, but he loved the work, and he knew he was hooked on publishing. Yes, things would get better. Just a few months ago he'd met his significant other. Pam was like nobody he'd ever met. During his entire four years of college his social life had been one superficial fling after another. No regrets, of course. It had certainly been fun. But Pam was different. Pam was like a part of him. He wanted to share everything with her. It really wasn't just the sex. Really. Okay, so they weren't exactly ready to get married, but maybe in a couple of years.... Yeah, he thought, *that* serious. Lately they'd been talking about living together. He was ready. Pam still needed a little persuading. Actually, it wasn't Pam. It was her parents. Kinda from the old school. Pam didn't want to hurt them. He understood that and respected it, but he was confident that in the end she'd make up her own mind.

The phone rang at about 6:45, barely five minutes after he'd entered the apartment. It had been a busy Saturday. He'd done editorial work all morning. In the afternoon he'd been out getting stuff he needed for his apartment. Never enough time during the week. Tonight, though, he'd relax. He and Pam would do something—probably take in a movie and then get something to eat. He didn't really care what as long as they were together. Anyhow, they'd decide as soon as he called her—right after he took this call. Maybe this was her now. No, too early. "Hello?... hello?..." He waited a few more seconds. "Hello?" Still nothing. He was about to hang up when he heard breathing. "Hello, who is this?" Then a click, and the line went dead.

\* \* \*

The shock wave of the ringing telephone caught her heart in mid beat... just as she was getting up to get some coffee. *Why do the phones here sound so damned loud?* Unlike most of her friends, she was not a phone lover. She used the phone as a necessary tool, but she'd never hung out with it. She doubted if she'd ever spent a half hour on the phone at any one time in her life. Pretty strange, she knew. Inevitably, the second ring came. She grabbed the receiver, "Pappas."

"Detective, this is Tony Marcantonio, at Harmon Hall. We spoke recently in my office..."

"I remember, Mr. Marcantonio. What can I do

for you?"

"I've just been given some very shocking news, and I thought you'd better hear about it. Unless you already have."

"Go ahead."

"Another one of my editors has been killed. Saturday night. Have you heard about it?"

"No, we haven't. How come we're just hearing about it now, on Monday?"

"Well, it happened in Jersey. Fort Lee. I figured you might not have heard about it, being out of your jurisdiction and all that."

"You're right. It's unlikely, and even if we'd come across it, we might not have connected the death to Harmon Hall. How'd this editor die, and who was it?"

"Shot by an unknown assailant according to the information I have. Editor's name was Tad Szczepanski. Came here right out of college. Three years ago."

"I take it the Fort Lee Police haven't got the killer yet?"

"Unfortunately that's true, detective."

"How'd you hear about this, Mr. Marcantonio?"

"One of my other young editors was a close friend of his. He just learned about this from Tad's girlfriend."

"Mr. Marcantonio, are you going to be in your office today in case we need to reach you?'

"Yes, I'll be here all day, detective."

"Okay, can you spell the name of that editor for me?"

"S-Z-C-Z-E-P-A-N-S-K-I. Tad Szczepanski." Gwen scribbled fast as Marcantonio continued, "Lived in Fort Lee in a place called Renaissance Towers. That's where he was killed."

"And you say this happened Saturday night?"

"Yes ma'am. That's what I was told."

"Okay, thanks for the call, Mr. Marcantonio."

As soon as she hung up, she looked around the cacophonous room for Flynn. Not seeing him she decided to call her father, knowing she'd catch him home. He rarely left the house anymore.

"Hello?" said Rip Pappas listlessly.

"Dad, you sound terrible. Are you all right?"

"Gwen? Yeah. I'm all right. 'Bout the same."

"You should hear yourself on the phone, Dad. You'll scare people off." She tried to sound lighthearted, knowing it would probably fall on deaf ears. Her father had grown increasingly despondent since his retirement three years ago. Then, with the first angina attacks his despondency had sunk into an even deeper depression. His spirits did, however, tend to pick up when she called. But she was never sure whether he was acting or really was lifted by the calls.

"What's up, Gwen? You don't usually call in the morning."

"I had a rare minute to breath. Besides, lately you've got me so worried. Have you had any more of those attacks?'

"No. I just feel kinda run down. No pep lately."

"Maybe you should get out, Dad. Go for a walk or something."

"In this neighborhood?"

"Hey Dad. You're a cop, remember?"

"I'm not a cop anymore. I'm an ex cop. A retired old fart. I'm not so healthy."

"God, I hate to hear you talk like that."

"I'm sorry sweetheart. Guess I'm just feeling sorry for myself."

"Maybe you are, Dad.You've gotta start doing something. You've got too much time on your hands. Too much time to think about yourself and every little ache and pain. You're not an old man, Dad. You're in your fifties; not your seventies."

"Yeah, but when your body starts to go, you don't feel like doing anything, Gwen. Someday you'll be old. I don't wish it on you, but it'll come sooner than you think."

After she'd hung up Gwen just sat, looking at the entrance to the squad room, as if hoping that someone or something would enter and change her mood. Lately she'd dreaded these calls to her father. Ever since her mother had died a year and a half ago, she'd seen him sink into the depths of self pity. A self-indulgent depression that made it hard for her to maintain the close relationship they'd once had. Then again, she thought, more confused than she'd felt in a long time, maybe she was being too harsh....

"Hey, what's up?" said Dawson, interrupting her reverie and startling her at the same time. "You look like you're off in space."

"Guess I was. It's my dad. Every time I talk to him he sounds worse."

"Well he did have a heart attack, didn't he?"

"Yeah, he did. But the doctor said he was doing fine. Said he could and should take light exercise. It's more than the heart attack, Dawson. He's just feeling sorry for himself. The more he gives into it, the deeper he falls into his depression."

"You sure you're not being too hard on the guy, Gwen?"

"Maybe. Maybe.... Hey, I'm glad you're back. I just got a very interesting call from that Marcantonio guy."

"Refresh my memory."

"One of the executives over at Harmon Hall. The Giants fan, remember?"

"Oh yeah," smiled Dawson mischievously. "The one you jumped on because he wanted to talk football."

"That's the guy. Anyway, he says another one of their editors was killed. On Saturday."

"No kiddin'. Where'd it happen?"

"Fort Lee. That's all I have now, but I think we should look into it, Dawson. Gotta be more than coincidence."

"Yeah, and Williamson couldn't of done this one since he's being held in custody. Very interesting. Very interesting. How'd Marcantonio learn about it?"

"Another one of his editors was one of this editor's best friends. Told him first thing this morning. But I have more news for you, Dawson. Williamson is not in custody. Not anymore. He was released on bail Friday afternoon—on his own recognizance—the day after we arrested him. Judge felt his chance of jumping bail was minimal. I just found out. Anyway, that means he's a suspect."

"I can't believe they released him. He was arrested for murdering Andy Mack, and you're right, he's now a suspect in the Szczepanski murder."

"The explanation I got was that, since everything we had on him was circumstantial, there was a lot of pressure from above to get him out until the trial or until we get more evidence."

"Who knows, he may have an alibi for the second murder. Hey, nice of the D.A.'s office to let us know. I guess I'm not surprised he got out, though. I'm sure he's got the best lawyers in the city. And I'm sure the Harmon Hall would like to see him get off. Doesn't look good for their president to be in jail."

"I don't know, Dawson. I heard that the company is dealing with him at arm's length. Afraid the stink of him will rub off, I guess."

"We better go see Marcantonio and this editor, Gwen. Then we talk to the Fort Lee police."

"Marcantonio's already expecting us."

\* \* \*

"Can you get this editor in here so we can talk to him...ask him, or her a few questions?" As Dawson addressed Tony Marcantonio, Gwen allowed her eyes to roam around the room. She couldn't help admiring the built-in bookcases that lined one entire wall of the office. She recognized a number of titles. Mostly bestsellers that had been published by Harmon Hall in recent years. Marcantonio punched in a four-digit number and spoke a few words into the phone.

"He'll be right in," said the editorial director pleasantly. Then, more seriously, he asked, "Do you think Tad's murder is connected with Andy's?"

Gwen chose her words carefully. "It's possible. If it isn't connected, it's certainly one hell of a coincidence. That's why we need to talk with your editor." Then the buzzer on Marcantonio's phone sounded.

"Send him in," said the burly executive. All eyes looked to the door expectantly. "Come in, come in, Jason. Detectives, this is Jason Margolies. He's all yours." Then he added, apparently realizing the implications of what he'd just said, "Relax, Jason. They just want to ask you a few questions."

Flynn spoke first, "Jason, I understand you were a close friend of Tad Szczepanski. Can you tell us how well you knew him?"

"He was my closest friend. Certainly my closest male friend. We were friends in college. Even after I got married last year Tad and his girlfriend and my wife and I did a lot of things together. We were planning on doing a lot of skiing this winter. Tad was one hell of a skier. I'm not as good as he is...er, was. God, I can't believe he's dead. Anyway, we were real close."

"How'd you find out he was killed?" asked Gwen.

"We usually, the four of us, that is...we usually do something together once or twice on the weekend. I kind of expected to hear from him on Saturday. When I didn't, I figured he and Pam wanted to be alone. Sometimes they do. They're not married so it's understandable. Anyway, when I hadn't heard from him by noon on Sunday, I gave him a call. No answer.

Got his machine. Coupla times actually. Finally I called his girlfriend's place figuring I'd catch him there. She's the one who told me. She was frantic."

"What time was that?" asked Gwen.

"Must've been about two."

Flynn asked, "What's Pam's last name, Mr. Margolies?"

"Loring."

"How did she discover he'd been killed?" asked Gwen.

"Oh God, that's the worst part of all this. Would you believe today is Tad's birthday? He'd be twenty-six. His mom and dad were booked on a flight to Paris today, but they wanted to do something for his birthday before they went. So yesterday they planned to drop in on him with a new sound system. They described it to me. CD player, tuner, great speakers. Sounded terrific. They'd asked Pam to join them. Tad didn't answer when they rang him, so they used the extra key he'd given them. They were always dropping in. You can imagine what it must of been like for them when they walked in and found their son lying dead on the floor."

"Do you know when he was killed?" asked Flynn.

"All I know is that the Fort Lee police apparently think he'd been dead for a few hours. Maybe from the night before. I don't know. You'll have to ask them."

"Now we have to ask you a question that may seem a little insensitive," said Flynn. "Can you tell us what you did from Saturday at say five in the afternoon through two A.M. yesterday. Normal procedure. I'm sure you understand."

"Give me a second to collect my thoughts," said Margolies. He closed his eyes for a moment and then proceeded, "Well, I left work on Friday at about five-thirty. Went home...."

"Where's that?"

"SoHo. When we didn't hear from Tad, my wife and I took in a movie. I can tell you what we saw, but I doubt if anyone other than my wife can confirm it. Saturday my wife and I both worked on stuff we'd brought home from work. Mine was a manuscript, part of a dictionary of computer networking terms. I don't know what she was working on. That was in the morning. In the afternoon we went to our health club for a couple of hours. Saturday night we went out to dinner with friends. The Streeters. They can confirm that. Sunday morning my wife and I did the *Times* crossword puzzle; then we went to the health club. When we got back to our apartment, I started calling Tad's place. You know the rest."

"Thanks Mr. Margolies," said Gwen. "I just need your phone numbers, both here and at home—plus your home address. That should about do it. Oh yeah, phone number and address for the Streeters, too. By the way, sorry about your friend."


They had left the Harmon Hall Building and were now driving north on the West Side Highway, toward the George Washington Bridge. Gwen, who was driving, turned to Flynn, who stared silently out the window, arms folded.

"Somethin' bothering you, Dawson?"

Flynn shook his head, but said nothing.

"Dawson, you're awfully quiet."

"Damn it, Gwen. Do you need conversation every minute of the day?"

"Whew, sor-ry."

"No, I'm sorry. It just got to me. This poor family. Can you believe it, Gwen? Mom, dad, and girlfriend find the poor slob as they deliver his birthday present. This one really got to me. And I didn't even know the guy." They were on their way to Fort Lee, New

Jersey. Normally the seven-mile trip would take no more than twenty minutes in the middle of the day, but today the New York City Department of Highways had blocked off one of the northbound lanes on the already pitifully inadequate West Side Highway. Since hitting the construction area, they'd covered less than a mile in fifteen minutes.

"I know what you mean," said Gwen. "And something doesn't sit right with this, Dawson. I mean, c'mon, two editors killed, from the same company, in a three week period. And we would never have known about it if it weren't for Margolies being his friend."

"I don't know about that. The Mack homicide and Carson Williamson's face have been splashed all over the papers for weeks. Somebody would've made the connection."

\* \* \*

Fort Lee was just on the other side of the bridge. It was the first town you came to on the Jersey side. The local detective in charge of the case was named Brian Hammond. He looked to be about forty-five. Average height, and better looking than most detectives, thought Gwen. With the possible exception of how Dawson must have looked ten years ago. He also seemed cooperative and more than willing to talk with his New York City colleagues. On the few occasions Gwen had met cops from out of town she'd gotten the impression they felt they had to prove something to their big-city counterparts. Hammond didn't seem to have that hang-up.

"Yeah, we got a call yesterday morning from the father. Can you imagine? I got a son not much younger than this kid. Just when you think you've seen it all.... So we get right over there. These highrise apartments. Doorman and everything. Nice place. At least I thought it was till this happened."

"What'd the doorman see?" asked Gwen.

"Nothin'. Stupid fuck says he got a phone call about ten minutes to seven Saturday night. Says some guy asked him if he had a car parked downstairs in the garage or outside. When the doorman said 'in the garage,' the voice said, 'Then you'd better get down here right away. A bunch of cars are on fire, and it's spreading fast.' Needless to say there was no fire."

"Did the doorman recognize the voice?" asked Dawson.

"Nah."

"So how'd it go down upstairs in the apartment?" continued Dawson.

"Small caliber pistol. Probably a 32. Two rounds through the heart. Both direct hits. Guy died instantly. Whoever did this knew what he was doing. Nobody heard a thing, so I'm guessing silencer."

"Any sign of a struggle?" asked Gwen.

"Well, the room was messed up a little, but it looked a little funny. Kinda phoney, if you know what I'm saying. Almost as if the killer wanted to make it look like there was a struggle."

"That's interesting," said Gwen. "That is really interesting. What do you think was the motive?"

"On the surface it looks like a robbery," said Hammond. "But if it was, it was a strange one."

"What d'you mean?" Gwen asked. "You don't think it was a robbery?"

"Well, his wallet was missing, but that's all," explained Hammond. "Usually when an apartment is robbed or burgled, a lot more than that is taken. And usually a burglary takes place when the tenant is away. Too many risks when he's home. Unnecessary risks."

"I get the feeling there's something else?" probed Dawson.

"Maybe. Why would Szczepanski let a perfect stranger into his apartment? In this day and age it doesn't make sense."

"You think he knew the killer?" asked Gwen.

"Either that or the killer had a hell of a line. There's another thing, too. Szczepanski's answering machine had like three hangups on it. May be nothing to it, but maybe the killer kept checking to find out when Szczepanski got home. Then, when his intended victim finally answers the phone, the guy moves in for the score."

Dawson considered for a moment, "Very possible. But, you know, I'm not at all sure Szczepanski knew the killer. The more I think about it, the more I doubt it was someone he knew. The guy was too young to have that kind of enemies. I know, if he was pushing dope, he wasn't too young. But he doesn't look to be the kind of guy involved with drugs. I could be wrong. You been able to check that angle out yet, Brian?"

"Yes. We already ran a check. The guy was clean as a whistle. At least as far as the records are concerned. No, I tend to agree with you, Dawson. The kid was a good kid from a good family. So if it was someone he didn't know, who could it be? I'm sensing that you two have some idea. You're not here just to help the Fort Lee police with our case load."

"We're nice people, but not that nice," smiled Dawson. "One of Szczepanski's fellow editors took a bullet three weeks ago. Right in his Midtown office. Two editors from the same company seems a little out of the ordinary, wouldn't you say, Brian?"

"Yeah, I'd say. So you think it's the same perp?"

"Good chance," said Gwen. "Frankly, there's still a lot we don't know about this case. Hey, a thought just hit me. If the killer made some of those hang-up calls to Szczepanski's phone, he was probably nearby when he made them. Let's assume for the sake of argument that he'd want to shoot right up to the apartment as soon as he knew Szcezepanski was in. No pun intended. Being it was Saturday night, there was a good chance Szczepanski'd be going out again. You with me on this, guys?"

The two male detectives nodded and mumbled that they were. Gwen continued, "Assuming that was the case, why don't we check all calls made on cell phones or pay phones located within a couple of hundred yards of the building—say from five-thirty to six-fifteen Saturday night."

"Is that doable, Brian?"

"I'll look into it. Let you know what I come up with."

# THIRTY

Markham's spirits couldn't be higher. He'd only been in charge of the company since Friday, but already he realized he was more fortunate than he'd ever dreamed he would be. Tacitly, and grudgingly, he paid respect to his incarcerated predecessor, Carson Williamson, who, Stuart now realized, had been doing a bang-up job running the company. The preliminary P & L for the fiscal year ending September 30 showed a whopping 21 percent gain in sales over the previous year, a year that had also shown major revenue growth. Profits were expected to be up close to 23 percent. Not bad for no effort on his part, thought Markham. Williamson had done all the work, and he'd reap all the benefit.

The best part of it was that Carr had left him the proverbial well-oiled machine. He was not going to have to bust his hump getting a beleaguered business back on its feet. No late night hours. No sleepless nights. No convincing a reluctant board that he had the answers to how to resurrect an ailing company. Nothing of the kind, because the company was far from ailing. It was thriving. Carr had handed him a smooth operation, and all he had to do was run with it. How could he have ever imagined three years ago when Carr got the presidency that it would actually work out for the best in the long run. Williamson was now out of the way, and he, Stuart Markham, was running the show. Beautiful.

His gaze returned to Walter Birchfield, sitting contentedly on the other side of the gleaming desk. Birchfield seemed unperturbed at being left out of Markham's private reveries. The director of corporate security appeared to be rather satisfied with himself. Well he should, reflected Markham. Well he should. Despite the man's vulgarity, he was obviously capable.

"Sorry, Walter. Just thinking. Things have

been so busy around here lately, I don't get much opportunity to reflect. Well now, let's get right to *our* business, so that I can get back to the business of running the company."

"Sounds good to me, Stuart."

"Walter, I've elevated the position of director of corporate security to the vice presidential level. As an officer in the company you'll receive an increase of thirty-five thousand dollars in salary. Naturally you'll also be eligible for participation in the bonus plan like every other officer. A few other nice perks, too. You'll find out about them later. Now you understand that the board has to approve this. They approve all officer positions, but I don't think there'll be any problem. I hope this promotion shows you how much I appreciate your services, Walter."

"Sounds good, Stuart. Sounds good. Just one question. This board approval thing. What happens if they don't approve?"

"They will. They will. Don't worry."

"If they don't," said Birchfield ominously, "it won't be my worry."

## THIRTY-ONE

It was late Monday afternoon when he got the call from his ex-wife. "Dawson, could you come over for a little while? I need to talk."

"Can you tell me what it's about, Julie? I'm really busy."

"It's about this guy..."

"Oh jeez, not that again. Is this the same guy? What's his name, Wade?"

"No, I haven't seen Wade in two months. This is a different guy."

"Why do you get me involved with this stuff? Is this guy hurting you or something?"

"Dawson, I thought you said we were still friends. No, he's not hurting me. Why would you say that? I just need to talk to you for a little while."

"Can it wait till tomorrow?"

"Yes, I suppose so," she said, sounding extremely disappointed.

"Never mind, I'll try to stop by after work today. Can't promise, but I'll try. Look, gotta go now. Bye."

The call from Brian Hammond came as soon as he'd hung up. Flynn greeted the call eagerly, hoping for anything that could help—anything tangible that he and Gwen could pursue. He and Gwen were convinced that Tad Szczepanski's death was related to the murder of Andy Mack, and since Carson Williamson, the alleged killer of Mack, was out on bail, the two killings could have been done by him. But Flynn thought that seemed pretty unlikely. He didn't think Williamson was that stupid. One thing he had to find out right away was whether Williamson had an alibi at the time of the Szczepanski killing. If he did, the publishing murders would appear a lot more complex than he and Gwen originally thought they were. The options were nothing if not confusing. If Williamson had an alibi, there were several possibilities that had to be considered. One possible explanation could be that Williamson had a partner who killed Szczepanski. That seemed pretty far-fetched, though. A second possibility was that Williamson was not the killer of Andy Mack and that the real killer was still running around murdering people. That, too, seemed hard to accept, since the best evidence they had pointed to Williamson as the killer of Andy Mack. Still, if Williamson had a good alibi he couldn't have killed Szczepanski. A third possibility was that Williamson hired a second killer to dispatch Szczepanski, with the express purpose of throwing the authorities off the scent. And a fourth possibility was that the two killings were, in fact, unrelated. That also defied the odds. He and Gwen had been around and around with these hypotheses with no clear idea of where to go next. But if Hammond's check with the phone companies came up with a caller, there was a very good chance they were on to something.

"So Brian, what've you got?"

"Hate to tell you this, Dawson, but we came up dry," said Hammond, sounding sincerely sorry. "Nobody called Szczepanski's phone from a Verizon, Cingular or Sprint cell phone Saturday night. Checked Verizon land lines and their cell phone people. Really sorry. I even checked the few phone booths in the area. Nada. Gwen had a good idea there. But no cigar my friend."

Flynn said, "Hold on a sec, Brian. He turned to Gwen and said, "Says he got nothing. Checked Verizon, Cingular and Sprint. Too bad."

Gwen's look of disappointment reflected his own. She said, "I know this is a long shot. Did he check T-Mobile or any of the cable companies. Some of them offer phone service now?"

"Brian, can you check T-Mobile and the major cable companies?. I know it's unlikely, but would you mind. Just to cover all the bases?"

Flynn heard a deep breath on the other end of the line. "Yeah, we'll check. Gotta go."

Gwen looked crestfallen. "So, where's that leave us? A big mystery with no clues. And soon, Farrell and Maggie Muñoz'll be all over us for bringing in Williamson. Not good, Dawson. Not good."

"What a Goddam shitty day. Maybe tomorrow will be better."

"C'mon, it's not that bad."

"Yeah, it is. My ex just called. Wants me to drop by."

"What is it this time?"

"Wants me to advise her about the latest jerk she's goin' out with. Can you believe that woman."

"Why do you bother, Dawson? I gotta say, you two have a pretty cozy relationship for a divorced couple."

"We really don't. I've never really forgiven her. Don't know why I bother to even talk to her."

"Never forgiven her for what?"

"I never told you?"

"No, and I never asked."

"It was about a year-and-a-half into our marriage. She told me she was pregnant. I was ecstatic. Julie wasn't happy, though. Seemed almost panicky."

"And?"

"A week later I came home one night and she was crying. Told me she'd just had an abortion. Christ, Gwen, I can't tell you how crazy I got. She went and did that without even talking about it first. I never forgave her. Our marriage went downhill fast after that."

"Did she explain why she did it?"

"Gave me some bullshit about not being ready for a child. About not knowing what to do."

"Maybe she was scared."

"Scared. What's to be scared?"

"Oh c'mon, Dawson. Don't act like such a man?

She could've been scared because she wasn't ready to stay home, and she saw that as the end of her life as she knew it; not the beginning of her life as a mother. It's a subtle thing, but the distinction could be scary to a woman who wasn't ready yet."

"I don't think so, Gwen. That's not the way I see it."

"How do you see it?"

"Julie is very into herself. To her, the baby was this thing that was going to interfere with her life. Anything that inconveniences Julie...well, let's just say she's a very immature person."

"Well, I don't know Julie, but I have to say that you make her sound pretty bad."

"Look, maybe I just feel a little guilty. All right."

"Hey, I'm not judging you. You were both young. And both human. Maybe you should cut yourself a little slack, Dawson."

"Hey, lady, can we change the subject? Bad enough I've gotta go over there in a little while. I don't wanna talk about her now, too."

Gwen looked hurt, "Pardon me for caring."

His expression softened, "Sorry, I've got a temper. Does wonders for your career." He remained thoughtful for a moment; then said, "So, where are we on this Szczepanski deal?"

"I think the first thing we should do is check to see if Williamson has an alibi for the second murder."

Flynn grinned, "You wanna ask him?"

"Not me."

"Me neither."

"I'll do it. What can he do but bite my head off. And, I suppose, there's no time like the present. I think I have his home number here somewhere."


"Hello."

"Hello, Mr. Williamson. This is Gwen Pappas,

the..."

"I know who you are, detective. Believe me, I know who you are. What do you want?"

"I really hate to ask you this, sir, but ..........well, it's my job. I have to. Can you tell me what you were doing Saturday evening from six o'clock till two A.M?"

Gwen waited expectantly, not knowing how Williamson would react to her question. Finally he said, "I was home with my wife and daughter. Where else can I go now? Why do you ask?"

"You haven't heard? Another editor from your company was found murdered."

"Oh my God, who?"

"A Tad Szczepanski, did you know him?"

"No, I can't say that I did. My God, that's terrible. How did it happen?"

"If you don't mind, Mr. Williamson, I'd like to finish with my questions." She knew it sounded cold, but one of the first things she'd learned at the academy was not to lose control of an interview.

"I know you people have your jobs to do, detective, but you don't let up, do you?" Gwen could hear the fatigue in his voice as Williamson continued, "Because of my arrest the board didn't waste any time in getting me out of my office at Harmon Hall. I don't really have a lot of options, detective. Home is where I spend most of my time now."

"I'm sorry about that. I really am." She took a deep breath, "I assume Mrs. Williamson will verify that you were home Saturday night?"

"Of course she will, damn it. She's here now. Hold on just a minute." The line went quiet, and Gwen looked over at Flynn and rolled her eyes.

"Hello." It was a woman. A tired voice. "This is Laura Williamson."

"Hello, Mrs. Williamson. This is detective Pappas. I'm really sorry to bother you. I know what you must be going through, but..."

"I don't think you do, detective. You have no idea."

"Look, Mrs. Williamson, this will only take a minute. I just need to know..."

"I know what you want. Carr just told me. Yes, he was here Saturday night from six to eight. In fact he was here from a little after five on. We ate at home."

"Thank you. I won't trouble you any more." She hung up and turned to Flynn, "That was not fun."

He grinned. "Okay, so he didn't do Szczepanski, at least he didn't do the job himself according to his wife. Can we believe her?..." He was interrupted by the ringing of the telephone.

"Detective, this is Carson Williamson again." It had been a long day, and Flynn was not eager to have a conversation with the man he and Gwen had arrested only a few days ago. He just wasn't in the mood for dealing with embittered complaints.

"Yes, Mr. Williamson, what is it?" Flynn looked helplessly at Gwen.

"As soon as I hung up an idea came to me. This second murder got me to thinking, and I believe I might have something you could use in your investigations."

"What's that?" Flynn could not decide whether to show interest or annoyance.

"Could you and Detective Pappas come up here. I'd rather tell you in person. Would you mind?"

"Could you hold for a minute, Mr. Williamson." Flynn turned to Gwen, "Williamson says he has something about the case that might be useful. Wants us to go to his house up in Rye. Wanna go?"

"Why not."

"Okay Mr. Williamson, we'll be up there tomorrow morning. Somewhere around nine." He hung up and turned to his partner, "Okay, pick you up at eight tomorrow morning for a nice drive into the country."

Gwen gave him a studied look. "Can you concentrate now, or are you thinking about Julie?"

"What's that supposed to mean?"

"I wasn't trying to be sarcastic. It's just that I know that it's bothering you, that's all. I understand. Really, I do. We can get back to this tomorrow morning."

"She'll wait. I'll get there when I get there."

"You mentioned before that you maybe felt a little guilty. I thought you said she was wrong to have the abortion without even asking you. If you still feel so strongly that you're right, why do you feel guilty?" Then thinking she might be going too far, she added,

"Dawson, If you don't want to talk about it, tell me to butt out."

"Nah, probably good for me to talk about it. Look, if you must know, since the divorce I haven't always felt so sure I was right. No, that's not exactly it either. I still think I was right about it, but let's just say maybe I understand her better. She was just a kid when we got married. Barely twenty-one. All of a sudden the idea of playing grown-up, especially grown-up mother probably scared the crap out of her. It's possible. Anyway I'm not as sure as I was a couple of years ago, so I hate to dump on her. But I gotta tell ya, Gwen, she's pushin' it when she asks my advice on these characters she goes out with."

"So there is a sensitive side to you, partner," grinned Gwen. "Don't worry, I won't tell anyone."

"Okay, so what do you want me to concentrate on?"

"Think about Williamson for a minute. We know he couldn't have killed Szczepanski himself, not if we believe his wife. Though can we believe her? Good question. Anyway, unless he hired somebody, sort of mafia style, to do the killing, that means there's a killer with a whole different agenda running loose. You and I've talked about this, Dawson. We both doubt that there could be two separate killers at Harmon Hall, especially with no connection to each other. Doesn't add up. The odds against that must be a billion to one."

"Yeah, I'm with you so far. Where you goin' with this, Gwen?"

"So I'm wondering who has it in for Williamson. You know what I'm saying?"

"I'm not sure I do. You and I both put our asses on the line by convincing Farrell and Maggie that Williamson's a killer."

"Yes, but suppose we were wrong. Dawson, it's better *we* discover we're wrong than Farrell or Maggie. And if Williamson isn't a killer..."

"We come back to: Who is?"

"Which brings us back to my original question: Who has it in for Williamson...enough to get him out of the way? And who would kill twice to achieve that result? Gotta be someone with a very big hate or an awful lot to gain—or lose."

"Okay, so we answer that, we got ourselves a killer. But this thing is really strange. Killing Szczepanski didn't hurt Williamson. If anything, it may have gotten him off the hook for the Mack killing."

"Exactly, but what if Szczepanski wasn't supposed to die. What if he knew something about the Mack killing, and the real killer had to get rid of him?"

Flynn pursed him lips in concentration and nodded, "Not bad, Gwen. Not bad. Got any idea who would want Williamson out of the way? Assuming it really isn't him."

"It would probably be some honcho. The peons wouldn't see Williamson as competition. Too high up. Has to be someone Williamson competed with, or was an obstacle to."

"Could also be someone Williamson stole a woman from."

"Yes, it could be. But from what we know of

Williamson the only woman in his life other than his wife was this lady lawyer, and she's single."

"That still doesn't mean there isn't another man besides Williamson in *her* life. It's a long shot, Gwen, but still a possibility. I like your theory better, though. Somebody in the company with either an ax to grind or something to gain. Let's proceed on that line for a minute. But keep the jealous lover in mind."

"Agreed. Now who would know a lot about the internal politics of Harmon Hall? I think we need to talk with somebody in the know."

"And somebody who's likely to be willing to talk. How about Jacqui Dyer? She seemed pretty knowledgeable, and definitely inclined to talk."

Gwen looked at Flynn with a knowing grin, "And not too hard on the eyes, either, right?"

"That has nothing to do with it," said Flynn, trying to look serious, and failing miserably.


When Gwen called Jacqui Dyer's office she learned that the editor had just left work and was headed for her health club. Armed with the address of the health club Gwen turned to Flynn with a mischievous grin, "She's on her way to her health club. Guess we should wait and see her tomorrow—after we get back from Rye."

"Why wait. The older this case gets, the harder it'll be to solve. We can see her at her health club."

"God, you are a lecher, Dawson."

He grinned, "That's bullshit. I'm a professional. C'mon, this won't take long."

"I thought you were going to see your ex tonight after work?"

"I'm not through work yet."

"Job gets tougher and more hazardous every day, huh, Dawson?"

# THIRTY-TWO

The health club on East Forty-sixth Street occupied three-stories of the nondescript building. As was the case with many successful health clubs in Manhattan, expansion had to be upward. Jacqui Dyer's club had expanded twice in five years. It was a full-service club offering racquetball, swimming, Nautilus, a wide variety of free weights and other trendy equipment, plus numerous aerobics classes. On entering, Flynn went up to the desk and read the name tag on the healthy looking blonde behind the counter. She looked to be in her early twenties. "Hi, Tina," he said, flashing his shield as he continued, "Detective Flynn, and this is detective Pappas." Tina's cheerful expression turned to concern.

"Yes? Is there some problem?"

"We need to see one of your members. Has a Jacqui Dyer checked in yet? She's supposed to be here."

Tina turned to a computer terminal at her side and within seconds said, "Yes, she's here now. Want me to page her?"

"No," said Gwen, "just tell us where you think she is, and we'll find her. Who knows, we may want to join." Gwen knew Flynn would be disappointed if they stayed in the reception area to interview Dyer.

"Well, I really don't know where she is. She could be anyplace...on any floor. You'll just have to start on the main floor and work your way up. Do you know what she looks like?"

"Yeah," said Flynn, thinking how hard it would be to forget Jacqui Dyer's appearance.

Tina called after them, "If you have any questions about the club..."

"We'll see you on the way out," Flynn yelled back. "Thanks, Tina."

As they made their way toward the rear of the

main floor they came to a glass wall beyond which could be seen a swimming pool. A sign on the door said people in street shoes were not admitted in the pool area. A quick scan told them it wouldn't be necessary, since Dyer was nowhere to be seen near or in the pool.

"Okay. Stop staring," said Gwen. "Half of them are fat anyway."

"Yeah, but the other half look pretty good."

They climbed the stairs to the second floor where the landing opened onto a large room that appeared to be organized by activity. Along one wall and spreading into the room were the Nautilus machines. A row of treadmills and stationary bikes faced floor-to-ceiling windows looking out onto Forty-sixth Street. At the other end of the room they could see and hear the metallic clanking and thumping of free-standing weights. By Flynn's quick estimation two thirds of the taut, glistening bodies in the room were women.

"Hey, Gwen. Did you ever see so much spandex in your life?"

"Yeah. Ain't it awful?"

"Lot of healthy people. This country's doing something right."

Gwen said, "Do you see her?"

"Not yet."

"I suppose you have to check out each woman?"

"Hey, it's the job."

"There she is. On one of those Exercycle. Whatever you call 'em." Flynn spotted the editor and noted with some surprise that she was one of the few women not wearing spandex tights or halter. What surprised him even more was that, in her loose-fitting black shorts and white T-shirt, she appealed to him more than the other women in their body hugging outfits.

As they approached her, Dyer recognized the two detectives and flashed a somewhat startled smile. She recovered quickly, "Detectives, you're not wearing your sweats."

"Unfortunately, Ms. Dyer, we're here on business," said Gwen. "Is there somewhere we can talk?"

"There's a refreshment area in the next room. If it's real crowded we can go to the reception area."

"The refreshment area consisted of four round tables, each with four chairs. At that hour they were the only ones in the room except for a man behind the counter, who seemed to be occupied washing and drying glasses.

"I suppose you're here about Tad's murder," said Dyer. It was hard to tell from her voice whether she was annoyed at having two detectives interrupt her workout.

Flynn nodded, "What can you tell us about it?"

"Not a damn thing. God, this has got to stop. Our whole company is scared out of their gourds. That's why I came over here so early. Gotta burn off some of these nerves. No, detective, I have no idea why Tad was killed. He was the nicest kid. God, that's all he was. A kid. It's not like it was with Andy. Nobody disliked Tad. Hell, everyone who knew him liked him a lot. He was kind of shy, so a lot of us didn't know him well. But, and don't take this the wrong way. He wasn't important enough to kill. He didn't have a job people coveted, and he had no power, no authority. I really have no idea why anybody'd want to kill him."

Flynn waited until Dyer had collected herself enough to focus on his next question, "Who would want to see Carson Williamson in jail?"

"I don't honestly know. He's always seemed like a decent kind of man. Oh, I know, to get where he is, he had to step on some toes. I'm sure he did, but his reputation is pretty good around the company. You're probably talking to the wrong person, anyway. I don't travel in his circles. I've met him a few times. Been in a few meetings with him. But we're certainly not friends.

More like acquaintances."

"Let me phrase it a little differently," said Gwen. "Who would benefit by his being out of the way?"

"Well, I suppose you'd have to say Stuart Markham. Looks like he's already benefited from Mr. Williamson's arrest. The board just named him acting president and CEO."

Gwen looked at Flynn. "That's interesting. That's very interesting."

"Well, I can't believe Stuart would kill to become president. I know business can be pretty cutthroat, but not literally. Besides, how would killing two editors help Stuart?"

"You did say he was just made president," pointed out Flynn.

"Yes, but I don't see the connection. Or maybe I should say connections. Why two murders? After Mr. Williamson was arrested for the first murder, and subsequently jailed, Stuart would have already had what he wanted. That's assuming he did this, and I still can't believe he did. But just for the sake of argument, how would the second murder help him? If anything, I would think it would tend to weaken the case against Mr. Williamson. I mean how could Williamson have committed the second murder if he was in jail? It suggests to me, and I know I'm not privy to what you guys know, but it suggests to me that Mr. Williamson may have been set up for Andy Mack's murder."

"Assuming you're right," said Gwen, "that brings us back to square one. Who would benefit by his being set up?"

"I see what you're getting at. It comes right back to Stuart, doesn't it?"

"Or anyone else who would have benefited by Mack or Williamson being out of the way," continued Gwen. "But Markham seems to be the only one who's actually come out ahead because of all of this.

Although, as we discussed before, now that Andy Mack is dead, it would appear that there's a good chance you'll get your project back." Dyer's eyes flashed anger, and Gwen held up a hand, "Wait, I know, you have an alibi for when the murder went down. I was just showing you how it's possible that more than one person could have a motive. We just may not be aware of all the motives. Can you think of anyone else we've overlooked?"

"No, I can't. As I said, maybe you're asking the wrong person. But getting back to what we were just talking about, how would Stuart Markham gain by killing Tad?"

"Good question," said Flynn. "You would think he wouldn't—unless Szczepanski happened to catch him in the act of killing Mack, or knew something damaging. Let me ask you this. Do you have reason to believe that Stuart Markham wanted to be president?"

"Does it snow in Alaska? C'mon, officer, what do you think? Most of these senior executives want the top job. They're ambitious. They love the power and the money. They love the attention."

"Okay, fine," said Gwen, "but do you know anything specific about Markham that would indicate he was hungrier than most?"

"Well..." Jacqui Dyer made a steeple with her extended fingers and closed her aquamarine eyes for a moment. Then she continued, "I remember when Williamson was made president three years ago, the articles in the press seemed to express surprise. A number of pieces commented that people in the industry...well-placed observers they were probably called...were surprised that Stuart Markham wasn't picked. I suppose if Stuart read those pieces, and I'm sure he did, well, who knows what he would have thought. I do know Stuart has a huge ego. But that doesn't make him a killer."

"Of course not, and we're not saying he is.

We're just asking questions." Gwen looked at Flynn. "I don't think we have anything else now, do we Dawson?"

"No, thanks for your help. Sorry to interrupt your workout."

"You guys really think Stuart did it, don't you?"

"You know we can't comment on that," said Gwen. "By the way, Mr. Williamson is no longer in police custody. He was released on bail Friday."

Dyer seemed genuinely surprised. "I didn't know that."

Gwen continued as if she hadn't heard Jacqui Dyer, "I would urge you to give us a call if you think of anything else. Two editors in your company have already died..."

"Company, hell, my department."

"Okay, so if anyone knows anything, or if the killer thinks anyone knows anything, it would behoove that person to contact us immediately. You should probably advise your staff not to stay late alone or come in early alone. Until we find the killer of Tad Szczepanski, it's possible that other people in your department are at risk," said Flynn.

As they left the building, Flynn turned to Gwen, "What do you think?"

"Frankly, I believe her. A very unlikely suspect, if you ask me."

Flynn frowned, "When they appear that clean I begin to get suspicious."

# THIRTY-THREE

"Christ, Gwen, did I have a night." Flynn rubbed his eyes as he unloaded on his partner. It was Tuesday morning, the morning after their visit to Jacqui Dyer's health club. They were heading north on I-95, on their way to meet with Williamson in Rye. Summer was hanging on longer this year than usual. The air conditioning in the unmarked car was struggling to keep up with the heat even though it was still early in the day.

"You look like you were up all night," grinned Gwen. "Must have been a helluva time. I thought you and Julie were finished."

"Gwen, it wasn't like that at all. I swear."

"Okay, fine. It's your business anyway."

"No, I mean it. It wasn't anything like that."

"I said fine. You don't have to explain your evenings to me. You're a big boy."

"When I tell you what happened...aw shit, you won't believe it anyway."

"Try me. Otherwise, let's just change the subject."

"I don't know... I..." he threw up his arms in frustration.

"You gonna tell me?"

"She wants to become a single parent. Wants me to be the father."

"She what? Hey maybe you shouldn't be telling me this. We're gettin' kinda personal here."

"You're the only one I'd tell. I have to tell someone. I know you won't yak to anybody around here. Damn! Of all the bone-headed things she's done, this one takes the cake. I know she's only doing it 'cause she feels guilty about the abortion. I told her that, and she started crying. Says she really wants a child now. She knows she's been too selfish. She's ready to be a mother."

"Maybe she is, Dawson. Maybe she is."

"You don't know her. She's immature. I mean really immature. This is so typical of her. Someone plants an idea in her head, and she can't let it go till she tries it. Or until she gets a new idea."

"Maybe that's the answer. Wait this out till she gets a new idea."

"I don't know. She's really fired up about this. Wants to have a baby."

"Well," she smiled mischievously, "being a donor can't be that painful." Then more seriously, "How was the sex when you were married? I'm only asking since you seem to want my opinion."

Flynn's face turned red, "It was very good, since you ask. At least it was until the abortion. Then it was nonexistent."

"So what's the problem if she persists? Moral, religious? It certainly can't be shyness on your part." She looked thoughtful for a moment, "Or is it your role after the baby is born?"

"See, I knew I came to the right person. That's exactly it. She doesn't want me to act as father after the birth. She just wants me to be the stud. I can't handle that, Gwen. I could not walk away from my own child."

"Then your answer to her is simple. Tell her no."

"That would devastate her. I told you, you don't know Julie. She's a very fragile personality."

"All the more reason you don't want her as a single parent. Fragile sounds to me like one step away from unstable."

Flynn screwed up his face as if trying to decide whether to agree. "I'm not sure I'd say that. Aw hell, I don't know. Anyway, thanks. I gotta wrestle with this on my own time. Back to business. I just got a call from Brian Hammond. By the way, he thinks you're one smart lady, maybe a little pushy, but smart."

"Pushy?"

"Only because you didn't give up on that phone call thing. He tried those other companies like you suggested, and low and behold T-Mobile had a record of a call to Szczepanski in that time slot." He grinned.

"So pushy paid off."

"I prefer persistent or tenacious."

"Whatever. Anyway, the bottom line is the phone angle paid off. He got us a name and an address of the caller." Flynn smiled, "Thanks to your pushiness, partner."

"Cute. All right, tell me about him."

"What makes you think it's a him?"

"Okay, okay. Whatever. Who is it?"

"You're right, it's a him. A LeRoy Rivers. Staten Island address. I think we should visit Mr. Rivers."

"Where's he work?"

"His cell phone application says he's a waiter at a place in the city called Pintello's. Upper West Side. On Broadway. Let's drop in before the lunch crowd starts. Hopefully we can get back to Manhattan before noon."

Williamson's colonial-style house wasn't hard to find. It was big and impressive as they'd expected, and set comfortably in a neighborhood of equally impressive homes. Flynn entered the circular drive and pulled up to the front entrance. Carr Williamson met them at the door, "Please come in." As Williamson led them into the living room, Gwen couldn't help but take in the understated elegance of the place. No sooner were they seated comfortably than a woman appeared carrying a tray. In her late forties, she carried herself with an easy assurance.

"I'm Laura Williamson," said the woman as she put the tray down on the enormous coffee table. "Please help yourselves to coffee." Gwen really didn't want coffee, but somehow felt that Laura Williamson would be disappointed if she didn't have some, so she poured herself three-quarters of a cup and sipped at it politely. Flynn poured a full cup and said to the woman, "Thank you." He then turned to Williamson,

"All right, sir, what do you have to tell us?"

Laura Williamson responded, "I'd like to answer that, if you don't mind, detective. To begin with, I know about Carr's affair with Kate Ferrara. He told me about it a couple of days ago. No, I wasn't happy. Not at all. What wife would be? But I love him, and I'm not going to leave him."

"Look, Mrs. Williamson, you don't have to tell us this."

"No, I want to say this. As you can imagine, Carr and I have had a great deal of discussion about this. I'm not going to tell you about all of that. But I do want you to know how I feel now. Despite what my husband has done, I love him. We've shared a lot together, and we're going to try to resurrect what we had in the past. We both want that. And I want to make one other thing clear. I'm not saying all this because I'm a desperate woman trying to preserve my financial security. For your information I had money when I married Carr, so that is not at issue. I'm defending Carr, because I know he couldn't have killed anyone. He has a very high regard for all life. He always has."

Gwen's face felt flushed, "Thank you for telling us that." She turned to Williamson, "You told us on the phone that you had something we'd be interested in?"

"Yes I did. For one thing, I'd hoped you'd be interested in hearing what Laura has just told you. The other thing was this: A friend of mine on the Harmon Hall board told me once that Stuart Markham had resented my getting the presidency of the company. In fact, I'm told he's continued to harbor resentment over the past three years. I also heard that in his early years at Harmon Hall Stuart supposedly fabricated a convincing, but phoney case against his then boss. Got him fired, and got himself appointed to replace him. I know none of this proves anything, but it does suggest that Stuart might be worth a closer look. Heck, maybe I'm way off, but please understand that I'm fighting for my life. As I told you from the start, I didn't kill Andrew Mack. And I certainly didn't kill young Szczepanski. I'm embarrassed to say I didn't even know who he was until this happened." He smiled wanly, looking first at Gwen and then Flynn, "Please help yourselves to more coffee."

Flynn couldn't help liking Williamson. He didn't want to believe the man was a killer. "Thanks, but I've had enough for today. I hate to ask you this, but didn't you once say to Mr. Wasserman that you'd like to see Andrew Mack dead?"

Carr looked shocked. *Herb!* "Herb Wasserman told you that?" He shook his head in disbelief, "Yes, I guess I did say that—in a moment of frustration. My God, detective, it's a figure of speech. Haven't you ever said something like I'd like to kill so-and-so?"

"Detective!" All eyes turned to Laura Williamson. "My husband didn't kill anyone. He made a mistake. A terrible mistake. Frankly he hurt me more than he'll ever know, but having said that, I also know that he's not a killer. Despite his hurting me, it is not in his nature to hurt people." She paused, as if reminded of something, "Certainly not intentionally. The killer is still out there. Please go find him...or her!"

Back in the car, heading toward Manhattan. Gwen spoke first, "You believe them?"

"They're pretty convincing. Still, they're smart people. They could just be good actors. But face it, Gwen, you and I started having second thoughts before we went up there."

"True, but Williamson was awfully eager to give us dirt about Markham. How nice is that?

"He is fighting for his life. Nice only goes so far."

# THIRTY-FOUR

Pintello's catered to a mostly young crowd—wanna-be actors and would-be yuppies. The menu of slightly glorified fast foods was eclectic, and by New York standards, inexpensive. Just inside the front door a waitress, who looked a lot like a cheerleader from Ohio, was busy putting place settings on one of the miniature tables that New York diners quickly get accustomed to. She looked up as Gwen and Flynn entered. "Sorry, we don't open till 11:30."

Flynn flashed his shield and said, "Is LeRoy Rivers here?"

The cheerleader's smile evaporated as she pointed to the rear, "He's probably in the kitchen. Something wrong?"

"We just need to see Mr. Rivers," said Gwen noncommittally. As they pushed through the swinging doors that separated the dining room from the kitchen they caught sight of an overly thin, almost gaunt waiter just finishing up what appeared to be a hurried lunch. Definitely not healthy looking, thought Gwen.

Flynn called out, "You LeRoy Rivers?"

The sickly looking waiter looked up, still chewing part of his lunch. "Yeah, who's asking?"

Gwen flashed her shield, "Homicide. Detective Pappas. This is detective Flynn. Is there someplace we can talk, Mr. Rivers?" As she spoke, an older man, apparently the owner or maitre d' stood up from tasting the contents of a large saucepan with what appeared to be a larger-than-life tablespoon. He stood, hands on hips, staring in exasperation at Rivers and his two visitors.

Rivers gave a furtive look in the direction of the older man, "There's another dining room downstairs.

He led them to some stairs leading down to the restaurant's basement. We can go down there."  As they reached the bottom step, Gwen could see they were alone.

"Okay, Mr. Rivers," said Flynn. "Can you tell us where you were late Saturday afternoon and Saturday night, till about two A.M.?"

Rivers looked from side to side, as if hoping somehow to be rescued. Flynn thought he detected a momentary trace of fear in the tired eyes of the waiter. "Why do you wanna know?" asked Rivers.  "What's this all about?"

"Part of an investigation. Just answer the question please," said Flynn firmly.

"I was right here, working," said Rivers.  Then he hesitated, realizing how easy it would be for the detectives to check his story with his boss upstairs, "Wait, I forgot. Not last Saturday. Last Saturday I got off 'cause I wasn't feeling so great."

"So where were you?"  asked Flynn.

Rivers mind raced in confusion. He was not overly bright to begin with, and he sought frantically for some kind of plausible activity that could be verified by someone, anyone.  But he knew there was no such activity for the time frame in question, and he was just smart enough to know that if he took any more time, the delay itself would be suspicious. "I just crashed in my apartment. Felt like crap," he said.

"Can anyone testify to that?" asked Gwen.

"Hell, no. I said I was home alone."

"Do you own a cell phone?"  Gwen held him in her gaze.

"Uh, yeah, I do.  Why?"

"You apparently made some calls to a Tad Szczepanski in Fort Lee last Saturday. Can you tell us what they were about?"

"I don't know any Tad...wha'd you say his name was?"

"Szczepanski. According to the phone company's records you made three calls to him between five-thirty and six-fifteen Saturday afternoon. Can you tell us why you called him?"

Rivers looked as if he'd gone over a cliff. For a moment nothing came out. Finally, "Must a been a wrong number. Yeah, I remember now, I was calling for a pizza, and I kept getting this guy's answering machine."

"But you live in Staten Island. That's in Jersey. Different area code. Seems unlikely you'd make that kind of mistake," said Flynn.

"Yeah, well I was over in Jersey, and I figured I'd pick up a pie on the way home."

"Wouldn't it be kind of cold by the time you got back to Staten Island?" pressed Flynn.

"Yeah, well I like this place in Jersey. Easy to heat up the pie when I get home."

"Can you tell us the name of the pizza place?" asked Gwen.

Fear returned to the face of LeRoy Rivers. "Jeez, I never paid much attention to the name. It's a place I pass on Route 46. I can get the name if you want."

"We'd like that, Mr. Rivers," said Gwen. "Here's my card. Please give me a call this afternoon with the name and address of the place. And don't leave the metropolitan area. We may want to speak to you again."

"Shit, I don't see why you need the name of this nothing pizza joint."

"Just call it in, please. And be sure it's today. If detective Pappas is not there, leave the information with whoever answers the phone," said Flynn, who realized what Gwen was hoping to learn. She knew there was no such pizza place. Rivers would probably now go to the yellow pages and find some pizza joint along Route 46 in New Jersey and feed that to

Gwen...thinking it would satisfy her. Chances are, though, the place would have a phone number quite dissimilar to Tad Szczepanski's. And if that were the case, it would make Rivers' dialing of a wrong number all the more implausible. If the number were clearly different, Rivers alibi would be shaky at best. Flynn already felt that Rivers was guilty, but he knew that they didn't have quite enough to bring him in. It wouldn't take much, though.

Outside the restaurant Gwen said, "That guy's guilty as sin, Dawson. I don't like not bringing him in. Did you see the fear in his eyes? He's scared shitless."

"You're right. Let's hang out here for awhile. Keep an eye on him. If we lose Rivers, we lose our best prospect, or certainly our closest link to who's behind all this. Let's grab some coffee and sit in the car for awhile."

They didn't have long to wait. Twenty-five minutes after they'd settled down with their coffee, Rivers emerged from the restaurant and immediately went to the corner where he began trying to hail a cab. Gwen's eyes were still glued to the window, "What d'ya think? Shall we grab him or follow him?

"Let's take him now. Leave him to me. You check with the restaurant to see what he told them." With that Flynn jumped out of the car and started across the street. Rivers was unaware of him as he approached.

Gwen found the older man she'd seen earlier in the restaurant. "Detective Pappas again, sir." The man nodded in recognition, crossed his arms stoically and stood there, waiting for her to say something. She didn't hesitate. "Can you tell us where Mr. Rivers just went?"

The man shook his head slowly, as if he were at his wits end. He spoke with a thick Eastern European accent. "You tell me. Frankly I hope he doesn't come back. That guy. He's been trouble from the start."

"Are you the owner?"

"Yes, and at times like this I wish I'm not."

"Your name?"

"Witold Nacinovich."

"So, why did Rivers leave—and just before your lunch crowd starts coming in?"

"He says he doesn't feel so good. That man, he's always getting sick. When he's here, he's not such a bad waiter, not bad with the customers anyway. But with me—he's a different story. I can never depend on him. Always calling in sick. Nobody's sick like this man." Nacinovich threw up his hands.

"Was he here Saturday?"

"He was here for lunch, but right after lunch he says he's feeling sick. Says he won't be able to work dinner. Saturday afternoon he tells me this. Ai yi yi.... One of our busiest times." The restaurateur shook his head again in frustration.

"Do you trust Rivers, Mr. Nacinovich?"

"No, I don't trust him."

"Has he ever stolen from you?"

"No, he never stole nothing...at least I don't think so, but he's, how do you say...sneaky. Something about him..."

"Does he ever get calls here at the restaurant?"

"Too often. He talks in quiet voice, like some people I remember in my home country, in the old days. No, this Rivers, if he doesn't come back, it's better I think."

\* \* \*

Back at the car Flynn had already cuffed Rivers and had placed his hand on the top of the head of the anemic-looking waiter, pushing him into the back seat of the car as Gwen returned. "I see our wayward friend is going to be our guest," she said.

"Yeah, says he was going home sick. Funny, he

didn't seem so sick when we saw him half an hour ago."

In one of the interrogation rooms back at the precinct the pasty faced Rivers sat facing Pappas, Flynn, and Lieutenant Farrell. He'd repeatedly told the three officers that he didn't want a lawyer. He maintained that he didn't need one because he was innocent. He wasn't doing too well without one, however. The hapless waiter was beginning to look as sick as he'd earlier claimed to be. "Let's try it again," said Flynn. "What's the name of the pizza joint you stopped in on Saturday night?"

"I told you. I don't remember. I said I'd get the name for you. You din't give me no chance."

"How were you going to find out, LeRoy?" asked Gwen.

"I was gonna look it up in the phone book."

"Well we have Jersey phone books here, my friend. You want to look it up for us now?"

"Sure," said Rivers, feigning a pugnacious attitude he didn't quite feel.

"Okay, LeRoy. In the meantime we're getting you a court-appointed lawyer.

Twenty minutes after providing Rivers with the appropriate Jersey yellow pages Gwen poked her head back into the interrogation room. "Find it yet, LeRoy?"

"Yeah. Here it is. Look, right here." He pointed to it with his finger. Gwen noticed that the nail, like those on all of his fingers, was bitten down almost to the quick.

"Jimmy's, huh. Let's see now. Phone number five five five, oh two two one. And...just a second...ah, here it is. Tad Szczepanski's phone number is. Hmmm...That's strange, LeRoy. Not one of these digits is the same. Not even close. Hard to believe that you would have dialed this number when you really wanted

Jimmy's Pizza."

Rivers started to sweat. He fidgeted in his seat. "Like I said, I made a mistake. Don't you ever make mistakes?"

Gwen gave him a pitiful look. It occurred to her that the man really was quite stupid. "I don't think you get the point Leroy. Nobody makes mistakes like that. Nobody. And no jury is going to believe you made a mistake. Now come on. Tell us what you did and who hired you. Maybe we can work something out. Make a deal. If you don't co-operate, we'll throw the book at you."

"A deal huh? What kinda deal?"

Man, this guy really is dull, thought Gwen. "Tell us what happened and who hired you, and we'll see what we can do."

Rivers only hesitated for a minute, "Okay, so I did the job. I was hired to do it. It was nothin' personal." He looked almost relieved. "Strictly business, okay?..."

"So who'd you do it for, Leroy?" pressed Flynn. "Who hired you?"

"Hey, all I know is I get this call from a guy I know. Says he's got a client who needs to get rid of someone. Quick and not in Manhattan. No trace." Rivers smiled wanly, "No trace. That's a laugh. Anyway, he says I gotta do it within twenty-four hours or don't do it. Job's worth ten grand. Well, I could use the money so I'm more than willing to do the job quick. Only problem is I gotta find the guy and do him with no witnesses, all in less than a day. Not as easy as you might think, believe me." Rivers looked up, as if expecting sympathy for the Herculean task he'd taken on.

"Okay, so you don't know who wanted the job done," said Flynn. "Tell us who called you."

A loud rap prevented Rivers from answering. Gwen went to the door and opened it. The tall, willowylimbed woman who entered had the kind of personality and presence that dominated a room. "Monica Watts," said the cocoa-skinned woman by way of introduction. I've been appointed by the court to represent Mr. Rivers. Gwen thought that she'd never seen a woman with such composure. She couldn't have been more than thirty-two or three, yet she was clearly no one to trifle with.

"I'd like to see my client alone for a few minutes if you don't mind," said Watts.

"I don't need a lawyer," barked Rivers. "Certainly no black lady lawyer."

"Look, Bucko. Let's you and I talk. There's no charge. Might even be able to help you."

"He's already confessed to the killing," said Gwen. "We were just starting to talk about who ordered the hit."

"I hope he didn't confess under duress."

"Hey, does he look abused?" exploded Flynn. "He got his Miranda, and he knew what he was doing. We'd like to continue talking to him when you're through. Hey, LeRoy, you talk to the lady. We'll be back."

A few minutes later Monica Watts found Pappas and Flynn and said, "Okay let's go back in."

"So LeRoy," said Gwen, "let's get back to what we asked you before. Who called you and asked you to do the job?"

While Rivers wasn't overly bright, he wasn't the dumbest person in the world either. He didn't quite know how much bargaining power he had, but Monica Watts figured if he had anything to trade, it was information. "What kinda deal do I get if I tell you?"

"Detectives, may I have a word with you outside?" asked Watts, somehow making her request sound like a demand.

Outside, Gwen said, "You're not serious about a

deal here?"

"Damn right, detective. You think you got my client, but without his help you got squat. Besides, you already offered him a deal. Convenient of you to forget that." Gwen felt her neck burn and her face flush. She'd underestimated Rivers. She'd also been caught pulling a fast one, something for which she would have jumped all over someone else. Watts continued, "You want the people behind this, and Rivers can give 'em to you."

"Hey, miss legal eagle. Withholding evidence is a crime. If he knows something, he damn well better cough it up."

"What're you going to do, arrest him?"

Gwen and Flynn exchanged looks. "Okay," said Flynn, "we'll see what we can do for your friend there. But he's got to give us a name and all he knows."

"What does *we'll see what we can do* mean?"

"Just that. If Rivers gives us a name and info we can use, we'll talk with the a.d.a. Maybe she'll go for second degree, reduced."

"Man-one," countered Watts.

"Hey, the creep already confessed to planning and executing a cold-blooded murder. Where do you get off with manslaughter?"

"You want the name or not?"

"Listen, Miss Watts," said Flynn. "We can make the case without him. He can save us a lot of time, but hey, he's a goddam killer. If you don't like our offer, we'll see you in court."

"You're bluffing."

"You're so sure, why don't you walk outta here?"

"Look, if you promise to ask the a.d.a. for the best possible deal, including that he'll at least consider the possibility of man-two, you've got yourself a deal." Flynn suppressed a smile. When a defense attorney phrased acceptance of a deal that way, it meant acquiescence to the terms offered. The request that he and Gwen ask the a.d.a. to consider manslaughter as one of her possibilities was just to assuage Watts' conscience. That way she could go home that night believing she'd pleaded for the best possible deal for her client. It was clear to Flynn that she didn't like Rivers anymore than he did, or she would have fought harder.

Flynn looked at Gwen. She nodded assent. "Deal. Now let's get this over with," said Flynn.

Back in the interrogation room Monica Watts spoke to her client, "LeRoy," she didn't say it with the same disdain that Flynn and Pappas expressed when they addressed Rivers, but there was no warmth in it either. "LeRoy, the detectives here have agreed to ask the assistant district attorney to consider reducing the charge to manslaughter if you tell them the name of the person who hired you and anything else that will help them."

"That the best you can do for me, lady lawyer?"

"I'd advise you to take it."

"Sure, why not? What've you got to lose?" Rivers was not going to roll over so easily.

"Look, LeRoy," said Gwen. "If you'd rather we stick to second degree, be my guest. We'll get the name without you. In the meantime, you can spend the time at Rikers thinking about the deal you might have had. Let's go, Dawson."

Monica Watts said, "Detectives, let me have another minute with my client."

When they'd reassembled back in the interrogation room ten minutes later, Rivers, in a lifeless voice, finally capitulated, "Wha d'you wanna know?"

"Who paid you to do the hit?" Gwen asked soberly.

LeRoy Rivers fidgeted for a moment; then took a deep breath. "Look, if I tell you, you gotta protect me.

If this guy hears I ratted, he'll fry my ass."

"You'll be safe, LeRoy. Believe me," said Flynn. "We'll keep you where he can't get to you." Watts leaned over to confer with her client for a minute. After a brief whispered exchange, Leroy shook his head resignedly, "Guy named Mickey D."

"What's the D stand for?" asked Flynn.

"Dunno. Goes by Mickey D."

"How'd he contact you?"

"Phone. Called me Saturday at the restaurant. Said he had a hit for me. He's sort of like an agent, if you know what I mean. Or a contractor. People like me are his subcontractors. Made it clear, though, that I had to do the job within 24 hours or no job."

"That's a lot of pressure for someone like you," said Flynn.

"Tellin' me. But the money was good. Hey, I got the job done within six hours. Not everybody coulda done that."

"How's it feel, counselor, to defend such an outstanding professional?" asked Gwen sardonically.

Monica Watts gave Gwen a withering look, but didn't respond.

"How do we find Mickey?" asked Flynn.

"Dunno," said the Willie Loman of hired killers. "He always found..."

"He always found you. Is that what you were going to say, Leroy?"

"Nah. What I meant to say was he doesn't like for people to be able to contact him. He's not easy to reach. He reaches you."

"But you started to say 'he always found you', like you did other jobs for him. Is killing people a regular sideline for you LeRoy?"

Rivers was beginning to perspire. "Hey, you kiddin' me? This was the first time. I was desperate." Flynn exchanged looks with Pappas and Watts.

"So how did you get paid, Leroy?" asked Gwen.

"He came by the restaurant and gave me half. Paid me the other half Saturday. Met him in this dive on Tenth Avenue. Jakes. I think he hangs out there."

"Is that where you'd contact him if you needed to reach him?"

"I spose. Like I said, he doesn't like to be contacted. He likes to do the contacting."

"Why did he want Szczepanski dead?" asked Flynn.

"I don't think he did."

"How's that?"

"Well, I think he got orders from above. Some big shot probably wanted this Polack out of the way. As I said, Mickey D's just a contractor or an agent. He arranges things."

"Did Mickey D. say anything about the big shot who ordered the hit?" asked Gwen.

"Nothin. I'm just guessin' there was such a guy. Mickey bein' a contractor and all he usually handles things for other people. Important people."

"How would such people reach him, then, if he doesn't like to be contacted, LeRoy?"

"Maybe some people have his number. Maybe they leave a message at Jakes. Hey, I dunno. It's not my problem."

"Oh, but it is your problem, LeRoy. It is your problem. We can't take your deal to the A.D.A. unless your lead pays off. That means we've gotta find Mickey D." Flynn leaned back and folded his arms across his chest. "This beginning to make any sense to you, LeRoy?"

"Now you see why I didn't want no lady lawyer—especially no black lady lawyer," Rivers turned to Monica Watts. "You didn't warn me about these cops pullin' a fast one on me. No Jew lawyer would'a let 'em get away with this. What the hell good are you?"

Monica Watts counted to ten before she spoke, "Mr. Rivers, you got good advice." She stuck her face in his. "Hey, bro, you can't expect the police to give you no deal if what you give 'em ain't no good."

Rivers stared at her, not knowing quite how to react. Figuring the deck was stacked against him, he said, "It is good, dammit. I just can't give you the guy's phone number. Like I said, he's not easy to reach."

"Well," said Gwen. "we're gonna give it a try. In the meantime, you're not going anywhere. We'll be in touch, LeRoy. Oh, and by the way, when the state pays for your attorney, you don't get to pick the religion or the color."

# THIRTY-FIVE

It was the first time the two men had met. Lousy way to meet, thought Carr Williamson.

The whole situation. God, what a comeuppance. Did he deserve this? All right, he'd been living the good life. Maybe a little spoiled. But did he really deserve this? His thoughts drifted back to a time long ago when he could go to his mother or his father for help or comfort. But the present stirred him out of that flash of reverie. He looked around the living room. No one there now, Carr. You're feeling sorry for yourself, but no one's going to put you on their lap and say there, there. Hey, you've spent a lifetime building yourself up as the consummate adult. You're going to have to deal with this on your own. That first night after he was arrested had been the worst. Alone in that dingy, depressing cell. Like some bad dream—a dream about somebody else. But it wasn't someone else. It was he who was locked up like a common criminal. He'd seen cells like that in a hundred movies. Read about them in novels. But people like him didn't end up in such places. God, what a stark contrast to the kinds of places he'd gotten used to in recent years. The best, the very best.

Was it the lack of comfort that bothered him most? Or was it the lack of dignity? In that damp cell, it had been hard to believe that less than 12 hours earlier he'd been a free man, commanding respect wherever he went. Oh how he'd taken all that for granted. People had fawned all over him. How clearly he saw it now. That it wasn't him; it was the office for Christ's sake. He promised himself that if he ever got out of the living hell he'd gotten himself into, he'd work to become a person worth knowing as a person. *Was this the kind of vow one made under adversity, only to forget when things got better?* God, he hoped he had more character than that.

He'd been so busy in recent years that he didn't realize how much he'd gotten used to the creature comforts. How much he'd taken for granted. The challenge of rising to the top of the heap had so preoccupied him that he'd just accepted the good life without really even understanding what he had. He certainly appreciated those things now. The cell had been cold and damp. Except for when one of the other prisoners complained. Then it became excessively hot, and unbearably stuffy. Creature comforts? A joke. It was a jail cell for Christ's sake! And the food. God, how spoiled he'd become. He'd never had such terrible food as he'd had that night. And what good would it have done to complain? Who was going to care whether a prisoner complains about the menu? He remembered reading in the magazine section of the *Times*—how many years ago was that—a piece showing how many of the recently constructed prisons around America actually looked pleasant, comfortable. He remembered the resentment he'd felt about these "country club" prisons. Clearly Rikers wasn't one of them.

At least he was home now—out of that cell—though home had become a new kind of prison. He shook himself out of his dismal reverie. The man opposite him, Bradford B. Tillson, a man in his mid-sixties, looked tired, almost disinterested—not very comforting to Williamson who had been hoping his new defense attorney would, through sheer legal and oratorical brilliance, extricate him from the depressing quicksand that was threatening to engulf and destroy him.

Little did Carson Williamson know that Tillson's fatigue derived from his getting home late the night before and not from professional burnout. But Williamson was aware of none of this. All he knew was that this person who was supposed to defend him looked like a man who long ago had lost interest in his profession, someone who was now just going through the motions. Tillson hadn't been his choice in the first place. The company's chief counsel, Warner Phillips, had recommended Tillson after informing Carr that he couldn't use the services of corporate counsel. "It wouldn't be appropriate," Phillips had said, trying not to sound self righteous. Williamson had resented it at the time, but realized when he calmed down that were he still running things, he would have made the same decision.

Mike Gwynn, Williamson's personal attorney, thought Tillson was an excellent choice. Couldn't praise him enough. Gwynn had convinced Williamson that he needed a criminal lawyer of the first water. This guy, Gwynn claimed, was in the league with Melvin Belli, F. Lee Bailey (when he was still practicing), and Jerry Spence. "Hell, maybe even Perry Mason." Gwynn, however, was far from inept. After all, he'd argued successfully to get Carr out on bail. But Gwynn still felt Carr would be better off with a top criminal lawyer. Now, as Williamson stared across the table at the tired eyes of Tillson, the haggard-looking attorney reminded him of some reject from a rest home. Unbelievable, thought Williamson. I'm paying this guy $100,000, even if he loses. What's his incentive? The $150,000 he gets if he wins? He doubted that would be much incentive at all if the downside were a hundred grand. Where did a lawyer get off charging that kind of money?

"Mr. Williamson," began Tillson, "I'm going to start by telling you what I know about your chances. Then you can tell me where I'm wrong or what I need to know to change those odds." His strong voice surprised Williamson. Tillson sounded better than he looked.

"Go ahead."

"From a jury's perspective, Mr. Williamson, you don't make a very sympathetic defendant."

Williamson stiffened, "Why do you say that?"

"To begin with, you've been cheating on your wife."

"You don't mince words, do you?"

"Look, if we're to have any chance at all, you're going to have to accept something. You've been arraigned on a felony murder charge. The law says that you'll go before a jury of your peers. That just isn't so. Most members of juries come from segments of society that view presidents of large companies as pompous, spoiled fat cats. Most of these people are workers—people who work for people who work for people who work for executives like yourself. Not a lot in common with people like you, yet believe it or not, these people are your best bets. At least some of them believe in the work ethic. But there'll be others who are on disability or out of work. Very few of them are going to view the world the way you do. They're certainly not going to start out being sympathetic. And when they find out that you've been having an affair with another woman, a younger woman at that, you'll receive even less sympathy. Certainly none from any woman juror. You can probably assume for starters that all the women on the jury will be against you."

"In other words, I've already lost?"

"I didn't say that. I said you start out behind. You're paying me to change the way the jurors think. But I want you to see what you're up against. It's going to be an uphill battle. If you have any chance, you're going to have to understand what you face and then begin to deal with it." Tillson paused for a moment. Then a thought came to him, "You probably think of yourself as a basically good guy. You're obviously a high achiever. Things have probably come easy all your life. You've had the respect of people in school, at work, socially. People, no doubt have sought your companionship. Wanted to be your friend. You may even think you're charming. Well, don't fool yourself.

Many of these jurors won't see you that way at all. The charm they'll view as deceit. The achievements will be attributed to back stabbing, viciousness, and greed. The respect they'll say comes from being the boss. You get the picture.

"You paint a very bleak picture."

"All part of your education, Mr. Williamson. All part of your education."

"Well, do we have any chance at all?" He hesitated; then said, "And Call me Carr."

Tillson smiled. "I wouldn't have taken your case, Carr, if I didn't think so." Williamson was beginning to feel a little better about Bradford Tillson. The lawyer continued, "But I must advise you that a lot will depend on what you tell me today and what success the police have in finding the killer of Tad Szczepanski. First, tell me if you killed Andrew Mack?"

"Of course I didn't," snapped Williamson. Then, remembering who he was talking to, "I'm sorry. How could you know. Look, I didn't kill Mack. Believe me, if I were going to kill anybody, he would have been the one. But I didn't."

"Good, I believe you. Now let's get on with it. The police report says you admitted that Mack was blackmailing you because of your affair with Ms. Ferrara. Is that correct?"

"Yes, yes. It's true."

"If you didn't kill Mack, who do you think did?"

"I have no idea."

"Look, we have to work together on this. I think if we dig in here you can probably come up with some possibilities...some people who either wanted to get rid of him, or..." and at this, Tillson paused dramatically, "or someone who had it in for you, or would have benefited by getting you out of the way. Try to think along those lines for a minute."

"This is going to take a little adjusting in my thinking processes. I may be one of those fat cats you mentioned before, but believe it or not, I don't have a conspiratorial mind."

"Perhaps not, but you're an astute observer of human nature...or you wouldn't have gotten this far in your career. I'm sure you must have some ideas that could help us here."

"Well, as far as Mack was concerned, I have no idea who'd want to kill him. Other than myself, that is, and I've already told you that I didn't." Williamson held up his hand, "Wait, I have heard that after Mack was promoted he alienated virtually everyone on his staff. I never did find out how he managed that in so few days, but he must have stepped on some toes enough to make somebody really angry. I'm sorry, I just don't know any more than that. You should probably talk with Tony Marcantonio. He's editorial director of the reference division where Mack worked."

"Yes, I know. I did a little homework on this. I will talk with Mr. Marcantonio, of course, but I'm curious as to why you suggest I see him rather than Stuart Markham, the editor in chief?"

Williamson was beginning to think he'd seriously underestimated Tillson. "You *have* done your homework. Okay, that's a fair question, and it may lead into the second possibility. I suggested Tony rather than Stuart because I don't trust Stuart. Never have."

"Why haven't you gotten rid of him then?"

"I've been tempted...many times, believe me. But I haven't because he's a hell of an editor-in-chief. Been responsible for getting Harmon Hall some of the best talent in the industry. And frankly, I always felt I could stay one step ahead of him. I have to say, though, that since this whole mess began, I've had second thoughts about that."

"I'm not sure I follow you?"

"Well, as you no doubt know, the board of Harmon Hall just appointed Markham acting CEO and president. Knowing how he always wanted my job, I can't help wondering if he didn't do something to get the board to install him."

"Like what, for instance?"

"Like I don't know. I do know, though, that he resented it when I was named president three years ago. Thought he should have had the job."

"How do you know this?"

"A couple of my friends on the board strongly hinted at this shortly after my appointment. Since then, I've been aware of Stuart's feelings whenever we've had dealings. I mentioned this yesterday, by the way to the police. Anyway, it's subtle, but snide, sometimes biting. He doesn't like me. But whether he did something about that," he threw up his hands, "Christ, I don't know. Maybe I'm getting paranoid."

"Maybe not.

# THIRTY-SIX

"Good evening. This is your Metropolitan Report for Tuesday, September 12th... It's almost two weeks now since book editor Andrew Mack was cold-bloodedly struck down in his midtown office. In what have become known as the Harmon Hall murders, police admit they still have not found the killer or killers of a second young Harmon Hall editor, Tad Szczepanski, who was killed last Friday evening. With these two killings, Harmon Hall, a major publisher of murder mysteries, seems to have found real-life grist for its mystery writing mill." TV anchorperson, Lou Colvin, smiled professionally as he delivered the latest in his series of provocative sound bites inspired by the two murders. Colvin continued, "Earlier today Lieutenant Gavin Farrell of New York's Midtown North Homicide Division, said that, while the police had not yet arrested anyone for the Szczepanski murder, Carson Williamson, president and chief executive officer of Harmon Hall was still free on bail, pending further investigation of the Mack killing. Listeners may remember that, in an unusual turn of events, Carson Williamson was granted bail at his recent arraignment—apparently because of his standing and reputation in the community. It is generally believed that judge Myron Aronson, at the behest of Williamson's attorneys and several prominent citizens, was convinced that Williamson, the chief suspect in the Mack homicide, was not a threat to the community. Farrell would not comment on the fact that the second killing took place within hours after Williamson was released. Nor would he say anything about the likelihood of there being two killers involved." Colvin turned to face a different camera.

"At a press conference today at city hall, the mayor announced that, last year, for the fourth year in a row, the number of homicides declined in New York City. While conceding that the homicide rate, still hovering around the 600 level, was still nothing to be proud of, he took credit for the decline and vowed that..."

Stuart Markham beamed in contentment as he sat half dressed on the edge of his bed catching the evening news. He looked at his watch. Seven ten. He had a benefit to attend at eight. One of the first of a long season. Better finish dressing. From the looks of things he could relax and enjoy the evening—more than he usually enjoyed these benefits. Now, as the acting head of Harmon Hall, people sought him out. He loved the attention. And since the police considered Williamson as the primary suspect in the murders, he could really savor his new-found celebrity.

    He smiled. The only really unsettling thing about the latest TV report, from his perspective, was the implication that mystery books were the sole category that Harmon Hall published. Hell, didn't they know that Harmon Hall published virtually everything.

Nine blocks away Howard Harmon stood up and switched off the television set in his den overlooking Central Park. The news report he'd just heard left him in a troubled state. On top of the constant barrage of media attention concerning the two murders, this guy Colvin had the effrontery to be flippant about two tragic deaths. Not to mention how it made Harmon Hall look. Grist for the mill indeed. This kind of irresponsible journalism was getting worse. Lately, more and more TV commentators had taken to being cute about tragedy and death. No wonder so many young people in America treated killing so cavalierly. In recent years it was rare to hear a news item delivered without some lame attempt at humor. Ratings were everything, and the news was now treated like any other form of entertainment. Entertainment value counted for more than accurate reporting. The ratings game was all important. Harmon shook himself out of his black mood. He didn't have time for such reflections now. Damn benefit to go to.

* * *

Markham studied the man sitting behind the massive mahogany desk. Markham feared very few men, no doubt because he deemed himself a keen, albeit cynical, judge of character and believed he knew what people were thinking in almost every situation. Because of this uncanny ability he'd been able to stay one or more steps ahead of most people he dealt with. But Howard Harmon was a horse of a different color. Damn, he hated it when he found himself resorting to such trite metaphors. Still, in this case it was an apt expression. The man across the desk was not just his boss, he was a giant of a man, a man who ruled an empire because he, too, was ruthless and had an unerring ability to read people's minds and anticipate what they wanted—sometimes before they realized it themselves.

"So," said the great man, "we survived another benefit. Unfortunately, there's a lot more of them ahead of us." He paused dramatically before continuing. "Well, Stuart, I'm sure you realize that I didn't ask you here to talk about the year's social calendar." His expression softened ever so slightly. Markham thought he detected a trace of a smile. "Stuart, I want you to become the new C.E.O. of Harmon Hall Publishing Company. This *acting* C.E.O. arrangement is awkward for both of us. I know it's hard on you, and people keep pestering me about when and whether we're going to make it permanent. I want you to know I'm meeting with the board this Friday with the express purpose of recommending that you be made president and

C.E.O.—no *acting* or temporary strings attached. You should know also that I was at first reluctant to take this action. I've come to like and respect Carr a great deal. I was hoping—naively, I now realize—that this mess he's involved in would go away. With the advantage of a few days of reflection under my belt, it now seems clear that it isn't going to go away soon. And even if it does get resolved and Carr is exonerated, his reputation will be sullied so badly that his effectiveness on the job will be questionable at best. Having come to that conclusion, Stuart, it now seems imperative that we remove any doubt as to who's running this company. And the sooner, the better. I assume this meets with your approval?"

Markham worked hard not to let his elation show on his face, "I'm delighted. And I thank you for your faith in me."

"Well, I'm sure you know that the hard part has just begun. You've inherited a very healthy company. That's the good news. The bad news is you've got yourself a huge public relations problem to contend with. And if that weren't enough, the morale of your staff has got to be terrible, what with people wondering who's going to be shot next. It's not going to be easy, Stuart. The sooner the police can find the killer of that second young editor, the sooner that cloud will be lifted."

Perhaps, thought Markham, but I'll take my chances with a staff morale problem because that'll gradually fade away.

# THIRTY-SEVEN

The stretch of Tenth Avenue from 30th Street to 50th is not exactly high rent. Whether you think of it as part of Hell's Kitchen or just a neighborhood on the West Side, it's not the best part of Manhattan. Jake's bar was on Tenth, not far from 38th. It fit right in with the local decor, thought Flynn. Not the kind of place you'd want to take a date, or anyone else, for that matter. They parked across the street, about a block south of the grim-looking dive. As they pushed their way into the poorly lit tavern, their nostrils were assaulted by the sour chemistry of yesterday's beer as it struggled to overcome years of accumulated redolence. This assault proved to be the first of several sensory endurance tests. First the aroma test, thought Gwen; then the vision test. It was dark, and the two detectives had to wait for their eyes to adjust. As forms began to materialize out of the dank murkiness, and their eyes began to confirm that the bar was easily as dingy and disgusting as they'd expected, Gwen vowed to herself that she would not even consider taking the taste test. No way was she eating anything in this place. She looked at Flynn, and he grinned. A quick survey of the room revealed that, other than themselves, there were only three people in the place: the bartender and two men at the bar, each with a half-drunk glass of beer in front of him. The man nearest to the door gave a quick glance in their direction as they entered and returned to studying the contents of his glass. The second man, who Flynn thought in a different era could have passed for a Barbary pirate or a Marseilles dock worker, kept his eyes on Gwen. She found it unnerving and finally, flashing her shield, turned her attention to the bartender. "You know a guy goes by the name of Mickey D?"

The bartender, a balding man of average height

in his late fifties, squinted, as if in deep concentration. He shook his head, "Don't mean nothin' to me." He turned to the two men at the bar, "You guys ever heard of a Mickey D?"

The man closest to the door shook his head without interrupting his concentration on his glass. The ogler said a quick, "Not me."

Flynn put his face in front of the bartender, "You sure the name doesn't ring a bell?"

"Yeah, I'm sure. Never heard of 'im."

"This your place?" asked Gwen.

The bartender snorted, "Yeah. Wanna buy it?"

"Dawson," said Gwen, "when do you think the health inspector was here last?"

"Hey, look, you two. I run a clean place here. No drugs. Gimme a break, will ya."

"Yeah, real clean. This place look clean to you Dawson?"

"Yeah, eat off the floor. Okay, uh...by the way, what's your name?"

The bartender fidgeted, looking first at the customer near the door and then at the other one. "Angelo. Angelo Poppi. Hey why you guys bustin' my balls?"

"Are we doing that, Angie? All we want is a name," said Flynn. "Angie, I'm gonna give you my card. You remember anything about Mickey D, you give me a call. Meantime, we'll see what the health inspector's schedule looks like. You think of something real soon, Angie, maybe we don't have to bother with the health stuff."

"Hey, I'm just trying to make a living. Give me a break."

"All we want is some information, Angie. Wrack your brain."

Flynn and Pappas realized as soon as they saw that the bartender wasn't alone that they weren't going to get anything out of him. If he did know Mickey D, and if

Mickey D was as bad as LeRoy Rivers had said he was, the two customers probably also knew who he was. No way was Angelo Poppi going to give out information when either one of those customers could tell Mickey D that he'd talked to the cops. As much as the bartender wanted to avoid trouble with the authorities, the primitive drive to stay alive was going to win out every time.

"Okay," said Gwen when they'd left, "if our friendly tavern keeper is going to be any use to us, we need a snitch. You know anybody who could be useful to us in this neighborhood, Dawson?"

"As a matter of fact, I do."

\* \* \*

The phone rang. It was the following morning, and Flynn, as he waited for his coffee to cool down enough to take his first sip, was going over in his mind a conversation he'd had the previous night with Julie. She was still serious about being a single parent, and she still wanted Flynn to be the father. No strings. She just wanted his genetic input, as she'd put it. Dammit, Julie, he'd said. How mechanical do you wanna make this? She'd come back with a comment about how she thought he'd be flattered. The phone rang again. He picked it up. After a brief conversation in which he did most of the listening he hung up and went over to Gwen's desk.

"Just heard from my snitch, Gwen. Says Mickey D hangs out at Jakes from about 12:30 to 2:00 or 2:30 every day. Says the guy may not stay there very long today...if Angelo tells him about our visit. He'll figure we might be back."

"Then we better be there before Mr. D arrives."

"We should probably wait in the car, a little ways down the street. The snitch can join us to help identify the sonofabitch. By the way, I got another call this morning—from Carson Williamson. Tell you about it in the car."

"Tell me about your snitch, Dawson?" Gwen leaned back in the seat as Flynn turned into Tenth Avenue.

"Billy?" Flynn laughed under his breath. "Billy's somewhere between 40 and 50. Hard to tell. A real upstanding citizen. Sometime security guard, sometime petty burglar. One hand sorta washes the other if you know what I mean. But he does know a lot of the people in the sleaze world. A real networker our boy Billy is. You'll meet him in a minute."

"Is he reliable?"

"You mean would I leave him alone in my apartment? Or would I let him date my sister? Uh, no. You mean does he give good information? The answer is an emphatic yes. He's not stupid; just dishonest."

"Then he's not so unique is he?"

"When you put it that way...Hey, you're gonna meet him. You'll like him a lot." Flynn had arranged to meet Billy on the corner of Tenth Avenue and 34th Street. They'd then drive north a few blocks on Tenth and park in order to have a clear view of Jake's. As Flynn eased the car over to the curb a slight man in jeans and a gray sweatshirt jumped into the back seat of the car.

"Billy, this is detective Pappas," said Flynn. He looked at Gwen, "This is Billy."

"Hey, a lady detective. It's a pleasure indeed," said Billy with an awkward attempt at gallantry. Gwen noticed his thinning sandy hair and his unhealthy pallor. She was not at all surprised that he was a denizen of a place like Jake's. She couldn't help but notice also that his sweatshirt had an accumulation of stains.

"Hi. You know this guy Mickey D, Billy?"

"Well I wouldn't say we're the best of friends. I guess you could say we're more like acquaintances."

"What's he do for a living?" asked Flynn.

"He's like a contractor, if ya know what I mean. Does jobs for other people. Guy's got no emotions. Do his own mother for the right price. Lately, though, he's more like a facilitator. Tries to find other people to do his jobs."

"Sounds like a mean character," said Gwen.

"Yeah, in a way he is. I mean, when a guy can do the stuff he does without flinching, I guess you'd call that mean. But he's strictly a businessman. It's not like he's got this ugly streak. Come ta think of it, I never even seen him mad. He's a smooth guy, lotta polish. Just does what people pay him to do."

"Okay," said Flynn, "He's a real pro. Look, I'm gonna pull in here, on the same side. Joint's only a hundred yards from here. How're your eyes, Billy? You see people clearly that far away?"

"Yeah, detective. I can see fine. I better go in and check. Maybe he's already in there."

"Naw, you stay here with detective Pappas. I'll go in and check. If you go in and out without spending any time there, and if we take him later, he'll have your number. You don't want that, do you Billy?"

"Good point, detective. Yeah, good point." Billy seemed relieved. Of course it had occurred to Flynn that, if Micky D were already in the bar, and if Billy were so inclined, he could easily alert the contract agent when he went in—supposedly to check.

"We wanna keep you healthy," said Gwen.

"Yeah, I know you both care about my health."

Three minutes later Flynn emerged from the bar, looked both ways, then walked over to where the car was parked and kept going on past it for two hundred yards before disappearing around the corner onto 38th Street. If someone from Jake's was watching, they'd see him disappear out of sight and presumably stop looking for him. Hopefully they'd assume the bar was no longer being watched. After another two or three minutes, Flynn returned to the car.

"Angie says he hasn't come in yet today. Says he usually does. Hopefully our friendly bartender won't give him a call and tip him off. I tried to put the fear of God in him, but I think he might fear Mickey D. more than God. By the way, Billy, how's Mr. D. usually travel when he visits Jake's? By cab, his own wheels?"

"On foot. He always walks over here from wherever he comes from. Should be coming from across the street. Hey shit, there he is now! There, see him?"

"Who? You mean that guy in the brown suit?" asked Gwen.

"Yeah, that's him." The man Gwen saw was probably in his early fifties, wearing a cheap shiny suit with a black t-shirt. With better and different threads, thought Gwen, the look would be considered trendy. And with a better haircut the man could look almost sophisticated. Mickey D just looked tacky. He was still on the opposite side of the street, about to cross when an older man said something to him. Mickey D stopped for a moment to exchange greetings. He seemed comfortable with himself, thought Gwen. Neighborhood hero. He waved goodbye to the older man, nodded to another and stepped into Tenth Avenue. Just as he did so the old man on the sidewalk apparently had another thought and yelled out at Mickey D, who turned and looked back. The black Lincoln Town Car had been accelerating for several seconds now and hit Mickey D square in the back, lifting his lean body off the pavement and onto a parked blue Honda Accord ten feet away. The Town Car continued on down Tenth Avenue and was swallowed up in traffic before Pappas or Flynn could get to the Honda.

"Holy shit!" said Flynn, "You get a plate number?"

"Smeared—deliberately I'd guess, " said Gwen. "Guy came outta nowhere. Not a typical hit and run.

Looks professional to me."

"Gotta be. Let's take a look at what's left of Mr. D."

The crumpled victim was lying on his stomach on the hood of the Honda. Gwen put her fingers on his carotid artery, checking for a pulse. "Hey, he's still alive. Mickey, can you hear me? I'm detective Pappas, NYPD."

The man's lips moved, but nothing came out.

"Mickey, who paid you to off the Szczepanski kid?" asked Flynn.

Gwen put her ear close to the barely moving lips. They moved again, in a barely perceptible whisper.

"I'm not..."

"Yeah, we know you're not the one who pulled the trigger, Mickey," pursued Flynn, "But who paid you to do the job?"

"I'm not..."

"You're not what, Mickey? You're not what?"

The dying man's lips fluttered ever so slightly. Nothing came out. He tried again. His lips moved soundlessly.

"I don't think he's got much left," said Gwen.

"Let me try. Mickey, just tell us who paid you?"

The mouth started to open one more time. Then the body expelled its last feeble breath and the lips closed. Gwen felt for a pulse. "Nothing. That's it for Mickey D."

# THIRTY-EIGHT

Lieutenant Farrell was doing the talking. He was responding to a report just delivered to him by Dawson Flynn. Gwen stood by silently as Farrell exploded, "You're telling me that less than 90 minutes ago your best chance of nailing whoever orchestrated all this was killed by a hit-and-run driver...and that you didn't even get a make on the driver...nor did you get a tag number. That what you're telling me, detective?"

"Look, I know how it sounds, but..."

"But what? I'll tell you how it sounds. It sounds like the Keystone Kops. That's how it sounds."

"Lieutenant, may I finish?"

"Go ahead."

"Look, the guy came out a nowhere. We did see the plates, but they were smeared with something. Guy knew what he was doing. This was no drunk. This was definitely a hit. Bet my shield on it," said Flynn, wishing as he'd said it that he'd chosen something else to wager.

"And you, Pappas," barked Farrell. "Did you see anything?" The lieutenant allowed himself to appear a little calmer, but he wasn't going to ease up too much.

"Same thing as Dawson. The plates were smeared with something, both front and back. I could tell that it was a guy. He had some kind of hat pulled way down so it was hard to make out his features. Wasn't young."

"White, black?"

"White."

"Okay, so we got an older white guy who drives a black Lincoln Town Car. Not much, but something," said Farrell. "Can either of you think of anything else, anything at all?"

"Well," said Flynn, "we learned a couple of things."

"What's that, detective?"

"That there definitely is someone behind this, someone who hired Mickey D, and someone who somehow found out that the heat was on Mickey D and decided to get rid of him."

"And," interjected Gwen, "we learned that whoever this someone is, he...or she...doesn't know how much we know. He didn't know we'd be in front of Jake's when he took out Mickey D."

"This someone we're talkin' about," interrupted Farrell, "may or may not be the same guy who offed Mickey D. The driver could've been more hired help."

"You're right, lieutenant," agreed Gwen. "Still, either way, whoever wanted the hit no doubt intended it to be seen as a simple hit-and-run. Never dreamed we'd be on the scene."

"Okay, so how do we find this guy?" Farrell, had forgotten to maintain his tough exterior.

"I've got an idea," said Gwen.

"Let's hear it, detective."

"As I see it, whoever's behind this is in a position of some power over at Harmon Hall. On the surface this guy must be a pillar of respectability."

"Detective," interrupted Farrell smugly, "We already arrested Williamson. You saying there are two high-ranking executives at Harmon Hall involved in murder?"

"Well," Gwen glanced at Flynn for support and hopefully a little understanding, "we might have screwed up with Williamson. He might not be a killer."

"Tell me I don't hear that, detective? You do remember how you two stood here in my office convincing me that Williamson was our man?"

"He still could be the guy who killed Mack, lieutenant," rallied Flynn, "but Gwen may have a point. It's not looking so definite now as it did when we arrested him."

"Like what's changed?" challenged Farrell,

becoming pugnacious again.

"Well it's unlikely that he killed Szczepanski. He was only out of Rikers a couple of hours. Hard to believe he could have planned and executed that with such short notice. Remember, he didn't know if and when he was going to be freed on bail. And we know he didn't do in Mickey D. We called his house right after Mickey was killed and he was home."

"Let's not be naive, detective. You never heard of someone pulling strings from behind bars? Or behind the scenes?

"Of course it happens, but usually it's mob stuff. Some big mob guy who's connected, knows how to arrange hits. I can't believe Williamson has that kind of connections or pull. I'm sure he's got connections, but not that kind."

"You're probably right," agreed Farrell, calming down again. "Look, all I'm saying is it happens. But you're probably right about this one. It still doesn't get Williamson off the hook for the Mack killing, though."

"No, it doesn't," said Gwen, "but it does at least raise some doubt. Hard to believe there are two executives at Harmon Hall running around killing people."

"Okay, reasonable assumption. So where do you go from here? Got any leads?"

"Well, whoever ordered the hit on Szczepanski had to know where he lived in order to arrange for it to be done in his apartment. Harmon Hall's a big company, and it's unlikely as hell that a senior executive would know where a relatively minor employee lived. But that executive could get that information from the human resources department."

"Okay, I'm with you so far."

"Well, I think Dawson and I should pay a call on the human resources department to see who requested that kind of info in the past two or three weeks."

"Okay. Keep me posted."

It was not hard to find Human Resources. Years ago it had been called Personnel and consisted of three people. Today, as Human Resources, it employed 42 and occupied 12 times as much square footage. A receptionist got up from her uncluttered desk and led the two detectives deeper into the department—past two job applicants conscientiously completing application forms, and numerous offices on the right and modular workstations on the left—back to what clearly was the largest and most important office in the department. It was a corner office, and the receptionist asked them to wait outside the door while she checked to see if the boss was ready to receive them. After poking her head into the office, she ushered them into the large room. A few undistinguished watercolors with sterile-looking floral subjects added splashes of color to the otherwise plain-looking room. The gray haired woman behind the desk was Harriet Stahl, director of human resources for Harmon Hall. Her face was pleasant, almost grandmotherly, though from her crisp, efficient manner it was clear to both Flynn and Pappas that she was anything but grandmotherly when sitting behind her desk. "I don't know if that kind of information has been requested in the past few weeks by anyone. A request of that type would not normally come to my attention, providing the person making the request had the authority to do so."

"Would any senior executive have that authority, ma'am?" asked Gwen.

"Yes, of course."

"Would there be a record of such a request, ma'am?" asked Flynn.

"There should be. Probably a Xerox copy of what was sent. Why don't we check." Harriet Stahl picked up the phone and punched in a four-digit number. "Marjorie, did anyone in the past few weeks request information on that Tad Szczepanski, you know the editor who was killed? No, I know payroll would be finalizing his account. That's not what I'm looking for. I mean before he was killed. Has anyone asked to see his file folder or asked for background information...his home address, for instance?" The director of human resources leaned back with the receiver to her ear and smiled benignly at the two detectives. Finally, she spoke, "Hold on a minute, Marjorie." She addressed the two detectives, "Nobody requested that information on Szczepanski per se, but one person, a corporate officer, did ask for a printout of routine information for everyone in the editorial department. That would have included addresses. Obviously Szczepanski would have been included. Do you want to see a copy?"

"Yes," said Flynn, "if you don't mind."

"Marjorie, bring me a copy of that, would you please. Right away. And Marjorie, what date was that request made? Last Friday. Thanks."

Harriet Stahl's features grew serious as she faced the two detectives. "It's kind of unusual for a senior officer to request printouts on a whole department. Usually if they want information on an employee they ask specifically for that information."

"Like what kind of information, for instance?" asked Gwen.

"Like what their last salary increase was...and when. Or to see their performance appraisals. Quite frankly, I'm not even sure what our policy is on letting managers see complete personnel folders. I doubt if it's come up that much. Still, if an officer of the company wants to see something, who's going to say no? For that matter, I'm not sure if I should be showing files to you people."

"Look, we can't demand it, but if you show them to us because we request it, all you're doing is helping with a murder investigation." said Flynn trying to sound sensible and logical. "If you don't help, you're impeding that investigation. Besides, we could get a warrant. But, that just takes time, and the faster we move, the better our chances of getting to the bottom of all this."

"So you think there are two murderers? Mr. Williamson and this other person?"

"I'm afraid we can't comment on that, " said Flynn in his professional police manner.

"Then you must think this other officer had something to do with it?" probed the director of human resources. This was juicier than she could have dreamed. "I can't believe..."

"Look," said Gwen, "you haven't even told us who this officer is."

Harriet Stahl's face took on a conspiratorial look. "Just a minute or two. You'll see for yourselves." As she spoke there was a knock on the door. A matronly woman with a kindly face peeked in. "Sorry Mrs. Stahl," said the woman somewhat sheepishly, "I don't understand it. I can't find any of it. Someone must have misplaced the hard copies, and Janet's not in today. She's the only one who could get that information from the system. She'll be back tomorrow and then we should be able to pull up copies of what you're looking for."

Stahl looked annoyed. She looked at the detectives, "Will that be all right? I'm really sorry."

Gwen shook her head in the affirmative, "Call me or detective Flynn as soon as they're available and we'll pick them up."

"I can have them messengered over to you. Would that be better?"

"Yes," said Flynn. "That'll be fine."

## THIRTY-NINE

"We may still have one more card to play, Dawson. It's a long shot, but remember Tad Szczepanski's girlfriend?"

"Yeah, that's right. Did any of the Fort Lee cops talk to her?"

"I'd assume so, but let's find out. Maybe Szczepanski told her something about Markham or someone else that will give us more to go on than hunches. Why don't I give Brian Hammond a call." A few minutes later she put down the phone. "The plot thickens. He did have a girlfriend. Name of Pam Loring. Brian says they haven't been able to find her. Hasn't been in her apartment since the day after Szczepanski was killed."

"Did they check with her parents?"

"Apparently she's not from around here. Comes from out West. Nobody knows exactly where. Anyway, she's disappeared. Which leads me to believe one of two things: Either she knows something and is scared to death that the killer knows she knows, or she herself was involved in the killing."

"My guess is the former."

"Me too. We've gotta find her, Dawson. She's the key to all this, I know it."

"Brian tell you where she worked?"

"Said she worked in a graphics arts studio somewhere here in town. He has the address. I can get it."

"Let's start there. Maybe somebody she worked with can help us find her."

Graphic Solutions was located in the tenth floor loft of a building built in the early years of the $20^{th}$ century that in its heyday couldn't have been much to look at. It was the low-rent part of Fifth Avenue just south of Eighteenth Street. To the east lay the Gramercy section of town. To the west, Chelsea. It wasn't a bad neighborhood. Many of the yuppies and wanna-be yuppies preferred this part of town to the more expensive, more pretentious Midtown area. When they reached the tenth floor, the elevator opened onto a dimly lit corridor. There were only two choices. The door to the left proved to be the correct one. The old-fashioned frosted glass window in the top half of the pale yellow door said Graphic Solutions. Gwen knocked. After a moment, the door opened a few inches and someone peered out. "Can I help you?" asked a male voice.

"Police," said Flynn, holding his shield to the crack so the man could see it. "We need to ask you a few questions." The door closed, a chain was released, and the door reopened revealing a man of average height and build, in his mid-thirties, wearing jeans and a gray sweatshirt.

"Something wrong, officers?"

"Homicide. Detective Flynn. This is detective Pappas." Flynn realized, as he always did, that the average law-abiding citizen was more than a little shaken when told that two homicide detectives had come visiting. He had to resist the temptation to put their minds at ease under these circumstances. As much as one part of him wanted to do this, his professional self reminded him that the shock impact was often helpful in an investigation. He continued professionally, "We'd like to talk to whoever's in charge here."

"I'm in charge. Name's Fred Gulik. I own this place. Why don't we go into my office?" It was easy for Gwen to understand why the studio was located on the top floor of the building. The entire street-side wall consisted of windows that rose from a wainscoting-like ledge to a height of about fourteen feet and wrapped around to form part of the ceiling. In addition to this gracefully arcing wall of glass, skylights punctuated the rest of the ceiling making the studio an ideal place for artists to work and create. "Now what can I do for you?" asked Gulik, feigning a composure he didn't feel.

"We need to ask you a few questions about one of your employees...a woman by the name of Pam Loring," said Gwen. "Is she here today, Mr. Gulik?"

"No, Pam hasn't been in since last Friday. And her boyfriend was killed Saturday night. At least that's what I've read. I guess that's why you're here. About him I mean?"

"I'm afraid so. Did Ms Loring tell you where she was going?"

"She just said she had to get away for awhile. She was really shaken up. She was planning to go out with Tad the night he was killed, you know. Then he didn't show up. Wasn't like him at all not to show. They were real tight. Totally out of character for Tad not to at least call her and explain. I mean, these two were so close they didn't do anything without telling the other one. She didn't know where he was or what happened until Sunday when she heard about it from Tad's parents."

"Do you think she might have gone to stay with her parents?" asked Flynn.

"Could be. She was very close to her parents, too. But she didn't say. At least not to me. She might have mentioned something to one of the other people here. She and Ursula are good friends. Should I get her in here?"

"If you don't mind."

Ursula Klingbiel, a stunning blonde woman who appeared to be in her mid-twenties, was self assured beyond her years sitting in Gulik's small office as she pondered the question Flynn had just posed. Finally she spoke, "She's from L.A. Always talks about going back home to see her parents for Thanksgiving and Christmas. I got the feeling her family was pretty well off, not that she ever flaunted it. Just the opposite. Seemed to want to live it down. She used to tell me how her parents kept offering to use their connections to get her good jobs, but she wouldn't have any of it. Wanted to be a success, but wanted to do it on her own. God, what I could have done with parents like that!"

"Did she ever mention any other relatives—anywhere—or friends that she wanted to visit?" asked Gwen.

"Why are you guys looking for her? Do you think she did it? Oh my God! You can't think that."

"We don't think that at all," said Flynn trying not to let the cobalt blue eyes distract him. "We think she might have information, though, that could help us find the killer."

"I don't understand. If you don't think she did it, what makes you think she'd know who did?" Suddenly she put her hand to her mouth. "Oh no! You don't think Tad knew and would have told her?"

"Yes, we do," said Gwen. "Since you ask, that's exactly what we think might have happened. That could be why she left town—if that's what she did. To get away and feel a little safer. But if she does have the kind of information we think she has, and if the killer knows this, we need to track her down as soon as possible. She could be in danger. Can you help us?"

"Well, as I said, she might have gone back to L.A. She used to say that she missed home, even though she and her parents didn't always see eye-to-eye. I know she cared about them." Klingbiel thought for a moment. "She called me Sunday after she and Tad's parents discovered the body. I guess Fred must have told you. She was upset, as you'd expect...she and Tad being so close and all. But there was something else, too."

"Something else?" said Gwen.

"Well, as I said, she was upset. God, upset was

too mild a term for it. She was shattered. But there was more to it than that. She was scared. She didn't exactly say that she was scared, but she acted as if she were. Yes, she actually seemed terrified of something."

"Did she tell you what it was?" asked Flynn.
"No, but she was scared. Believe me."
"You wouldn't happen to know her parents names, would you?" asked Gwen.
"Yes. Hold on a second. Yes...Edna and Carl. Big bucks from what Pam tells me. They travel a lot. Nothing to do but spend money. Must be nice."


He knew that there was always the possibility that someone could finger him in connection with the Szczepanski thing or, more likely, the Mickey D. thing. But neither was very likely.

He felt a little bad about Szczepanski. Probably a nice kid. And if it could have been avoided...but there was really no other way. There really wasn't. Now Mickey D—he was a different story. Shit, the guy was a slime ball. World's a better place without him.

He couldn't believe how many loose ends had developed. He'd thought he'd wrapped everything up neatly by taking Szczepanski out of the picture. Then the police got on the trail of Mickey D, and he'd had to take care of that problem. That should have been it.

But it wasn't. He'd just now learned that Szczepanski had a girlfriend. One of the female editors at Harmon Hall had said that she heard that, after Szczepanski died, the girl planned to leave town, go out to California where her parents lived. He knew what that meant. Either she was going to leave town because the death of her boyfriend hit her hard, or, more than likely, she'd leave because Szczepanski, before he died, told her what he'd seen and heard near Mack's office. She'd leave town because she was scared shitless.

Fortunately, she probably hadn't left yet. The editor thought she was flying out this afternoon.

The only course he had, then, was to fly to L.A. himself—right away—this afternoon, if possible.

What a pain this was becoming. But facts are facts. She's leaving town, and she hasn't spoken with anyone yet, but certainly not for long. She'd either come back here and talk to someone, or she'd stay out there and call someone here. Either way the girl was a problem.

He knew he could track down the airline and flight number. He'd already found out the girl's name, and a quick search on the Web had produced her parents address. A Carl Loring. Some kind of Hollywood producer. He recognized the name. Fortunately, the parents were out of town on their own trip. He'd called the house out there and gotten their Mexican maid. His expression showed disdain. He'd barely been able to understand her, but he'd finally been able to learn that the Lorings wouldn't be back in L.A. till the following night. So......., if he worked fast"

# FORTY

Five-thirty in the afternoon. Traffic heavy, but moving. Beverly Hills was northeast of the airport, but she actually had to travel in a northwesterly direction for six miles or so on 405 before taking Santa Monica Boulevard and heading east. Off to her left a huge vermilion sun hung suspended—poised for its end-of-day plunge into the Pacific.

Nothing changes. One of the reasons she'd wanted to get out of L.A. in the first place had been the urban sprawl. Oh sure, New York was the heart of one vast sprawl itself. Actually greater New York had more people than greater Los Angeles, but somehow you weren't as conscious of being surrounded by the enormous sweep of suburban insignificance that forced people in L.A. to feel like human specks moving across some enormous galactic surface.

In L.A. you felt more like a tiny island in the midst of a vast sprawl—probably because L.A. was so dependent on the automobile. In L.A. it seemed as if your whole life revolved around either your car, other peoples' cars, or the freeways. Not so in New York. It wasn't as if she weren't aware of the New York's defects. God knows, it had its share. But that feeling of vastness, of urban sprawl... Yes, sprawl was a good word for it. This is exactly the way it was the last time she was home. Still, it was familiar territory, and she was eager to see her parents. Hadn't seen them since Christmas. Almost a year.

They used to be such a close family, too—until she'd moved east. They were still close, of course. Talked on the phone at least twice a week. But she did miss being with them. Even now that she was practically home, she'd have to wait till tomorrow to see them. They were away on one of their frequent trips. They loved to travel. This time it was Italy. The South. They'd been to Rome and the northern cities before, but never below Rome. Anyway, they'd be home tomorrow afternoon—late. She couldn't wait. She would have been more excited about their trip, though, if her reason for coming home had been pure-and-simple homesickness. Unfortunately that was not the case. The real reason was fear. She now believed Tad had been killed because he'd seen the person who killed Andy Mack. When Tad had told her about seeing this person coming out of Mack's office, she'd pooh-poohed it, telling Tad that he was jumping to conclusions. Not about seeing the person, but about the person's clandestine visit being tantamount to being guilty of murder. Tad had stuck by his guns, though, and subsequent events proved he was right. Unfortunately. She was now convinced that Tad was not killed by some random burglar. Tad had seen the killer, and the killer would eventually figure out that she existed and that Tad had probably confided in her. She could be next. This was like a nightmare that you couldn't wake up from.

She had a key to the house. Once she got settled in, she'd have time to think about her next step. Who was she kidding? She'd already thought about it a 100 times before she left New York. She'd gone over it 200 more times on the plane. She only had three options as she saw it: Tell her folks? Call the New York police and tell them what she knew? Or tell the L.A. police and let them communicate with New York? She'd probably tell her parents first and get their opinion as to which of the other two choices made the most sense.

In the meantime she was glad to be back in Southern California. It had never looked so good. The weather today was exceptionally good. The air was clear. Much better than she'd remembered from her last visit. One of those rare days when there was enough breeze from the ocean to clear the L.A. basin and remind people of why they'd originally moved to Southern California in the first place. At LAX she'd rented a mid-size

American car from Avis. Not a bad car either. Must be true what they were saying about American cars. They were getting better. This one seemed fine. She'd enjoy it a lot more, she realized, if her mind weren't occupied with her own survival. If her parents had been home she wouldn't have rented the car. They would have picked her up. But this was fine. While she was in L.A.—and she had no idea how long that would be—she'd need a car.

She'd already taken the Santa Monica Boulevard exit. Traffic was no worse. Slightly better, if anything. Now a left onto Beverly Drive. This would take her north through Beverly Hills.

She'd forgotten how pretty this part of L.A. was. She didn't think of herself as a spoiled brat. It wasn't her fault she came from a well-off family. Not that it mattered to some of her friends who came from more modest backgrounds. She supposed one reason she'd gone to New York was to prove that she wasn't spoiled. That she could make it on her own. Beverly Drive at this point became Coldwater Canyon Drive. Not far ahead she'd take a right onto Mulholland.

That blue car has been in the mirror for quite awhile. This was an area she loved. The rolling hills that turned brown by mid-June. The stunning homes and exquisite views. The beautiful landscaping. The downside, of course, was the constant threat of brush fires—fires that could advance mercilessly through thousands of acres in a day, showing no more respect for a multimillion-dollar home than they did for a dry leaf.

She was on Mulholland now, admiring anew the neighborhood she'd taken for granted until recently. Not far from home now. Even though the house would be empty, she couldn't wait to get there. Funny, the blue car made the turn onto Mulholland. Wish he'd turn off—or pass. Oh well, she'd be home in five minutes. Road getting narrower now. Canyon on the right, and a pretty good drop on the left side of the road. That's what she liked about Mulholland, though. Right in the middle of this populated residential area, Mother Nature had a presence. A small presence, but still a presence. Good, the blue car is passing. Glad to see him go. Now he's abreast of the car. Looks just like the car she's in. "Hey! Watch what you're doing." The other car was inching closer to her car. She had to move to the right or he'd hit her. Wasn't even her car. All she needed now was to bring the rental car back with dents in it. She slowed the car, hoping the other car would go on by. He didn't. He, too, slowed down, keeping pace with her speed. Her right tires were now two feet onto the dusty shoulder of the road. "Hey, you jerk! Watch out." As she spoke the other driver held up his wallet with what looked like a shiny object in it. Looked like a badge. Yes, it was a badge. "Damn! A cop. Where's the uniform?" The driver of the other car pointed toward the side of the road, indicating she should pull over. "What the..." She hadn't been speeding. She hadn't gone through any lights. Well, that last stop sign... But she wasn't driving fast. And there was no traffic. Why doesn't he go after real criminals? The driver kept motioning towards the side of the road. He looked pretty serious. "What the hell." Better get this over with, she thought resignedly.

The roadway at this point had become a narrow isthmus with canyons on each side. Barely enough shoulder to allow for her car. And no guardrails either. The cop's car pulled to a stop behind her. Watching in her rearview mirror she saw his door open. He approached the left side of her car with that cocky deliberate gait that most traffic cops effect. He bent down and put his face to the window. "Afternoon ma'am."

"Afternoon, officer. I wasn't speeding. And I know I didn't come to a complete stop back at that sign, but..."

"That's not why I stopped you, young lady. Your brake lights don't work."

"Oh, I didn't know. Really, I didn't. This is a rental car. I just picked it up."

"I know that, ma'am. That's why I'm telling you about the problem. Maybe I can help you. Probably just a fuse. Should be under the dash there. Mind if I take a look?"

Already relieved that the officer seemed less intent on giving her a ticket and more inclined to help, she slid over to the right as the kindly officer got in and slammed the door shut. Oddly, though, he made no move to look for the fuse box.

"Now young lady, we've gotta talk. You see, I'm not a traffic cop. I'm an L.A.P.D. detective. We got a call from the New York City police asking us to give them a little help on a case they're working on."

Pam was beginning to feel uncomfortable. Something didn't quite ring true. "Then why did you say my brake lights were out? Why didn't you just come right out and tell me you were a detective?"

"Wasn't sure you'd cooperate, ma'am. Now let's get on with this. Won't take long."

"What do you want to know?"

"You were pretty tight with a young man back in New York named Szczepanski, right?"

"He was my boyfriend." Her eyes narrowed. "Why do you want to know?"

"It's possible he may have known something that would help us find his killer. Did he tell you anything that might be helpful to the New York police? Anything at all?"

"Yes... he did."

"Have you told anyone else what Szczepanski told you?"

"No, but..." As soon as she'd uttered the words she realized that, if this guy were not a cop, she'd made a serious mistake.

"That's good. Very good. Now tell me what he said to you."

She didn't like this guy at all. Something about him.... Still, he'd shown her his badge. She hadn't gotten a good look at it, though. How stupid. Could have been a cheap imitation. She should ask to see it now—up close. Mind racing now. What if it were a fake? What would he do to her then? Hit her over the head. Shoot her. Kill her because she knew he wasn't a cop? Don't overreact. But he might. Still, if the shield were real, she could relax.

In her few years on earth she'd already learned that one's worst fears were seldom realized. Far better to meet a problem head-on. She took a deep breath and proceeded to tell the man everything Tad had told her. The man listened attentively without interrupting. Near the end, he shifted in his seat and sat up straighter. She was just finishing her story, "...but Tad said he looked sort of guilty coming out of the office. Like he didn't want to be seen. Tad said he couldn't tell what the pictures were of....." The phoney policeman was not a sentimental man. But he was a father. He looked at the young lady sitting to his right—trembling with fear. She wasn't much older than his daughter. A shame. Kind of sad really. Still, he had no choice. He would try to make it quick. He feigned a serious, puzzled expression. "Hmmm. That is interesting, ma'am. Well, I want to thank you for your time. Maybe I can help you with your brake lights anyway. They really are out, you know. Show you how to change the fuse. Look down here." In desperation she grasped at the sudden display of kindness. She bent down, craning her neck to look where he was pointing. He continued helpfully, "Under the dash. No, a little further...under the radio and behind. There you go. Perfect. She still didn't see anything.

The brilliant flash of white light was sudden, and became blackness just as suddenly. With it Pam

Loring's fears disappeared—along with her hopes. He'd timed the blow perfectly. He'd wanted the blow to be either on the top of the head or the front. From where he sat behind the steering wheel, the best he could manage was a blow just above the occipital lobe. He hit her again—just to be sure. It wasn't necessary.

# FORTY-ONE

The uniformed cop stood waiting for Flynn to get off the phone. Dawson was explaining to his ex-wife, as patiently as he could, why his refusal to act as a stud was not an indication that he didn't care about her life. "Julie, will you please listen for a minute. Why can't you see that I'm not the only guy who would hesitate at what you're asking? I do care about you, but I'm not going to do this. If I'm gonna be a father, I'm gonna be a father. I'm gonna see my kid every day. No, no, no. You wouldn't. You say that, but you wouldn't. Look, Julie, you've never been good at anticipating what's gonna happen next. You think you'll let me, but you won't. Okay, so what happens if you remarry. Look, you say that now, but you might. My guess is you will. I'm sorry, but the answer is no. I gotta go now." He looked up at the uniformed officer waiting patiently and held up his hands, palms upward. "I'm sorry, Julie but I have to go now. We'll talk. Bye." He looked expectantly at the cop.

"There's a lawyer here wants to see you or detective Pappas," said the officer. "Says he represents a Carson Williamson. Got a whole entourage with him. A private dick and coupla scruffy types. Look like street people. Wanna see 'em?"

"Yeah, Ernie. We got a room I can use?"

"Interrogation two, next to the lieutenant's office is free. I'll bring 'em in there."

Flynn waited until the quartet had filed into the interrogation room. As he opened the door he found himself facing three men and a little girl, a child he estimated to be no more than eight years of age. One of the men—Flynn estimated to be about thirty-five or forty—was dirty and dressed in shabby, threadbare clothes. It appeared that he was the father of the little girl. A second man of about the same age was better dressed. The third man was immaculately fitted out in what was clearly an expensive navy blue suit. The man carried himself with an elegant assurance that made his identity an easy guess for Flynn. "You Carson Williamson's attorney?" asked Dawson.

"Yes. Tillson. Bradford Tillson. This is Wayne Davis, a private investigator who works for me, and this is Robert Spicer and his daughter, Emily. I believe we have evidence here that can exonerate Mr. Williamson. I hope you can spare us a few moments, detective Flynn?" Tillson asked the question in a way that suggested that he clearly expected the detective could.

"Yeah, sure. Coffee?"

"Thank you, I don't think that will be necessary...unless." He turned to the others. Davis nodded his head no. Emily said nothing. "I'll have a cup," said Spicer. "Regular." Flynn opened the door and yelled out, "Hey Ernie, can you bring us a cup of coffee? Regular. And ask detective Pappas to join us when she comes in. Thanks, Ernie."

Minutes later, Gwen arrived and was introduced. Robert Spicer slurped his coffee contentedly.

"May I begin?" asked Tillson.

Flynn looked at Gwen, "Sure, go ahead."

The lawyer looked first at Gwen and then at Dawson, "When the two of you questioned my client in his office a week ago, he told you that he had an alibi for the time when Andrew Mack was killed. He told you that he was on his way in to work and that he had given some money, to wit, ten dollars, to a homeless man and his daughter. The problem in verifying this at the time and subsequent to that time has been that the man and his daughter could not be located. We're here today to tell you that they have been found. Mr. Spicer and his daughter are those people."

"So far so good, Mr. Tillson," said Gwen. "As I recall, Mr. Williamson claimed that the two homeless people were on the sidewalk on Park Avenue between 46th and 47th. Mr. Spicer, were you and your daughter at that location on the date in question?"

Spicer looked up from his half-finished coffee. "What?" He seemed distant.

"Can you tell what block you and your daughter were on the morning Mr. Williamson says he saw you?"

"Park Avenue between 46th and 47th Street. Like he says."

"You're sure of that?"

"Yep."

"How do you know that, Mr. Spicer?" Flynn kept his voice as unintimidating as possible. "What I mean is, how do you know you were there and not some other place on that specific day?"

"Cause it was a Wednesday, and we hung out on that block every Wednesday."

"You weren't there yesterday, or last Wednesday, either," said Gwen. We've checked.

"I know it. We haven't been there in two weeks. Now we spend Wednesdays on the corner of Madison and 49th. In our situation, you have to change your locations pretty often. After a while people get tired of seeing you. And when they get tired of seeing you they stop giving you money. You know what I'm saying?"

"Yeah, we hear you," said Flynn. How can you be so sure you were there the day Mr. Williamson says you were?"

"Because we were there every Wednesday for two months. That's about as long as you want to hang out in one spot before you move on. We never missed during those two months. We'll probably stay at the Mad Av spot for another two months unless we don't get enough. Some locations are much better'n others. You have to try them out. Sort of market research, if you know what I'm saying. Mondays we hung out on

Fifth Avenue between 51st and 52nd. That's the west side of Fifth. Tuesday we hung out across the avenue. Wednesdays we were on Park between 46th and 47th, like I told you. Thursdays we ..."

"Okay," smiled Gwen, "we get the picture. Mr. Spicer, how long have you and your daughter been living on the street?"

"Almost two years now," he looked down as he responded.

"Do you mind if I ask you how you ended up there? You don't have to answer."

"I lost my job almost four years ago. My wife couldn't handle it. Oh, she tried for a while, but she likes the good life. Hell, she wasn't that happy before I was laid off. After about six months, she left us. Never even tried to contact us after that. I did odd jobs while I sent out my resume, but...nothing. I don't sell myself too well, case you hadn't noticed."

"What kind of work did you do, Mr. Spicer?" asked Gwen.

"I was a programmer. Worked for this hi-tech outfit on the Island. With the crummy economy we had a few years ago, they got in trouble and had to lay a lotta people off. I was one of the lucky ones."

"So after your wife left you, what happened then?" asked Gwen.

"One day I got a letter from the bank saying they were gonna put the house up for sale—since I hadn't made my mortgage payments in months."

"Didn't they give you a chance to pay up the money you owed?"

"Yeah, but I didn't have anything left. My wife had cleaned out our joint accounts. The little I got from odd jobs just kept food on the table and gas in the car. So here we are. The American dream fulfilled. Look, I can't blame my wife entirely. I'm not a very aggressive guy. Most guys in my situation would have come up with a job. Now that we're out here on the street..."

Robert Spicer looked down at himself and then at his daughter. "now that we're on the street, I'll never get a job. Who'd even interview me now?"

Gwen turned to the others in the room as if to say, here's a well-spoken, intelligent person, a person more or less like any one of us. Can't we do something to help these people? Anything?

Certainly one good thing would come out of all this, she thought. Robert Spicer's credibility would be excellent. Homeless he and his daughter might be, she thought, but his mental ability was unimpaired. He was not some rambling drunk or some babbling druggie, or worse yet from the standpoint of credibility, some pitiful psychotic prematurely released from one of New York State's institutions to satisfy the cost-cutting promises of some politician. No, Robert Spicer was credible, and thanks to his servitude to the freedom of the streets, Carson Williamson would gain true freedom.

Tillson beamed, "Satisfied, detectives?"

Dawson turned to Gwen, "I am. How 'bout you?"

"I am."


It had not been hard to convince Maggie Muñoz that Williamson should be released. Oh, she gave them a hard time at first. Made sure they ate a little crow, and made it a point to remind Gwen and Dawson that she'd been reluctant to arrest the publishing executive in the first place. When it came right down to it, her only reason for hesitating to dismiss charges against Williamson had been that dismissal was tantamount to admitting she'd made a mistake in calling for his arrest in the first place. She accused Flynn and Pappas of sloppy police work, impeding her career advancement, and whatever else she could think of, but ultimately the facts forced her to recommend dismissal. The D.A.

concurred and within 24 hours a judge had ordered that all charges against Williamson be dropped.

# FORTY-TWO

"Mr. Williamson, I have good news for you." The aristocratic face of Bradford B. Tillson beamed as he spoke to his client. The expression of incredulity that greeted his words told Tillson that Carr Williamson needed convincing. "I told you when we first met that we had chance. Well, one of my freelance investigators finally tracked down your homeless man and his young daughter. They've both confirmed your story, that is, that you gave them a ten dollar bill the morning that Andrew Mack was killed." The stress lines in Williamson's face seemed to soften, and his eyes turned moist with emotion.

"This is the best news I've had in weeks. Thank God."

"You can also thank my investigator for his persistence. He's damned good."

Then, because it seemed too good to be true, and he didn't want to lose the two people who could corroborate his alibi, Williamson, concern in his voice, asked, "Do the police know about this yet? Have they spoken to the police?"

"As soon as my investigator found them he called me, and I told him to meet me at the precinct—with the man and his daughter. At first they were afraid to go to the police station—most of the homeless are reluctant to have anything to do with the authorities, if they can help it. But my man is good, as I told you. He's a very sensitive person, considering the nature of his work, and he can be very persuasive." Tillson smiled, "I mean that in the very best sense. He convinced them that they could save an innocent man, a man, incidentally, who had been nice to them. This hit home, and they finally agreed to go with him. Fortunately he didn't have to use money to persuade them. Makes their testimony all the more convincing."

Initially Williamson was elated, feeling a great burden lifted from his shoulders. The exhilaration, though, quickly dissipated as he considered what kind of freedom he would be returning to. No longer was he CEO of Harmon Hall. Oh, he could demand some recompense from Howard, but the venerable chairman of the parent company was not going to risk further chaos at Harmon Hall by firing Stuart Markham after just promoting him. Reinstatement was out of the question. He was pretty sure of that. Howard would justify the status quo by pointing out that regrettably, he, Carson Williamson, was too controversial just now to run Harmon Hall. Howard would feel badly about the situation, but he was too much of a pragmatist to let sentiment get in the way of good business.

And what else could he, Carson Williamson, look forward to? Living happily ever after with Laura? That remained to be seen. He'd told her about Kate, and admitted it was a mistake—his pathetic version of the now tiresome midlife crisis excuse for infidelity. She'd been hurt. Badly hurt. Yet even in her pain she'd been more loyal to him than he'd been to her.

Obviously Kate was out of the question. He'd thought he'd loved her. He still found her attractive, interesting. But it had been wrong. What bothered him now was the why. Why did he come to the right conclusion? What brought him to his senses? Was it simply because he finally realized Laura was everything she'd always been, and that was plenty? Or was it that in the desperate straits he'd found himself lately, his sense of order required that he shed complications? Or perhaps did the stress and adversity he'd found himself in somehow subconsciously lead him to the conclusion that he'd better show his best side to the world. Did he somehow unconsciously see that he couldn't afford any more controversy or enemies if he had any hope of surviving? Was he just being "political?" He didn't think so.

When the two detectives met with him, they told him what he'd already learned from Tillson—that he'd been exonerated by the Spicers. The detectives had been apologetic, if not contrite, about having arrested him erroneously. He'd accepted their apologies halfheartedly. They'd as much as said that they now believed Stuart Markham was the real killer. Asked him if he had any reason to believe Markham would want to kill Mack? Anything he hadn't already told them. He'd told them that he'd never liked or trusted the new CEO, but that they already knew that. He reminded them that Markham had resented it when he, Williamson, had been named president. He'd definitely gotten the impression that the two detectives were convinced Markham was behind all the killings. He'd also gotten the impression that they were reluctant to move ahead with an arrest for fear they'd screw up again. Not a very comforting thought. As long as the real killer remained at large most people would still wonder whether he, Williamson, really was guilty.

## FORTY-THREE

"Damn!" Flynn looked up from his coffee. They were in a coffee shop on Third Avenue. "We got nothing, Gwen. Nothing. Williamson's home free, and rightly so. Man, did we screw up on this one."

"We didn't really mess up on Williamson, Dawson. We followed the evidence. As things developed, we learned we'd gotten ambiguous and misleading clues. We fixed it as best we could. Nobody would've done any better."

"I'd like to believe that. Small comfort to Williamson who lost his job and maybe his family."

"Hey, if he loses his family, don't hang that on us. He screwed up— literally and figuratively."

"Okay, so we can sleep nights. Funny thing is, we don't have a killer, and Stuart Markham, our best prospect, has now got Williamson's job. We've got shit for evidence. Every time we think we got something he gets rid of it."

"Has it occurred to you, Dawson, that the reason we can't pin anything on Markham is that one of our other suspects is the real killer? Maybe we should take another look at Paul Manwaring. Or Tony Marcantonio or Fern Mallory. Maybe even Jacqui Dyer? Do you remember how much anger there was in Jacqui Dyer?"

"C'mon Gwen, do you think the love of my life could kill anyone?" Flynn smiled impishly.

"Probably not. But I think we should dig a little deeper anyway. And how about Marcantonio. Real macho type. Mack drove him crazy. Remember how embarrassed he was by the little pain in the ass. And some temper. Who knows how much anger or ego we're dealing with here?

"Maybe we've been way off base, and Manwaring's our guy? I mean everyone knows how violent a rejected lover can get? I'm gonna run a background check on these people, just in case there's anything there we might have missed."

It was a gray Friday morning in Westchester—the kind of day that promised only unpleasant choices. It was still September, and the temperature had dropped overnight to thirty-four degrees, an unusually cold temperature for this time of year. Wasserman appeared to be reading the *Times*, but his wife could tell that his mind was elsewhere. He'd been glued to the same page for ten minutes. She was sure his thoughts were about Carr Williamson. News of his exoneration had been on the ten o'clock news the night before. She pretended to busy herself with things in the kitchen, but she couldn't help but notice that her normally cheerful husband, was anything but happy this morning. Finally, folding the paper in his typically fastidious way. he swallowed the last of his coffee and started to get up. She decided she couldn't hold back any longer, "Are you going to contact him, Herb? He's your friend."

"Estelle, how can I? What do I say to him? I ratted on you to the police. Gave them evidence that may have helped to get you arrested?"

"Not evidence, information. You did what you thought was right."

"Evidence, information. Call it what you like. How do you think it looked to Carr?"

"You did what you thought was right, Herb. You did what you thought was right."

"You're not thinking, Estelle. How would we feel if the tables had been turned?"

"I understand, but how do you think he'll feel if you avoid him like the plague? You have to try."

*  *  *

Heather Barnes had known Kate Ferrara since their

days at Wellesley. They'd been roommates the last two years. Upon graduation Heather had hiked around Europe for a year with two other friends. Kate had been invited to join her, but she'd begged off. She was too anxious to get on with her career. So while Heather was in Europe, getting to know herself—and a number of young European men—better, Kate had gone on to law school. They'd both ended up in Manhattan—Kate as an attorney and Heather as an account executive for a medium-sized ad agency handling, at one time or another, everything from analgesics to computer software to Japanese auto imports. They'd both done well in their respective fields, and they'd made it a point to keep in touch, meeting for lunch or dinner six-to-eight times a year. Tonight it was dinner in SoHo, at Mezzogiorno. The young waiter-cum-actor had just brought their drinks to the table, leaving the menus to be considered at their leisure.

"So who's the latest love of your life, Kate?" Heather Barnes lifted a glass of excellent Clos-du-Bois chardonnay to her lips. "Last time I saw you, you said you were seeing this big corporate muckety-muck, but couldn't say who. Very mysterious I recall."

"God, where do I begin. You are behind. The last few months have taught me more about life, and maybe less about love, than my previous thirty-six years. Guess there's no harm in telling you now because it's over. You know what they say, Heather. Never date a client, because you'll get hurt. And never date a married man because you'll get burnt. Well I violated both rules. And I threw in an older man to boot. It was great while it lasted, but you won't believe how it ended." She proceeded to tell her friend about Carr and all that transpired at Harmon Hall. Heather was flabbergasted that Kate had been involved with everything she'd been seeing on TV and reading in the papers. She'd followed the news of the Harmon Hall killings, and she'd been aware that Williamson had been arrested and had lost his job as president and CEO.

"Come to think of it, the papers and TV did hint at Williamson being blackmailed about some affair he was having, but I don't remember your name ever coming up. I would have remembered that. And you know you would have heard from me if it had come up."

"Thank God, it didn't. Carr never went to trial, so the police never had to release any of the evidence. I'm sure if it had gone on much longer, though, the media would have gotten their clutches on something. There were pictures and everything. Taken by this creep, Mack. What a nightmare."

Heather Barnes looked compassionately at her friend for a moment or two. Then her expression changed, "So what did he say? That he didn't love you anymore?"

"You go for the details, don't you, my friend?" said Kate, shaking her head. "Oh what the hell. No, he told me that he still loved his wife, even though he didn't know for sure whether she still loved him... Oh, shit, Heather. He dumped me!"

# FORTY-FOUR

Maggie Muñoz ran her fingers through her hair. "Let me get this straight. What I'm hearing is that you've got another president of Harmon Hall you're thinking of arresting, only this time you've got even less evidence than you had the last time—and that one didn't stick. Is that essentially it, detectives? You got some sort of vendetta against successful people, or is this just part of some social engineering campaign to bring down the upper class?"

Gwen shook her head slowly, "Look, Maggie, I know how you must feel..."

"I don't think you do, detective. I don't think you do. In case you don't know it, the D.A.'s office is a very competitive place. They don't allow many mistakes. How do you think the D.A. classifies issuing an arrest warrant for murder for one of the top business executives in publishing? A man who just also happens to be a buddy of the mayor. You think that kind of screw-up is good for upward mobility?"

"We understand," said Flynn. "It hasn't been too good for our personnel file, either." He glanced sheepishly at his partner. "But, these things happen. Don't tell us it didn't look like a good arrest to you when you authorized it, Maggie. I know you wouldn't of gone for it unless it made sense to you."

"Okay, okay, so we all fucked up. But I gotta tell you, you got nothin' to justify an arrest of this Markham guy. I mean, what've you got? A motive. Maybe. But how are you gonna prove it, and how're you going to prove Markham killed Mack in order to make Williamson look like the killer? I'll grant you that maybe he did do it, but I don't expect Markham to fess up on that. Do you?"

"No, but..." Gwen didn't get a chance to finish her words.

"But nothing, detective. Why the hell should he

confess to that? I doubt very much if we're ever gonna find witnesses to his innermost thinking."

"Look, Maggie," said Flynn, "we're almost certain Markham arranged for the killing of Tad Szczepanski. Mickey D was right on the verge of telling us that. I know he didn't get the words out but..."

"Come on, detective. You're telling me that you know what this sleaze was gonna say before he was run down by a hit-and-run driver? Amazing. Simply amazing. You must be psychic."

"Cute. Very cute. Hey, Maggie, aren't we on the same side here?" pressed Dawson.

"We are, detective, but you've gotta give me hard evidence; not educated guesses. C'mon, don't you see that?"

"Okay," said Gwen, "we think—you'll pardon my use of the word *think*." Muñoz frowned, but kept silent. Gwen continued, "We think that Szczepanski's girlfriend may have known that Markham was involved. She's disappeared. Hasn't been seen since Szczepanski's murder. It's a good bet that she went to her parents' place out in L.A. We've got the authorities out there checking into it now. If it turns out that she can and will testify that Markham was involved, is that enough for an indictment, Maggie?"

"Could be. I'll have to hear what she has to say first. I'll give you a tentative maybe on that one."


Two hours later Dawson Flynn received a phone call from detective James Sanchez of the L.A.P.D. "Detective Flynn, I'm afraid I've got bad news for you. That girl you asked us to check on...Pam Loring."

Flynn took a deep breath and closed his eyes, "Yeah, what've you got, detective?"

"She died yesterday in a suspicious car incident. Either deliberate murder or a freak hit-and-run."

"What happened?"

"She was driving this rental car and went off an embankment up on Mulholland Drive. Kind of a treacherous spot, but I don't remember many accidents at that location in the twelve years I've been on the force. Not that bad if you don't speed. Everyone around here knows it's dangerous, so they go pretty slow.

"So why do you say it was a suspicious incident?"

"We've got a witness who says it looked like she was pushed off the road... by a car just like the one she was driving. Witness claims this car pushed her car until it went down an embankment. Medical examiner said it looked very much like one blow to the head was made by a blunt object, almost as if it happened before the car went over the side. Way I see it, even if she wasn't deliberately hit on the head, the whole thing is still pretty fishy because the second driver took off."

"You didn't get the second car I take it?"

"No, took off like a bat outta hell according to the witness."

"Doesn't sound like an accident," said Flynn. "You said the missing car looked just like the rental car the Loring girl was driving?"

"Yes. And I know what you're thinking. That it, too, could be a rental. We've already checked all area rental car agencies for the names and addresses of drivers who rented cars like that."

"What'd you come up with, detective?"

"Two people from Seattle. One from L.A. One from Denver. One from Tokyo. And one from New Jersey. I can fax you the list."

The first five names on the list all checked out. The sixth name was for a Martin Smith of Maplewood, New Jersey. A check of the phone company revealed no Martin Smith listed for the address given. A check with the local police revealed what Flynn already feared—that there was no such address in Maplewood.

"Whoever was driving that car, Gwen, was probably the same guy who was driving the car that killed Mickey D right here in little ol' New York. The sonofabitch behind this is slick. Must of had a phoney driver's license. We're dealing with a pro. Damn! That was our last lead."

"Dawson, if that was our last lead, Markham gets away scot-free. He not only saves his ass, he gets the big job he went after, and eliminates Williamson as his competition. The guy made a mockery of the system, and is probably laughing all the way to the bank right now. Damn!"

"At least we got Williamson off."

"That's the least we could do. Hell, we're the ones who screwed up in the first place."

"There has to be something we overlooked, Gwen. The thought of that arrogant bastard living like a king when he's killed or arranged for the killing of four people gets to me. I can't let this die."

"The system will force us to let it die. The D.A.'s office won't go for spit without a hell of a lot more than we've got. And the lieutenant won't go out on a limb on this one—and for the same reason. And you can't blame them, Dawson. Look, we gave it our best shot."

# FORTY-FIVE

"Dawson, the stuff from Harriet Stahl just arrived. Remember, the personnel files, and who requested them. Maybe there's something there. By the way, you know those background checks we did on Dyer, Mallory, Marcantonio, and Manwaring?"

"Yeah?"

"I'm beginning to see some interesting patterns."

"Like what, for instance?"

"I'm waiting for two more documents. Should have them within the hour. When I get them and after I've had a chance to look at what just came over from Harriet Stahl, I'll go over what I have with you."

"Gotta hand it to you, Gwen. You don't discourage easily. Frankly, I think you're wastin' your time."

"We can't just quit on this, Dawson."

"Gwen, we've worked our asses off on this case. You've been around long enough to know that you don't win 'em all. Sometimes it's better to cut your losses and move on to the next one. In my opinion, this is one of those times. We got other cases piling up, you know."

"Dawson, you're talking like this is some kind of game, and we're just keeping score. Look we know we're close to breaking this case. Just because we're dealing with a killer who happens to be a lot smarter than the usual murderer doesn't mean we can't nail him."

"Or her," grinned Flynn.

"I think we both know it's a him."


Williamson picked up the receiver on the second ring.

"Mr. Williamson, this is Gwen Pappas, I'm one of the detectives..."

"I know who you are. What do you want?"

"Detective Flynn and I have some information that we think you'll find interesting. It's good news, and frankly we wanted to share it with you because we both feel pretty bad about all you've been through."

"Tell me what it is, detective," said Williamson trying not to sound too icy.

"When we were investigating the death of one of your editors at Harmon Hall, a fellow by the name of Tad Szczepanski, the trail led to an underworld character by the name of Mickey D. Mickey D was a known contract man, and we almost got him to talk about who hired him when he himself was killed by a hit-and-run driver."

"I remember. I followed events back then pretty carefully, as you can imagine. When your Mickey D died, so did my chances of going free. Or so I thought at the time."

"Well sir, we had other leads at the time, but each one of them seemed to be eliminated just as we got close. Whoever killed Mickey D and Andrew Mack seemed to be able to stay one step ahead of us."

"Yes, I've noticed. You still haven't made any arrest since you pulled me in almost two weeks ago."

"That's what I'm trying to tell you. We're going to make an arrest soon, and Detective Flynn and I wanted you to know about it in advance. I'm violating department procedure by telling you this, but we really feel we owe you one."

"All right, detective, tell me who you're going to arrest?"

"I'm afraid we can't tell you that, though. However, you'll know soon enough."

"Detective, maybe you *can* you tell me one thing?"

"What's that?"

"If all your leads disappeared, how come you're able to make an arrest now?"

"Frankly, things started to break all at once. Some of the background checks we've been doing turned out to be pretty productive. And, get this. It turns out that our friend Mickey D never died in that hit-and-run. Somebody died, but it wasn't Mickey D. The only people who could identify the body were this bartender over on Tenth Avenue and a paid informer we used to use. We found out that they were both paid by Mickey D to I.D. another low-life character in the area that Mickey D was willing to sacrifice in order to make us think he was killed in the hit-and-run. Apparently this unfortunate deceased knew enough about Mickey's arranging of the Szczepanski killing to make his demise doubly convenient. Got rid of a possible leak and took the heat off Mickey D. I won't bother you with the details, Mr. Williamson, but somebody else let the cat out of the bag. We learned about it from one of our paid informants, and we found Mickey D. He's been singing ever since. For a pro, our Mr. D had awfully loose lips once he knew we had him. Anyway, the person we're going to arrest hired him to handle the killing of Tad Szczepanski."

Less than two hours later, in the Harmon Hall Building, Tony Marcantonio walked toward his boss's office, his mind spinning. He walked with a purpose. He tried hard to keep his pace moderate and deliberate. He felt a little like a kid just before opening his Christmas presents. Or was it more like a kernel of corn just before it popped. Or more accurately still—exploded? Got to keep the emotional temperature down. Too close now to blow it.

He'd never liked Markham, but he did respect his abilities. And now that the man was secure in the presidency, his own fortunes would take a turn for the better. Very likely that's why he was being summoned to Stuart's office now. No doubt Stuart was about to tell him that he'd been promoted to the position of editor-in-chief, the position he, Markham, had vacated just a few short days ago.

As Marcantonio entered the office he noticed that Markham was not sitting behind his desk. "Over here," said the familiar, albeit offensive, voice. Tony craned his neck to the right and found his boss sitting over on the far side of the spacious office in his tastefully understated couch, behind his understatedly elegant coffee table. The new CEO was bending over a framed painting. Tony noted that it was the valuable, but garish Rauschenberg that normally hung just to the left of the hideous and even more valuable Jackson Pollock.

"What's the matter, Stuart? Cleaning staff didn't show up last night?"

"No, no. Nothing like that, Tony." As usual, Stuart failed to acknowledge humor, "When I came in this morning," he continued, "I noticed that this picture was askew. I went to straighten it—I can't stand it when paintings aren't straight." He grimaced, "As I started to straighten it, it fell right into my hands. The wire on the back came loose. Well, I can attend to this later. Let's get down to our business. Come, sit over here and be comfortable."

Uh oh, Tony didn't like the sound of this. It wasn't like Stuart to worry about the comfort of those he summoned. This is not the good news he'd expected. Markham moved from the couch to a nearby easy chair, pointing as he did so to the couch. When Tony had settled himself, he looked up at Markham, "What's on your mind, Stuart?"

When Gwen came running in, Flynn was on the phone pursuing a lead on a suspect in a liquor store killing that had taken place over the weekend on the west side. Gwen poked her head in front of him, frantically waving her hands to get his attention. He motioned that he'd be off in just a minute, but she kept gesticulating, clearly not satisfied with waiting. With an annoyed look, he excused himself, and, holding his hand over the phone, said testily, "What the hell is it that it can't wait two minutes?"

"We've gotta get over to Harmon Hall, and fast. Our killer may strike again. I'll explain to you in the car."

# FORTY-SIX

Markham peered at Marcantonio over the reading glasses perched halfway down his aquiline nose, "Tony, I've made a decision about who's going to replace me as editor-in-chief. And let me tell you, it hasn't been easy."

"I was sort of hoping it would be easy, Stuart."

"Yes, yes, I know you've wanted the job, and you do have most of the qualifications for it." *Except that you're not very bright, and you're a loose cannon of the worst order. Other than that you're perfect, Tony.* "As I deliberated, I weighed your qualifications carefully, and I matched them up against what I see as the editorial needs of this company."

"Yes, Stuart?..." urged Marcantonio anxiously. He could feel the blood rushing to his neck. He felt flushed and ready to burst. *Get to the goddam point, Stuart. Get to the point.*

"This, I realize, is a rather circuitous way of explaining to you that I finally decided to go outside to fill the job." Markham gazed out the window aloofly as he droned on, totally oblivious of the effect he was having on Marcantonio. "I'm delighted to say that I was able to recruit Jordan Blair away from S & R. A real coup, don't you think? He was ready for a change anyway. You know what they say about S & R. A good place to start a career and a good place to get experience, but certainly no place you'd want to stay. So the timing was perf..." His eyes came back to Marcantonio and casually homed in on the man's florid, distorted features. He suddenly realized that Tony wasn't taking the news well at all. He looked as if he were about to explode.

It finally dawned on Markham that he'd best try to calm Marcantonio down a bit. "Now, Tony, I hope you realize that I think the world of you, and..."

CRASH! The sound was deafening. Tony

Marcantonio had just slammed his fist down in the middle of Markham's beloved—and extremely valuable—Rauschenberg, leaving an indentation the size and shape of his rather large fist.

The color drained from Markham's face, "My God, Tony, look what you've done, man! That painting's worth over a million dollars. I could kill you for what you've done."

"No you couldn't, Stuart. You're a bastard, but you don't have the guts to kill." Tony Marcantonio had come unglued. His features had morphed into a mask of madness that made Markham recoil in horror. Tony stood menacingly—looming over Markham like a terrible, dark presence. "That job should be mine, Stuart. It should be mine. You owe me. You owe me," he shrieked. "You wouldn't be president if it weren't for me!"

Markham pulled back from the looming editor, regaining enough presence to reply weakly, "What do you mean, I wouldn't be president if it weren't for you? You're insane, Tony. You need help."

"No, Stuart it's you who needs help. You needed help to become president, and you need help now. How the hell do you think you became president anyway?" Marcantonio's eyes emitted a frightening otherworldly iridescence. "If I hadn't gotten rid of that annoying little queer, Andy Mack, and if I hadn't set it up so that it looked like Williamson was the one who did it, do you think you'd be president today?"

"You what?" Markham's eyes widened in disbelief. "You're not saying...?"

"Yes, Stuart, that's exactly what I'm saying," His voice had taken on a strange, unreal quality. "I killed Andy Mack, and I made it look like Williamson did it. I did it so that you'd become president, Stuart, and appoint me to replace you as editor-in-chief. And this is the thanks I get." The tendons in his neck stood out like the roots of a giant oak. "How in the name of

Christ could you go outside—after all my years of loyalty? Of covering for you? I can't believe you did this." His eyes flashed wildly.

As appalled as Markham was to see Marcantonio lose control of himself, he was at heart an opportunist. And for a moment his opportunistic side came to the fore, overcoming even his sense of self preservation, for he sensed the possibility of feathering his own nest. Or more accurately, preserving it. His inclination was to conspire with Marcantonio to preserve their shared secret, thus maintaining his own job as president and CEO. But then his racing mind recalled that Williamson had just a few days earlier been exonerated, so he immediately gave up the idea. Instead, he seized on the only option left to him. "Tony, this is unbelievable. You've got to turn yourself in."

Marcantonio stared at him, as if trying to decide what to do next. Markham, knowing he was dealing with an unstable man, and never comfortable with a void in the conversation, became uncharacteristically nervous. "You're insane, Tony, you're out of your mind." This was not the thing to say to Tony.

Marcantonio's eyes flashed crazily, but his words came out ominously quiet, "No, Stuart, I've never seen things more clearly."

Markham continued on his reckless course, "Not true, Tony, or you'd realize that I'd never have considered you for the job. Never in a million years. If I had, I'd be the lunatic." He knew the moment he said it that he'd allowed hubris to dominate his better judgment.

Tony's already deranged psyche snapped. His face reddened. The veins in his neck pulsated, and the tendons looked as if they were going to snap. His athletic body lunged toward his boss. He clasped his ham-like hands around the other man's thin neck and began exerting viselike pressure on his windpipe, his strong thumbs doing most of the work. Markham flailed his arms wildly; then grasped ineffectually at his attacker's wrists. It was futile. Marcantonio was too strong.

Stuart Markham could feel himself losing consciousness.

# FORTY-SEVEN

"Is he in there?" yelled Flynn.

"Yes, but..."

"Is Marcantonio with him?"

"Yes."

"Have you heard anything?"

"Yes, it sounds like they're arguing, but you can't just barge in there." Cathy rose from her chair and moved toward the closed door that led into Markham's office—somehow hoping to protect her boss from the unannounced incursion of the two detectives. Flynn and Pappas brushed past her and on into the office. They sized up the situation immediately, and Flynn raced to the two struggling figures. Marcantonio was so caught up in his demented rage that he was totally unaware of the two detectives. Flynn was stronger than the average man, but it wasn't easy for him to pry Marcantonio's powerful hands away from Markham's neck. Gwen quickly pulled out her nine-millimeter service pistol and, as Flynn finally wrested one of Marcantonio's hands away from Markham's neck, rammed the muzzle into the crazed man's back, "Freeze or I'll shoot."

Marcantonio didn't respond, and Gwen agonized over whether to pull the trigger. She'd never shot anyone before.

Then Marcantonio's body went limp. Apparently something finally registered. The hand that was still clutching Markham's neck dropped loosely to his side. He stood silently, as if having just awakened from an hypnotic trance.

Markham bent over forward, clutching at his throat, gasping for breath, making strange clucking, sucking sounds. Gwen leaned down to talk to him, "Are you all right, sir? Can you breathe?"

He continued panting, trying to catch his

breath, "I think so," he gasped. "Don't let that maniac near me."

"We've got him. Just take it easy. We've got him."

\* \* \*

"That's ridiculous," said Marcantonio. "I'm an editor; not a killer."

"Look, you already admitted to Mr. Markham that you killed these people. How can you deny it now?"

"You're not going to believe that bastard, are you? He'd lie about his own mother."

"Okay, so you want to play it that way. You said you don't need an attorney. Sure you don't want to change your mind?"

Marcantonio responded defiantly, "I said, I don't need a lawyer."

Flynn tilted his chair back, opened the door and yelled out, "Angelo, bring him in now, will ya."

A uniformed officer with a prominent paunch hanging over his belt entered the crowded interrogation room, gently pushing a middle-aged man with a receding mane of slick black hair. The man's exophthalmic eyes darted from one face to the next, as if searching for someone familiar, someone who could get him out the mess he found himself in. "Ladies and gentlemen," said Angelo, "this is Michael DiSalvo, better known to certain elements on the street as Mickey D."

Flynn tried to contain a smile, "Thanks Angelo. Sit down Mickey. No, not here. Over there. No there. Good. That's good. Now, let's get started. Tony Marcantonio, Mickey D. Mickey D, Tony Marcantonio. I realize the introductions are unnecessary. Mickey, would you tell the nice folks here who hired you to do in Tad Szczepanski?"

"He did." DiSalvo pointed in the direction of Marcantonio. Marcantonio tanned features blanched as the contract agent spoke.

"He's lying. I don't even know him."

"Please be quiet, Mr. Marcantonio." Flynn continued, directing his attention to DiSalvo, "Please describe the arrangement Mr. Marcantonio made with you?"

"Somehow he got my name." DiSalvo smirked cynically. "Mr. Clean has some interesting connections. He tells me he needs to get rid of somebody works at his company. Guy named Szczepanski. Doesn't care how so long's it takes place away from the Harmon Hall Building and so long's it looks like it was an accident—or part of a robbery. I say, can do. But it'll cost. How much, he says. I tell him fifteen grand. He says, okay, but it's gotta happen soon, like within 48 hours. I says that'll cost you twenty. He says, okay. Doesn't even haggle. I then ask him where this Szczepanski lives. He gives me an address over in Fort Lee."

"This is bullshit," erupted Marcantonio. "I don't know what motive this guy has for saying this, but he's lying."

"He's already confessed to hiring LeRoy Rivers to kill Tad Szczepanski," said Gwen. "Since he's already confessed to this, I tend to believe him when he tells me that you hired him to do the killing."

"So he admits arranging a hit. What's that got to do with me? You're taking this guy's word against mine?"

"In this case, I am. Where's he gonna get your name unless you contact him?"

"I never saw this guy before in my life."

At this, Mickey D rose from his seat and lunged at the dejected publishing executive. "Why you no good sonofabitch!"

"Hey," exploded Marcantonio, "somebody get this guy off me." Dawson and Gwen made a move toward the manic Mickey D, Angelo burst through the door to help. DiSalvo was quickly pulled off Marcantonio, who brushed himself off vigorously—as if he'd just been attacked by a swarm of roaches.

Dawson put his face in front of DiSalvo's, "All right, Mickey, my man, can you control yourself now?"

"Yeah, get on with it. But keep that lying bastard away from me."

Flynn looked at Marcantonio. "Who's Pam Loring?"

"I have no idea."

"Where were you last Wednesday, Mr. Marcantonio?"

"Probably in my office. Why?"

"We have evidence that you flew to Los Angeles that day. American Airlines verifies this. Are you sure you were in your office?"

Marcantonio swallowed, "That's right. I had to fly to L.A. I'd forgotten for a moment. So what?"

"According to American, you returned from L.A. that same night—on the red-eye. Is that correct?"

"Yes."

"Why would you fly out and back on the same day?"

"I...uh...had to meet with someone. But I couldn't afford the time to stay out there. Was a rush meeting."

"Please tell us who your meeting was with, Mr. Marcantonio. And where you met."

"Look, why are you asking me all these questions? What difference does it make who I met with?" Tony Marcantonio was desperately trying to come up with something plausible.

"Just answer the questions, please."

"His name has slipped my mind. And, as it turned out, he never showed up. I just turned around and came back. I can't tell you how annoyed I was." Marcantonio was beginning to sweat. Why hadn't he anticipated this?

"That has got to be about the lamest answer I've ever heard," barked Flynn in Marcantonio's face. "I'll tell you why you flew out and back in one day. You flew out to kill Pam Loring before she could talk. Before she could tell someone that her boyfriend, Tad Szczepanski, had seen you snooping around Andy Mack's office. That's why you flew to L.A., isn't it Tony. Isn't it?"

"No," screamed Marcantonio. "No, no, no. That's not true."

"Then maybe you can explain the car you rented—from the same place Ms Loring rented her car? And how it has dirt on the tires and undercarriage that matches the dirt on her car. That dirt comes from Mulholland Drive, where you killed her and forced her car off the road into a ravine. As a matter of fact, while you're at it, maybe you can explain why you requisitioned the personnel file on Tad Szczepanski just before he was murdered in his Fort Lee apartment. Could it be that you needed his address to give to Mickey here?"

The benighted editorial director was perspiring. "I...would like to call my attorney."

It took over an hour for his attorney to make it to the precinct station. Within an hour of his arrival all the bluster had gone out of Tony Marcantonio, and the attorney was talking about a plea bargain.

\* \* \*

Gwen pulled the sheet up over her breasts. She was leaning against two down pillows propped up against the headboard, holding a glass of white wine. She allowed a trace of a smile as she leaned over and planted a kiss on Flynn's cheek. "This was probably not a good idea, Dawson."

He grinned back at her, "It's not exactly

regulation, but it seemed pretty good to me."

"Me too. But Melissa's not going to be too happy."

"I uh...slightly exaggerated my relationship with Melissa."

"You mean you're not seeing her?"

"Uh, not exactly. Let's just say that things are not great between us."

They'd gone back to her apartment after wrapping up most of the paperwork. Marcantonio was safely in a cell, and they'd gotten Markham to a hospital. They'd also arrested Walter Birchfield for obstruction of justice. To wit, withholding information on a homicide. The interrogation of Marcantonio had been easier than they'd expected. He'd been ready to unload. He hadn't held back much, as far as Gwen and Flynn could tell.

"We deserved a little R and R, Dawson. This was a pretty exhausting case. And a pretty bizarre one, too."

"Yeah, can you imagine the intrigue going on in this one company. I mean, to the outside world, Harmon Hall looks like the typical American capitalist success story. Go to college, work hard, and make money. But look what was goin' on behind the scenes, Gwen."

"Yeah, Williamson gets caught with his pants down—literally—and this little worm of a blackmailer, Andy Mack, extorts a big job and a big project out of him. Then two of Williamson's senior executives get wind of it. Markham snoops around Mack's office and finds these incriminating photos. Szczepanski catches him in the act of snooping and reports to Birchfield, who proceeds to blackmail Markham into giving him a big promotion. Birchfield then tells his buddy, Tony Marcantonio, what he's learned about Markham. Marcantonio sees his chance to move up to editor-in-chief, a position he'd never get as long as Markham

301

held it. And he knew that Markham wasn't going anywhere as long as Williamson was running the company. Hell, it doesn't get any sleazier than this, Dawson."

"Ain't it the truth. Still, it probably wouldn't have occurred to Marcantonio to kill Mack if Andy hadn't made such a pain in the ass of himself. He was so damned blatant about his new position and about how secure he was, that he constantly rubbed Tony's face in it—sometimes right in front of the staff. I mean, talk about 'In your face.' He made it very clear that Tony couldn't do anything about it. Practically thumbed his nose at him. That was the wrong thing to do to Marcantonio. There was probably no more macho guy in the whole company than he was. On top of that, he had this violent temper that erupted whenever he felt threatened. Which was just about any time someone disagreed with him. God, some of that stuff I got from Harriet Stahl in Human Resources said one time he punched a guy out at a convention. Some salesman from another company or something. Of course, before he killed Andy, he first snooped around his office—I guess he was looking for something, anything he could use as leverage against Mack. Apparently he didn't find anything, so he went for the permanent solution. Tony is one very sick puppy, Gwen."

"I hope to hell he doesn't get off with a year or two in some mental hospital and then get released because some soft-headed shrink says he's 'cured'. The man's a walking killing machine, Dawson. First he shoots Andy Mack; then he arranges through Mickey D for the murder of Tad Szczepanski. Then, to cover that homicide, he personally mows down the Mickey D look-alike. And finally he flies to California to take Pam Loring out of the picture. A busy, busy man. And a very dangerous one."

"He almost got away with it, too."

"Let's not forget the other sleaze in this cesspool."

"You mean Birchfield?"

"Yeah. I know he didn't kill anyone, but he encouraged both Marcantonio and Markham. He wasn't even sure which one was the killer."

"It didn't really matter to him, Gwen. He was blackmailing both of them. He pretended to know, and even though they both denied killing Andy Mack, neither of these bastards dared call his bluff because he had enough on the both of them to make them cooperate."

"Actually what Markham did wasn't so bad. Yes, he snooped in an employee's office, but it's not enough to let yourself be blackmailed over."

"That is unless you want to stay in the good graces of Howard Harmon, the man who can put you on top of the world."

"Well, the man had a guilty conscience, and he's an ambitious son of a bitch. From his standpoint it was easier to keep Birchfield quiet—and loyal—by simply giving him a promotion." Gwen looked over at Flynn. He seemed quiet.

"What's the matter?"

"I was just wondering where this is headed?"

"Where what's headed?"

"This. You, me, Gwen. I know, it's just R and R but..."

"You want it to lead to something?"

"Jeez, I don't know. It wouldn't be the first time I had a relationship that went nowhere."

"I'm not sure this is a relationship, Dawson. I mean..."

"Look, we've been working together for weeks now. I know you better in some ways than I know my ex. And this...this was pretty good...wasn't it?"

"Yeah, Dawson. It was pretty good."

# FORTY-EIGHT

The view hadn't changed in the intervening years.

A morning mist rose from the Seine, softening the outlines of the ancient Louvre off to their left and transfiguring the river and the Ile de la Cité further to the east into soft impressionistic images of the most beautiful city on earth. They stood near the stone rail in the middle of the Pont Royal, a bridge that was over 300 years old, and as they looked toward the east, they could just make out in the distance the tops of the two towers of Notre Dame, whose first stones had been laid in 1163. No, the view hadn't changed. Not in the last 22 years. Probably not too much in the last 800 years.

"Carr, the last time we were on this bridge we asked a Parisian to take our picture. Let's do it again."

He looked at her, feeling the same warm feeling he'd felt 22 years earlier, "Think we can find the same guy?"

Laura feigned a frown of exasperation and turned to look for a likely candidate. She approached a thin, well-dressed Gallic-looking man of about 35 as he walked toward them, "*Pardon, monsieur. Voudriez-vous prendre notre photo, s'il vous plait?*"

The man looked at her for several seconds before he responded, "*Certainement, madame. Mon plaisir.*" He grinned as he continued, "But I would have done it if you'd asked me in English, too."

"I guess I don't sound like a Parisian, do I?"

"No, but your French is good," said the man sincerely.

"Your English is amazing!"

"Thanks, I'm from Boston. Been here six months. My company sent me over. Great place."

Carr leaned back against the stone rail of the ancient bridge, laughing, "My wife picked you out of all the pedestrians on this bridge because you looked so much like a Parisian."

The bridge experience was typical of their first three days in Paris. One marvelous, happy moment after another. Mostly people experiences. As Carr had hoped, Paris had been rejuvenating.

The pale November sun finally broke through the mist, bringing with it a new hope, much like the hopes that people in this city had experienced a million times before—for this was the city of light. The city of dreams.

They smiled sheepishly at each other, each sensing that the other was probably thinking the same thing: that they were acting like a couple of love-struck kids. A nice feeling. A comfortable feeling. For Carr it was cleansing. For Laura, healing.

It had been his idea to come to Paris. This was where it had all begun for them. They both knew Paris. Knew it was a place where much of what's good survives. Despite, or perhaps because of, all that this great city had gone through, it was a place where love endured. Where love survives—just as Paris itself survives.

Carr reached out with his hands, and she accepted them, slowly drawing him closer. They kissed, at first tentatively, like the two young lovers they so resembled. Then, more passionately. After a moment, Carr pulled back a bit and looked into her eyes. They were moist as she spoke, "You really were a bastard. You know that, don't you?"

"I know that. I know you're a saint for taking me back."

"Maybe I am, or maybe I just know and love the real you. You may be a bastard," she said as she looked out over the Seine, but you're my very special bastard."

"I guess that's a compliment."

She smiled impishly, "I guess it is."

"I didn't feel as if I had many redeeming

qualities when I was sitting in that jail cell at Rikers."
    "You'll forgive me if I don't cry. As I said, you were a bastard."

## FORTY-NINE

"Estelle, look at this." Wasserman folded back the pages of his *Times* and laid the paper on the kitchen table for his wife to see. "Here," he pointed. She read for a moment and looked up.

"How will that affect Carr, do you suppose?" she asked. "Will he lose his job again?"

"I wouldn't be surprised. That's the way these things usually play out. Talk about bad luck."

"Ironic, maybe, but he's had more than his share of good luck, if you ask me. He got off easy, Herb."

"Come on, Carr was innocent...and he still lost his job. Not to mention spending a night in jail for something he didn't do."

"He cheated on his wife, Herb."

"You're still angry with him because of that. Okay, so he's guilty of his little fling. You know Carr, Estelle. You used to like him. Come on, what's got into you? He and Laura are back together again, and everything's fine."

"Isn't that just like a man."

"Look, I know she was hurt, but they've apparently worked it out. Come on, give the guy a break. He made a mistake, but he's still a good guy. I think in your heart you know that."

"I suppose I do. Anyway, this article doesn't make it sound too good for him, Herb." Wasserman picked up the paper and reread the item:

New York- Media giant Harmon Communications said yesterday that it had made an offer to buy Tangent Publishing Company, one of the leaders in the book publishing business. Two key executives involved in the possible acquisition have been rivals in the past. Four years ago, Carson Williamson, now president and CEO of Tangent, was named CEO at Harmon Hall

Publishing Company, a major subsidiary of Harmon Communications. Stuart Markham, then editor in chief and now Williamson's successor, at Harmon Hall, was believed to have been disappointed, and more than a little put out that he was not selected for the top post. Feelings between the two apparently worsened during Williamson's tenure at Harmon Hall. Ironically, in the wake of the much-publicized Harmon Hall murders, Williamson was ousted and replaced by Markham. Speculation has it that, should the reported acquisition take place, Williamson would once again be out of a job. A high-ranking executive at Harmon Communications said that he expects to see Markham heading up a greatly enlarged publishing company consisting of Harmon Hall and Tangent.

Wasserman put the paper down on the table. "Remember last year when we heard Carr had landed the job at Tangent?" He shook his head as he recalled his sense of disbelief at the time, "Talk about a Phoenix rising from the ashes. I never expected him to get another big job. Even though he was exonerated, I couldn't believe any company would risk it."

"I know, but you've said yourself, Herb, more than once I might add, that Carr is one of the most brilliant businessmen you've ever known. Look what he did at Harmon Hall in the three years he was there. Didn't they have their best profits ever? He must know how to run a business. Obviously the board at Tangent felt it was worth the risk."

"Obviously. And I was happy for him when he got it. Even though we haven't been close since I ratted on him."

"You didn't rat on him. You did your civic duty."

"I could've waited longer. I didn't have to contact the police when I did."

"It's easy to be hard on yourself now, Herb. At the time, though, we both felt you might have waited too long. I know, it is a shame you two aren't as close as you used to be, but the whole thing was weird. Look at the job Carr's got now. At least he wasn't permanently damaged. "

"If this Markham guy gets Carr's job again, I'd have to say you're wrong about that."

\* \* \*

"Carr, I assume you've read the business section of today's *Times*?" Howard Harmon's booming voice resonated in the receiver at Carr's ear.

"Yes, Howard, I have indeed. Your contact at the *Times* must be publishing your copy verbatim."

"Pretty close. Close enough for our purposes," said the chairman of Harmon Communications with a detectable lilt in his voice. "I think we're going to have fun with this, Carr."

"I'm sort of looking forward to it myself." Williamson reflected on the extraordinary events that had begun unfolding in the past few weeks. Almost exactly three weeks ago he'd received a call from his old boss, Howard Harmon. The thrust of the conversation had been that the board of Harmon Communications wanted to expand their presence in book publishing. They had become convinced that, while printed books might not represent a major growth opportunity in the twenty-first century, the companies that published those books did. The idea was that, regardless of the medium, whether it be print on paper, or any of the new electronic media, publishers would control the sources and supply of information. In the age of the electronic superhighway, it made sense to have a greater presence in book publishing. Information was now a commodity—in some ways an industry in and of itself, and book publishers still controlled and processed a significant chunk of that information. Maybe the binding would change—it already had started with the emergence of the "electronic book" or as some called it, new media—but the message would still be sought after, regardless of how it was presented. Tangent Publishing Company was a natural target for any acquisition efforts that Harmon Communications might expend. As might have been expected, Williamson had been less than enthusiastic about his company being acquired, especially by the company that had tossed him out on his ass just one year ago. When he expressed his feelings to Harmon, the great man had laughed. Williamson remembered thinking at the time, "This conversation is going from bad to worse." And yet Harmon had once again shown the quality that put him several cuts above other successful men Williamson knew. It was the quality of being unpredictable. Unpredictability coupled with a marvelous sense of timing. And he'd come through again on that memorable phone call. "Carr, forgive my laughing, but please hear me out. I think you'll find what I have to say extremely interesting." Williamson remembered taking a deep breath as he successfully kept from exploding. "I'm all ears."

"I want you to run the new publishing operation. You'd be in charge of both Harmon Hall and Tangent. Can I count on you?"

"Howard, you fired me a year ago. Why do you want to give me a bigger job now?"

"I told you then why you had to leave. You were cleared, and that's good enough for me. You did a superb job at Harmon Hall We need you to run the new operation."

Carr asked, "What about Markham?"

"I can't wait to get rid of the bastard. I've known a lot of unpleasant people in my time, but Stuart Markham is just about the weakest excuse for a human being I've ever had the misfortune to know. The sooner I can replace him, the better. Do you want the job, Carr?"

"I'm flattered, Howard, I truly am. And I'm ninety-nine percent certain my answer is yes. Can I have the weekend before I give you a firm answer?"

"Of course, but I need to know Monday."

"I have to ask you one thing."

"Yes, what is it?"

"You want me for this job, even though you're obviously aware that I had a brief affair a little over a year ago. I always thought you felt pretty strongly about such things?"

"Damn right I do I take a dim view of such things. Fired a good man once for the very thing you did."

"Then, if you don't mind my asking...?"

"Why am I overlooking your affair with that young lady lawyer? To be honest, Carr, it wasn't easy. But if I've learned anything in my forty-plus years in business, it's not to be sanctimonious, and not to be rigid. It finally came down to the fact that I like you a hell of a lot better than I like that other guy. I also believe that every man's entitled to one mistake. And I guess, if I'm really honest I'd have to say that you're too good a manager to let get away. This new company needs you."

\* \* \*

It had not been easy for him to make the call. He'd waited, hoping Harmon would call him. No call had come. Finally, curiosity and ambition had won out over pride.

"Howard, I know you plan to make the official announcement about the Tangent acquisition soon." He paused, hoping that his brief hesitation would be enough to prompt his boss into telling him what he hoped to hear.

"Yes, Stuart, that's right. I do."

The sonofabitch isn't going to make it easy for me, sighed Markham. "I know, Howard, that with all that's on your mind it's probably been difficult to find the time to get to it, but you and I haven't even discussed my role in the new expanded publishing operation."

"Yes, Stuart, I have been busy. I planned to call you later today. I'd like you to come over to my office this afternoon...so that we can discuss your future with the company. Shall we say two-thirty."

At 2:25pm Markham presented himself to Carmela, the great man's assistant. The intervening four hours since the phone call that morning had passed for Markham the way time drags for a child waiting for a birthday. How could Howard do anything but place him in charge of the newly expanded publishing operation? Relax, he told himself. This is what you've been working up to your entire career.

"He'll see you now Mr. Markham," said Carmela. "Go right in."

Harmon was seated behind his huge desk, talking in muffled tones to someone on the telephone. "All right. That'll be fine. I'll call you later. I have a visitor now. Bye." As he put down the receiver, he turned his attention to Markham. Markham was encouraged by the smile on the chairman's broad features.

"Sit down, Stuart. Please sit down. I asked you to come over here because I wanted to be the first person to tell you this."

"I appreciate that, Howard. I'm looking forward to what you have to say." Markham smiled, trying not to look too pleased with himself as he sat back and waited for Harmon to speak.

"Stuart, the board of Howard Communications has, at my urging, asked Carr Williamson to be the CEO of Harmon Publishing Enterprises, the new publishing group that will include Harmon Hall and Tangent. It's a big job, and we feel Carr's the best man for it."

"You're joking, of course, aren't you Howard?"

The question came out as little more than a whisper. Markham suddenly found it hard to breath.

"No, Stuart, it's no joke, believe me. Though God forgive me for indulging one of the more adolescent emotions I've felt in over half a century. I do believe I'm enjoying it."

"I...I don't understand. You're enjoying this. Telling me that I won't be getting the job. You're enjoying it?"

"Absolutely. Oh, and by the way. You won't be keeping your present job, either. I don't think the company could survive much more of you. I know I couldn't."

The harder he tried, the harder Markham found it was to catch his breath. He didn't know whether he was hyperventilating or not, but the sensation was terrifying. This couldn't be happening to him, Stuart Markham, the man who his entire life had lived by his wits, had outsmarted virtually everyone he'd ever dealt with. All his life, by dint of his superior intellectual powers he'd been able to toy with most people. From his earliest recollection he'd been aware that he possessed this raw cognitive ability that enabled him to think circles around all but a tiny percentage of the people he knew. But now... now...a few more seconds passed. He gradually collected a semblance of his composure. He wasn't going to faint. Finally—it had seemed like an eternity—but it must have only been a very short time, finally he was able to speak. "Obviously, Howard, you've harbored ill feelings toward me, apparently for some time now. I think you owe me an explanation."

"Stuart, I don't owe you a thing. But because I feel like it I will tell you why, since your ego apparently precludes any kind of introspection on your part. As the young people say, you haven't got a clue, have you?" Harmon leaned forward. He looked directly at Markham. "Over the last year I've watched you closely. While the company hasn't done badly, it hasn't done all that well under your direction, either. I deliberately chose the word direction and carefully avoided the term leadership, because, in my opinion, you're not a leader—or at least not the kind of leader we want running Harmon Hall. Your performance, incidentally, has not gone unnoticed by the board. You know what I'm talking about, Stuart, for we've discussed your record at the helm of Harmon Hall on a number of occasions. During the past year, I've observed what kind of man you are. Conniving, manipulative, and deceitful are words that come to mind at the moment, but I'm sure I could think of a few more if you gave me a couple of minutes."

"Now wait just a minute...."

"No, Stuart, you wait just a minute. This is long overdue.

When we put you into this job I thought you'd do fine. I frankly didn't think you'd ever fill Carr's shoes, but I expected you'd develop your own style and do a good job. I should point out that there were two or three on the board back them who warned me against you, but I wouldn't hear of it. I suppose I was blinded by your reputation as a fine editor. Unfortunately, I hadn't seen the side of you that some people had."

"I gather, Howard, that there's no hope of persuading you to change your mind?"

"Not a chance."

**End**

If you enjoyed **Murder on Third Avenue** you'll probably like some of the following titles by Richard Scott:

**The Reluctant Assassin** (A Tony Dantry spy novel)
**The Eager Assassin** (A Tony Dantry spy novel)
**The Second Assassination**  (An historic mystery novel)
**Salem, the Novel**  (Historic fiction at its best)

**About the Author**

Richard Scott is a retired editor, writer, and publisher, having been president and publisher of the David McKay Company and president and publisher of Fodor's Travel Publications. He's also been managing editor of *American Bookseller* and *Bookselling this Week*. In the 70s Mr. Scott was co-host with Isaac Asimov, Brendan Gill, Nat Hentoff and others of the talk show *In Conversation*. The show ran on radio station WOR in New York and eleven other stations around the U.S. He's a former trustee of Historic Salem, Inc. and of the Salem Athenæum in Salem, Massachusetts. He lives in Salem. You can contact him at richard.scott2000@comcast.net.

Made in the USA
Middletown, DE
24 August 2024

59120653R00191